THE GIRL FROM GALLOWAY

1845: Since following her heart and moving from her comfortable home in Scotland to the harsh mountainside of Ardtur, County Donegal, Hannah McGinley hasn't had the easiest life. But surrounded by her two children and her loving husband Patrick, she has found happiness. When her daughter returns home with news that her school may close as one of the teachers is moving away, Hannah feels compelled to take the vacant post. With the schoolmaster Daniel having lost his sight, Hannah knows that he won't be able to manage the children alone. But the money from teaching is poor, and as the potato crops begin to fail all around them, times are getting tougher still. Will Hannah be able to help her family *and* save the school?

ANNE DOUGHTY

THE GIRL FROM GALLOWAY

Complete and Unabridged

MAGNA
Leicester

First published in Great Britain in 2019 by
HQ
An imprint of HarperCollins*Publishers* Ltd
London

First Ulverscroft Edition
published 2020
by arrangement with
HarperCollins*Publishers* Ltd
London

The moral right of the author has been asserted

This novel is entirely a work of fiction. The names, characters and incidents portrayed in it are the work of the author's imagination. Any resemblance to actual persons, living or dead, events or localities is entirely coincidental.

A catalogue record for this book is available from the British Library.

ISBN 978–0–7505–4834–2

Published by
Ulverscroft Limited
Anstey, Leicestershire

Set by Words & Graphics Ltd.
Anstey, Leicestershire
Printed and bound in Great Britain by
T. J. International Ltd., Padstow, Cornwall

This book is printed on acid-free paper

Author's Note

In 1845 Ireland was ruled by Queen Victoria. Irish Members of Parliament went to London and represented all thirty-two Irish counties. The only internal divisions in Ireland were the ancient provinces: Ulster, Leinster, Munster and Connaught.

Donegal is the most northern and westerly county in the northern province of Ulster, which is made up of nine counties. Every school-child could recite them in geographical order: Armagh, Down, Antrim, Londonderry, Tyrone, Fermanagh, Donegal, Cavan and Monaghan.

Throughout the period of our story most people in all four provinces spoke Irish, unless they had come from Scotland or England in the first place. Many Irish speakers from Donegal went to Scotland each year to help with the harvest. There they learnt a second language, which they called Scotch, but we would call English.

1

Ardtur, County Donegal
April 1845

Hannah McGinley put down her sewing and moved across the tramped earth floor to where the door of the cottage stood open through all the daylight hours, except in the coldest and stormiest of weather. She stood on the well-swept door stone, looked up at the pale, overcast sky and ran her eye along the stone walls that enclosed their small patch of potato garden. Beyond the wall, the hawthorns partly masked the stony track, which ran down the mountainside.

There was no sign of them yet. No familiar figures walked, ran, or skipped up the narrow rocky path leading steeply up the mountainside from the broader track that ran along the lower contours of the mountain. Below that, the final, bush-filled slopes dropped more gently to the shore of Lough Gartan. The only movement she could detect in the deep quiet of the grey, late April afternoon were flickers of light reflected from the calm surface of the lake itself, just visible between the still-bare trees and the pale rise of smoke from the cottage of her nearest neighbour.

Dotted along the mountainside above the lake, clusters of cottages like Ardtur itself huddled together in the shelter of the mountain, its brooding shape offering some defence against the battering of westerly winds from the Atlantic, westerlies that brought both mildness and heavy rain to this rugged landscape.

She moved back to the hearth, hung the kettle over the glowing embers of the turf fire and took up her sewing again. She paused to push back a few strands of long, fair hair that had escaped from the ribbon with which she tied it firmly each morning. Touching the gleaming strands, she smiled to herself, thinking of her daughter. Rose was as dark as she herself was fair, her eyes and colouring so like Patrick, her husband, while Sam, a year younger, pale-skinned and red-haired, so closely resembled her father, Duncan Mackay, far away in Scotland where she had been born and grew up.

They were good children, always willing to help with whatever task she might have in hand; Rose, the older, patient and thoughtful; Sam quick, often impatient, but always willing to do as she asked. Even now, though he was lightly built and only eight years old, he would run to help if he saw her move to lift a creel of potatoes or turf, or to pick up the empty pails to fetch water from the well.

She thought for a moment of her everyday tasks and reflected that she had not become entirely familiar with the harsh, yet beautiful place where she'd lived for the ten years of her married life. It surprised her that she still woke up every morning thinking of the well-built, two-storey farmhouse in Galloway and the view from the south-facing window of the bedroom

2

she had shared with one of her older sisters. Then, she had seen a very different landscape: green fields and trees sloping gently towards the seashore, rich pasture dotted with sheep, well cared for and prosperous, the delight of her hard-working father who loved his land as well as or perhaps even better than he loved his God.

Duncan Mackay was seen by many as a hard man, one who did not suffer fools gladly, shrewd in his dealings, strong in his Covenanter beliefs and not given to generosity, but, to his youngest daughter, Hannah, he showed a gentleness few others ever saw. It was Hannah's sorrow that in making her own life she'd had to leave him, widowed and now alone, her brothers and sisters married and moved into their own lives, two of them far away in Nova Scotia. Only her youngest brother, Matthew, running a boat-building yard on the Galloway coast close to Port William, was near enough to make the journey to their old home near Dundrennan, once or twice a year.

She knew her father still grieved for the choice she had made, though he had long ago accepted the quality of the man she'd married. But it had been hard for him. Patrick McGinley was a landless labourer, one of the many who took the boat from Derry, or Belfast, or the small ports nearest to the Glens of Antrim and went over to Scotland and the North of England to provide extra labour on the farms through the long season from the cutting of grass for silage, to the final picking and storing of the potato crop.

From early May till late October, or even November, if there was other farm work that

3

needed doing, the 'haymakers' came. They lived in a barn cleared out for them each springtime, and worked on the land, labouring from dawn to dusk in the long summer days, and they sent home money each week to support their families on rough hillsides with tiny holdings like this one. The only source of food was potatoes from the small patch of land behind or beside each cottage and what could be bought with the earnings of the few women who had the skill to do embroidery such as whitework, or sprigging.

For three years Patrick had come with a group of men and boys from Donegal, all good workers, as her father freely acknowledged. While they frequently worked on neighbouring farms, their base was Mackay's, the farm south-east of Dundrennan, the one her father had bought after long years of working with his brother in the drapery trade in Dumfries.

Her father had always wanted his own farm. His elder brother, Ross, had once told Hannah that even as a small boy in their home in the far north-west of Scotland, he had talked about it. He'd explained to Ross when he was still a boy that he wanted good soil and fine pasture so he could keep cattle or sheep, that would be plump and well fed, not bony like the few animals they had on the poor piece of land they rented from an English landlord they had never seen.

Years later, Ross and Duncan arrived barefoot and penniless in Dumfries, two victims of the Sutherland clearances; they'd been turned out of their croft and land in Strathnaver, with only the clothes they wore and what few possessions they could carry. As they tramped south looking for a means of survival, it seemed that Duncan's dream had remained intact.

Hannah would never forget the way her father told parts of their story over and over again, throughout her childhood. Every time they sat down to eat, he would give thanks for their food, even if it were only a bowl of porridge. He reminded them time and time again that he and their uncle Ross had travelled the length of Scotland on 'burn water and the kindness of the poor', with no place to lay their heads but the heather on the hill.

★　★　★

By the time the Mackay brothers arrived in Dumfries they were famished, their boots long disintegrated, their clothes tattered, stained and faded from sleeping in the heather, being drenched by rain and exposed to the sun. When they'd seen the notice in a draper's window asking for two strong lads, they'd tidied themselves up as best they could and tried to look robust, despite their thinness.

The shop, in the main street of Dumfries, sold fabric but its main purpose was as a collecting centre for woven materials brought in from outworkers who spun, or wove, in their own homes — small cottages with a tiny piece of land, a potato garden, or a cow, as their only other support. The older man, the draper who ran the business, needed strong lads to hump the bales of fabric coming in from the home workers, the bundles of handkerchiefs and napkins going out to merchants in England and the heavy webs of woollen cloth going much further afield. The brothers were weak with hunger, but both now in their twenties and knowing well how much depended on it, they managed to heft the heavy bales as if they were merely parcels.

They got the job. The hours were long, but there was a loft to sleep in and a daily meal as part of their small income. Neither of them knew anything about fabric, about the mysteries of spinning or weaving, but they learnt quickly, grew stronger in body and more confident in mind. According to Ross, even in those first years when they earned very little, Duncan had already begun to save for 'his farm' from his meagre salary.

Hannah's father took pride in telling her how they had helped the older man to expand the business and make it so very profitable that he regularly increased their wages. Some five years later, he offered them each a share in the business as well.

With no son of his own and well pleased with their commitment to their work, Mr McAllister, the draper, regularly said that when he retired he hoped they would be able to buy the business from him. In the meantime, he did all he could to make that possible for them.

He was as good as his word. A few years later, when Sandy McAllister finally decided to retire, the two brothers bought the business and Duncan then sold his share to his brother. With the money released and his savings Duncan then bought a small, neglected farm just a few miles outside Dumfries itself.

Hannah had never known that first farm. But her father had told her the tale of how it had been owned by an old woman, long widowed, her sons all in America. Although the sons had sent her money, it was only enough to buy food; she had none left over to pay for labour.

She had watched the few small fields fill with rushes and weeds, her only comfort the memory of happier times with her husband and children, They'd never had much money but the boys had been fed and clothed and walked barefoot to the local school. There, they became star pupils. By the time Duncan Mackay bought the farm from the old woman's executors, and learnt the story of its previous owner, her sons were wealthy businessmen in Detroit who barely noticed the small sum of money from the sale of their old home, their inheritance from a life long-forgotten.

★ ★ ★

The fire was burning up more brightly since Hannah had added a few pieces of fresh turf, but there was still no sound of children's voices. It was too soon to make the mugs of tea that welcomed them home at the end of their day. She spread the patterned damask on her knee, smoothed it out and began hemming the last side of the napkin as her mind wandered back to her father's stories of his younger days.

Duncan Mackay's second farm was much

further away from Dumfries. It was there that Hannah herself was born, the seventh and last child of Duncan and the former Flora McAllister, the daughter of the draper who had taken Duncan and Ross barefoot from the main street in Dumfries, fed them and given them boots and clothes for their new job.

Duncan loved Flora dearly but he had so wanted a son he could hardly contain his impatience in the tiny farmhouse where his three daughters were born one after the other. He was overjoyed when his first son was born, to be followed by two more. Hannah, as everyone used to tell her when she was a child, was 'the surprise' — an unexpected, late child born many years after her nearest brother. It was always Hannah's sadness that she never knew her mother. She had died within a year of her birth, perhaps — as so many women were in those days — worn out by the daily drudgery of work on a farm and the continuous demands of miscarriages, pregnancies and births.

She pushed away the sad thought and remembered instead her three older sisters: Jean, Fiona and Flora, who had all taken care of her and played with her, the wide gap in age making her almost like their own first child. She had been loved and cherished by all three of them. What surprised all of them, as baby Hannah got to her feet and walked, was the way in which she attached herself to her father from the moment she was steady enough to follow him around.

Later, they had each told her how she followed him wherever he went, unless he explained kindly, which he always did, that it was not safe for her to be with him just then and she must go back to her sisters.

But it was not Hannah's devotion to her father that surprised her good-natured sisters the most; it was their father's toleration of such a young child. From the point at which Hannah could walk they began to see a very different man from the fair, hardworking, but very impersonal father they themselves had known in their growing years.

Now in his sixties, her father had no one to share the solid, two-storey house with. It was once such a busy place, full of life and activity, its small garden rich in flowers, her mother's great joy, which her sisters had gone on caring for in her memory throughout Hannah's childhood. They often brought bouquets and posies into the house to add colour to the solid furniture and plain whitewashed walls.

Her sisters were now long married and scattered, her brothers Gavin and James were in Nova Scotia, and she, her father's youngest and most beloved daughter, in Donegal, his only contact the letters Hannah wrote so regularly. At least Duncan could rely on the yearly arrival of his son-in-law, Patrick, still coming to labour alongside him with some neighbouring men from Casheltown and Staghall who had been haymakers all their working lives.

Hannah still remembered the first time she'd seen Patrick, walking down the lane to the farm, one of a small group hired for the season to take the place of her absent brothers. Lightly built, dark-haired with deep, dark eyes, tanned by wind and rain, he moved with ease despite the weariness of the long walk from the boat that had brought them from Derry to Cairnryan.

Her father had greeted them formally, one by one, showing them into the well-swept barn where they would live for the season.

'This is my daughter, Hannah,' he had said, more than a hint of pride clear in his voice. Patrick had looked at her and smiled. Even then it had seemed to her as if his eyes were full of love.

She was just seventeen and working as a monitor at the local school, the one she herself had attended. It never occurred to her, when she offered to help the small group of harvesters with learning what they called 'Scotch', that she would also become fluent in another language and through it, come to love a man who listened devotedly to all she said but thought it wrong to speak of his love to a young girl who seemed so far out of reach.

Hannah dropped her work hastily now and reached for the teapot warming by the hearth as a sudden outburst of noise roused her and grew stronger. She made the tea, set it to draw, and stood watching from the doorway as the small group of children of Ardtur ran up the last long slope, their shouts and arguments forgotten, as they focused on open doors and the prospect of a mug of tea while they relayed the day's news.

'Oh, Ma, I'm hungry,' said Sam, rolling his eyes and rubbing his stomach, the moment she had kissed him.

'You're always hungry,' protested his sister, as she turned from hanging up her schoolbag on the lowest of a row of hooks by the door. 'You had your piece at lunchtime,' she said practically, looking at him severely. 'I'm not hungry. At least not very,' she added honestly, when Hannah in turn looked at her.

'Well,' said Hannah, unable to resist Sam's expressive twists and turns. 'You could have a piece of the new soda bread. There's still some jam, but there's no butter till I go up to Aunt Mary tomorrow,' she added, as he dropped his schoolbag on the floor.

Sam nodded vigorously. Then, when Rose looked at him meaningfully, he picked it up again, went and hung it on the hook beside Rose's and sat down at the kitchen table looking hopeful.

'So what did you learn today?' Hannah asked, as she poured mugs of tea and brought milk from the cold windowsill at the back of the house. She knew from long experience that Rose would tell her in detail all that had happened at school while Sam would devote himself entirely to the piece of soda bread she was now carving from the circular cake she had made in the morning's baking.

'Can I get the jam for you, Ma?' he asked, as he eyed the sweet-smelling soda bread she put in front of him.

'Can you reach?' she asked gently.

'Oh yes, Ma. Da says I'm growing like a bad weed,' he replied cheerfully. 'Look,' he went on, jumping up from the table and standing on tiptoe to open the upper doors of the cupboard. He stretched up, clutched a jam jar firmly in his hand and studied the contents. Hannah saw his look of disappointment and was about to speak, but then he smiled.

He'd seen the jar contained only a small helping of the rich-tasting jam she'd made from the bowls of berries they'd helped her to pick the previous year but now, as he looked at it hungrily, Sam was already reckoning there would be more next season. By September, he would be bigger; he could reach places he'd had to miss last year. He would also be able to get at places where the big boys had got to before him.

He sat down in his place, unscrewed the lid and scraped out every last vestige of the sweet, rich, dark jam and then spread it carefully over his piece of soda bread.

He heard nothing of what Rose had learnt at school that day and didn't even notice the small envelope she fetched from her schoolbag and handed to his mother.

2

The April evening was well lengthened from the shorter days of March, but it was still growing dark when Hannah heard Patrick greet a neighbour, as he walked up the last steep slope of his journey home from Tullygobegley, where he'd been helping to reroof a farmhouse that had fared badly in the winter storms.

The children were already asleep. Hannah moved quickly to the open door and held out her arms. She'd only to watch him for those last few yards to know that he was tired out, his shoulders drooping, his arms hanging limp by his sides. He'd admitted to her earlier in the week that it was heavy work, humping slates up a steep roof, exposed to the wind and rain. Now, as he put his arms round her, kissed her and held her close she could see he was quite exhausted.

'Bad news, astore,' he began, speaking Irish as he always did when they were alone. 'The job will finish the end of the week. No money then till yer father sends the passage money for me an' the other boys,' he said anxiously.

'That's not bad news, my love,' she said warmly, drawing him over to the fire and closing the door behind them. 'I'm pleased to hear it. Have you forgotten I've four weeks' pay due to me sometime next week when your man from Creeslough comes for the napkins?'

'Aye, I had forgot,' he said, looking up at her,

his face pale with fatigue. 'Sure, what wou'd we do if ye hadn't hans for anythin' an' you never brought up to a rough place like this?'

She saw the anxiety in his face, the dark shadows under his eyes and suddenly became sharply aware that sometime in the next few weeks the letter would come with the passage money. Her heart sank. When the letter came, they would be separated for months.

Parting never got easier. No matter how hard she worked on the piles of napkins, the cooking over the hearth, keeping the floor swept, the clothes clean and mended, when he was here, she knew at the end of the day there would be the warmth and tenderness of the night. It never ceased to amaze her how despite their exhaustion they could still turn to each other's arms for comfort, an enfolding that quickly turned to passion.

When the letter with the postal order came from her father, her days would be the same as they were now, but there would be neither comfort, nor passion, nor shared laughter, just note-paper in the drawer so she could write a little every day, as he did, for all the long months till the first chill of autumn stripped the yellow leaves from the hawthorns and the birds feasted on the red berries.

'You must be hungry, love,' she said quickly, as he released her and sank down heavily in his armchair by the hearth. 'It's all ready over a saucepan. Do you want to wash?'

'Oh yes, indeed I do, for I'll not bring the dust of that roof to our bed,' he said firmly.

He stood up again with an effort and went out by the back door to the adjoining outhouse, where he'd set up a wash place for them all with a tin basin on a stand, a jug for water and hooks on a board attached to the wall for the towels.

She heard the splash of the water she'd left ready for him as she poured a glass of buttermilk to go with his meal. She checked that his food was properly hot, carefully lifting the saucepan lid that covered the large dinner plate set over the simmering water below.

She thought then of her sisters who had used this same method of ensuring their father's meal was hot. He always intended to be in at a certain time, but in this one thing that most reliable of men was unreliable. It was almost a joke between Duncan and his daughters, the way he would assure them he'd be in by such and such a time, and then, invariably, he would find yet one more job he must do before he could possibly think of coming in for his meal.

Hannah picked up her sewing and watched quietly as Patrick ate in silence. He had never spoken much at the table in their time together, but these days, she knew it was not the long shadow of his own father's strict rule about not talking with food on the table; it was simply tiredness. At least when he went to Dundrennan he would be doing work he enjoyed, and her father, though he expected a lot, would not expect any man to work harder for him than he would expect to work himself.

Patrick cleared his plate, pushed it away from him and crossed himself. 'That was great,' he said. 'It would put heart in ye. Did they have a good day at school the day?' he asked, as he moved his armchair nearer to hers.

She put her sewing back in its bag and took his hand.

'They did indeed,' she replied smiling. 'Rose got all her spellings right and Sam managed to give out the slates this time without dropping any,' she said laughing. 'But there's more news than that,' she went on more slowly, suddenly concerned that he was so tired he might be anxious about what she was going to say next.

'Oh, what's that then?' he asked, a flicker of a smile touching his lips.

To her surprise and delight, she saw his blue eyes light up.

'Sure, ye know I always need a bit of news to pass on to the boys tomorrow,' he said, his tone lightening as she watched him.

'Well, it seems Daniel's niece, Marie, has been walking out with a young man from Creeslough direction and they've named the day.'

'Ach, sure, that's great,' he said. 'That'll be a bit of a gatherin' at some point or other,' he said cheerfully. 'They'll maybe have a kitchen racket at Daniel's.'

Daniel's house was not only the place used as the local makeshift school he presided over, but also a popular place for gathering to hear the best stories and songs shared between friends of an evening.

'Yes, it is good news,' she agreed, 'but it will be hard on Daniel. She'll be living down in Creeslough so she'll not be able to go on

16

working with him in the schoolroom. He can do so much and everyone says it's like he's got eyes in the back of his head, he's so sharp, but he *is* blind. How can you teach children if you haven't got at least one pair of eyes in the room, and a woman as well as a man when there's wee ones to look after?'

'Ach dear, it would be a great loss if that wee schoolroom were to be no more. Sure, where wou'd our childer go? I know there's been talk of getting a National School up here for years now, but nothin's ever come of it. If it weren't for Daniel being an educated man there'd never have been anywhere up this part of the mountain where they could go. How could he do anythin' at all on his lone? Sure, he can talk away, an' teach them their history, and tell the old stories and hear their readin' till the cows come home, but what about the writin' an' the figures? Sure, Marie must have done all that. How cou'd he do anythin' where he had to look at their work?' he asked, his voice suddenly weary again.

'They did seem to work very well together,' Hannah said slowly, her unease returning, now it had come to the point where she'd have to tell him about the note Marie had sent with the children.

'Would you like a mug of tea?' she asked, getting up and hanging the kettle over the fire.

'That would go down well,' he said, watching her carefully as she moved about the room fetching mugs and milk.

He always knew when she was thinking about something, for she moved more slowly and kept

17

looking at the kettle as if she expected it to start singing at any moment when she knew perfectly well it would take a while. He waited till she had put his mug in his hand and then said: 'Are you worried there'll be nowhere for our pair to go?'

She couldn't help but laugh, for he had taken her by surprise. So often, it was she who read *his* thoughts, but this time he had tried to read hers. It didn't matter that he hadn't got it quite right. It just somehow made it easier for what she needed to say.

'Daniel was wondering if I would come and give him a hand,' she replied. 'Apparently, I told him once years ago that I was a monitor back in my own old school in Dundrennan. He has an extraordinary memory,' she said, shaking her head.

'An' wou'd ye like that?' he said quickly, his eyes widening. 'Sure, it wou'd be company fer ye when I'm away,' he went on, brightening as she looked across at him.

'It wouldn't pay very much, Patrick,' she said cautiously. 'Certainly not as much as the sewing.'

'Aye, I can see that might be the way of it,' he said, nodding slowly. 'Sure, none of the families up here has much to spare. There must be childer Daniel takes in that can't go beyond their pieces of turf for the fire. I know some of them bring cakes of bread and a bit of butter for Daniel himself,' he said, shaking his head, 'but that would be because there was no tuppence that week, or whatever it is these days, that wou'd otherwise be forthcomin'. How does Daniel manage at all? Sure, everyone knows the

18

masters of these hedge schools don't see a penny when times are bad and Daniel wou'd never be the one to turn a chile away if it hadn't brought its few pence.'

Patrick himself had never been to school and he'd never figured out why people called these local places where children could learn to read and write 'hedge schools'. But Daniel's house, which he used for the school, was not typical. Most of the other schools in the area were far less robust: abandoned cottages, or caves, or even old cattle pens with a bit of a roof thrown over. But then, there was a time when running a school would have got you into trouble. There were laws against schools, like there were laws against celebrating Mass.

'Maybe yer da will give us all a bit more money this year, if the price of cattle keeps going up,' he offered cheerfully. 'Are you thinking about doin' it?' he asked directly.

'Well . . .'

'Well, indeed. What wou'd stan' in yer way if you had a mind to do it? Sure, Sam and Rose wou'd be there with ye . . . and sure, what'll they do if Daniel has to give up? Though you could teach them yourself like you taught me, couldn't you? Sure, you're a great teacher and me no scholar,' he ended sheepishly.

Hannah laughed and felt her anxiety drain away. She remembered again how she'd offered to help her father's harvesters to write their letters home, and how, in the process, she had ended up learning Irish. Patrick had been a diligent pupil. He had learnt not only how to

19

read and write, but also to make his way in English. It might well be English with a strong Scottish accent but it still stood him and his fellows in good stead when work called from south of the border around Carlisle, or even Lancaster.

She could still see the scrubbed wooden table in the farm kitchen where they had normally sat at mealtimes, covered with reading books in the evenings. Her own school, where she was then a monitor, had let her borrow what she needed for when she taught the haymakers, while her sister, Flora, the youngest of the three older sisters, still living nearby in those years, had bought jotters and notepaper for her pupils out of her egg money until she and her husband, Cameron, moved to take up a new job in Dumfries.

'My Irish isn't that great,' Hannah said feebly now, remembering her own difficulties when she had first begun to teach the Irishmen and found they had so very little English to begin with.

'An' when have I ever not been able to understan' you?' he asked, his voice gentle, his eyes looking at her directly. 'I'm for it, if it's what ye want. Sure, why don't we sleep on it,' he added, standing up and putting his hand on her shoulder.

★   ★   ★

It was still dark next morning when Patrick picked up his piece from the kitchen table and kissed her goodbye. She walked out of the cottage with him, pausing on the doorstep as

20

they looked up at the sky.

'That's better,' he said, slipping his arm round her and pulling her close for a few moments.

It was a fine-weather sky, the sunrise clouds tinted pink, the air calm with a distinct hint of mildness. As she stood watching him make his way down towards the lough, she found herself hoping that the mildness might go on to the end of the week. If it did, then the last few days of the roofing job would not be as taxing as it had been, especially during the last weeks when the turbulent west wind had made the exposed site bitterly cold and the pitched roof more hazardous.

He stopped and waved to her as he reached the bend in the track. Beyond this point he would be hidden by a cluster of hawthorns and the last group of cottages before the steep slope to the main track. She stood a moment longer till he was out of sight and then, already thinking of all she had to do, she turned and went back into the big kitchen.

She stood for a moment looking at the table, the empty bowls and crumbs from her breakfast with Patrick, as if they would help her to decide what to do. Certainly, she would always want to help Daniel in any way she could. Patrick was indeed keen for her to have company in the long months when he was away, but he had paid little attention to the possible loss of her earnings from the sewing.

This winter he had found quite a few jobs locally, but there were other years when there was no work of any kind. Then the only income was from her sewing. Without her sewing money and the savings she had made while he was away, she couldn't have kept them in food and turf.

If she went to help Daniel teach, with the house still to run and the children to care for, the hours to spend sewing would be very hard to find, even with the better light of the long, summer evenings.

She glanced out of the open door as if there was some answer to be found out there. The light was strengthening and a few gleams of sunlight were reflecting off the whitewashed cottage walls. Whatever her decision would be, there was no need to delay her visit to Daniel.

She made up her mind to go up to Casheltown and see what Daniel had to say. She knew she needed to wake the children right away so that she had extra time to fit in washing and dressing herself, something she usually left till after they'd gone and she'd done the dustiest and dirtiest of the morning jobs.

They were both fast asleep in the tiny bedrooms Patrick had partitioned off from the single, large bedroom of their two-room dwelling, the bedroom where they had begun their married life, in October 1835, ten years ago this coming autumn.

Sam woke up the moment she touched him, threw his arms round her and hugged her. Rose was always harder to wake and was very often involved in some complicated dream that, given any possible opportunity, she would talk about until they were both ready to leave. This morning, Hannah knew she would have to discourage her usual recital if they were all to leave the house on time.

They did manage it, though as Hannah pulled the front door closed behind her, she was only too aware of all the tasks she had had to leave aside. Out of her normal morning's routine, only the making up of the fire had been done.

Stepping into the brightness of the April morning, she set aside the crowding thoughts and focused on Rose and Sam who were now telling her what they were going to do with Miss McGee today and what story the master had promised them if they all did their work well.

Hannah listened carefully but as they picked their steps through the broken stones of the track and turned right towards Casheltown, she found herself looking up at the great stone mound, once a fortified place, that looked out over the waters of Lough Gartan. She thought of her own very different walks to school in the softer green countryside of Galloway. There, the sea was almost always in sight, the fields a rich green, the school itself a sturdy, stone building with separate entrances marked Girls and Boys, and a patch of land at the back where the older boys learnt gardening.

She remembered Flora taking her by the hand on her first day and walking her briskly along the familiar lanes to the school where she herself had been a pupil some twelve years earlier.

Suddenly feeling sad, thinking of her brothers and sisters scattered 'to the four winds' as her father often said, she was glad when a girl in a tattered shift ran down from a nearby cottage and greeted them all cheerfully.

As Mary O'Donoghue fell in beside her, Hannah gathered her straying thoughts and asked the children how many scholars there currently were in their school.

Neither Rose nor Sam were very sure about the number, but Mary, a year or two older than Rose, was quite clear about it. There were fifteen on the roll, she said, when they were all there, but mostly they weren't all there at the same time. She explained that often pupils couldn't come if they were needed at home, for driving the cow to the fair or planting the tatties.

'But that's a good thing, Mrs McGinley,' she went on, as Rose and Sam fell silent. 'If they were all there, the wee ones would have to sit on creepies. Mr McGee doesn't like that, but there's only room for twelve on the chairs and benches.'

Hannah nodded her agreement. The low, homemade stools might be all right for listening to a story, but they certainly weren't suitable for any written work, or even reading aloud comfortably. She was surprised that there could be any thought of fifteen in a kitchen not much bigger than her own.

Moments later, as they turned off the main track and walked the short distance up to Daniel's house, she saw Daniel himself waiting near the open door. He was greeting each child as they appeared.

'Hannah, you're welcome,' he said warmly, holding out his hand to her before she had even opened her mouth.

She was completely taken aback. Of course he

knew her voice, and he was well known for knowing everyone's footsteps, but how did he know she was there when she hadn't yet said a word?

'Good morning, Mary; good morning, Rose; good morning, Sam,' he went on briskly, then, taking her arm, he led her towards the stone seat where he sat so often when the evenings grew lighter.

'I'm heart glad you were able to come,' he said, as the three children ran into the big kitchen that served as the classroom. 'I'd be even more glad if you could see your way to helping me out, but we'll not say a word about that yet. Marie is going to start the work indoors and then she'll come out and tell you how we manage between us and what we each do. I don't want to give you a false picture. It's hard work, I confess, but then you've never been afraid of that or you wouldn't have married your good man. Is he still working on that house up at Tullygobegley?'

★   ★   ★

They sat and talked as old friends do, for Daniel was one of the first people she had met when she came to Ardtur. Patrick had taken her to meet him one evening when they'd been back only a week or so. She'd found a house full of people, not one of whom she yet knew, but Daniel welcomed her warmly, made her sit beside him by the hearth and introduced her new neighbours one by one with a story about each of them, or a joke. Then he had told a long, traditional story after which he encouraged his visiting neighbours to sing, or to recite.

There followed many evenings at Daniel's house before the children were born. When he had someone with a violin, or a penny whistle, he'd insist the young ones take the floor. Once, indeed, to please him, she had taken the floor herself with Patrick to learn 'The Waves of Tory'.

She would never forget that evening: being passed from hand to hand by young men in shirtsleeves, dipping her head below raised arms, making an arch herself with a new partner, and all the time the lilt and dip of the music mimicking the flowing waves.

Hannah's regular visits to Daniel were interrupted when she had her first miscarriage and then again when Patrick went back to Scotland. It was only a week after his departure when Daniel himself came to call on her. He told her that he still expected to see her, Patrick or no Patrick, whenever she could spare the time.

So she had walked up there on her own, or joined with another neighbour from Ardtur, for the long months when Patrick was away in Scotland. And so the year turned and Patrick returned. But it was only after two more miscarriages that she finally managed to carry Rose to full term. Then, there could be no more evening visits for her until Patrick was at home over the winter.

But Daniel made it clear that he was not prepared to be deprived of her company for all those long months. If she could not come to him in the evening because of little Rose, then he

26

would come down and visit her in the afternoons. That is what he then did, almost every week.

Sometimes he brought a book and asked her to read to him, sometimes they just talked, but always he asked her about 'home', her father, her brothers and sisters, their lives, their travels and their families. Slowly and very intermittently, he told her something about his own unusual background and how he came to have a formal education that included Latin and Greek.

It was while Rose was still a baby that he came one afternoon to tell her of a decision he'd made. He said that since a young man who took pupils had left the adjoining townland quite unexpectedly, there was now no school anywhere nearby. He had decided that unless he did something himself, a generation of children would grow up on the mountainside who could neither read nor write. He was going to start a school and he needed her advice as well as her encouragement.

3

As the morning passed and the sun climbed higher, Hannah felt the warmth on her shoulders for the first time that year. Her spirits rose as, first Daniel, and then Marie, came to sit beside her on the stone bench a little way from the open door of the cottage, where the table and benches had now been rearranged and set up to serve as a schoolroom.

She was aware of the murmur of children's voices. Like the hum of bees, it reflected the pattern of the morning's activity, the sound oscillating but never intruding on the conversation she was having with whichever of the two teachers was sharing the stone bench with her.

It was Daniel who came first, joining her after he had conducted the roll call. She had heard him clearly as he called out the names and then less clearly as he asked his questions about the pupils who were missing. He explained later that he always asked those present about the absentees, whether they were needed at home, or on the land. If they were ill, then he wanted to know who was looking after them and whether there was any question of a doctor having to come.

Daniel's first comments to Hannah when he joined her on the bench were on what they were trying to do with the children, encouraging them to speak out, to pay attention to other people, to ask questions and find out things for themselves. Marie, who came a little later, offered her detailed descriptions of each of the pupils, including Rose and Sam.

Hannah listened with growing interest and admiration. She was impressed by the way in which they dealt with the range of ages and abilities in the children who had come to them. There were several little girls barely five years old and some big boys already twelve. They were the ones most often absent if there were potatoes to be harvested or produce of any kind to go to market.

Daniel and Marie had managed to work out an overlapping pattern where the older children helped the younger ones and encouraged them to read aloud and recite the poems Daniel had taught them. At the same time, those who'd been present were asked to share what they'd been doing with those who'd been absent. Everyone was persuaded to talk about what they'd been doing at home, what visitors had called to see them and what answers they'd had to questions they'd been given by way of homework, things they could ask their parents, or other members of their family.

Daniel and Marie both said in their different ways, when they took their turn to talk to her, that they'd not realised to begin with how good it was for their pupils to be required to help each other in this way and what beneficial effects the shared activity had produced.

'Shyness has little educational value,' Daniel declared, when he sat down again after he'd taken a session on spelling. 'These children need to be able to communicate with other people whatever their rank or status. We're trying to develop their confidence. That way they can begin to educate themselves, however many, or few, their school years might turn out to be.

It was Marie who shared with her the surprise they'd had when they discovered Daniel's inability to see could be turned to good purpose. Each new achievement of an individual, or a small group, was brought before Daniel, for it had emerged very early on, that once a child grasped fully that he could not see, then he or she saw for themselves the need to explain exactly what they'd done. The effort of explaining, telling him what letters, or words, they had learnt, what information they had found out at home, had meant that among other benefits there were no problems of behaviour, nor of bullying, such as might occur in a traditional school.

Hannah had to smile when Daniel referred to his own memory and what a resource it had been to him. She remembered so well when she and Patrick first visited his home on their arrival together from Scotland how amazed she had been listening to the first of the long, complicated stories he told.

Now, it seemed, Daniel used the gift to benefit each one of the pupils.

When they had to report to him on some lesson they had learnt, or information they had found out, he would respond by offering encouragement, then remind them of something else they had recently achieved. He'd continue by telling them a joke or asking a riddle. He would then ask more questions. He'd encourage their answers and if they didn't have one, he'd ask them to go away and try to find one. They could ask other pupils if they wanted to, parents, or people they knew, or they could begin by looking up the indexes in the small selection of books they'd been given by a visiting English lady.

At one point, Daniel admitted freely that when they began their work in the schoolroom they'd been concerned his blindness would be a serious problem and put too great a burden on Marie, but they'd quickly come to see how facing the problem had actually shaped a way of working they might otherwise never have discovered.

Shortly after noon, the pupils all came outside carrying the pieces they had taken from their satchels. Hannah waved to Rose and Sam, then watched Mary O'Donoghue as she left her piece with Rose and came to ask the three adults if they would like mugs of tea. She and her friend then went and made it, Mary carrying it back outside to them on a tray, her friend carrying the milk jug separately so it wouldn't spill on the clean tray as they moved over the bumpy ground.

Hannah was impressed and said so. Daniel smiled and said nothing. Marie and Hannah sat watching today's class of twelve finish up the last crumbs of their lunch and begin their half hour of playtime. Some of them walked down to the lough shore in the hope of seeing the swans, others fetched a book and sat reading in the sunshine, and some played marbles on the flattest piece of ground they could find. Two of the older boys came and said they were sorry they had to go now. They explained they were needed at home to help plant the new crop of potatoes.

Hannah studied the two boys as they talked to Daniel. Scantily dressed, but robust, they smiled at him as he listened to them and then gave them a message for their parents.

'Tell them,' he said, pausing for effect, 'you've divided up a whole bag of big numbers with Miss McGee this morning and planted a few rows of new words forby. If you do as well with your potatoes, you'll have plenty to put by for the winter.'

Hannah had to smile when he got each of the boys to repeat his message until he was sure they had it word-perfect. Then he told them both to be sure to come tomorrow, even if it wasn't for the whole day.

'Thank you, sir,' said one. 'We'll do our best,' said the other, and they ran off cheerfully to pick up their battered satchels, which now contained only a pencil and an exercise book, all trace of the morning's piece having disappeared. As they said their goodbyes she suddenly felt quite overwhelmed by sadness.

She was back in the grey stone school in Dundrennan where her sisters had sat before her. In that school, there were plenty of pencils and pens and a monitor to fill their inkpots when they practised their writing in copybooks. Behind the teacher's desk there was a cupboard full of books, as well as those they each had in their satchels. There were proper wooden desks, and chairs, and maps, and pictures, hung around the walls. But in that Scottish school, where she herself had worked for three years as a monitor, the children were often too anxious to speak, even when asked a question during lessons.

'*Silence was golden*' indeed, in that school. If pupils were ever caught talking at any time except 'playtime' they would most certainly be caned.

But then the master, Mr McMurray, was a rigorous, older man who had no great love of children. In his youth he had wanted to be a minister but he had failed in his examinations to get enough marks in theology. The mistress was an elderly spinster whose favourite word was 'discipline'.

The contrast between the two schools was stark indeed. While the parents of children in the small farms around Dundrennan were not particularly well off, their school was entirely free of charge and no child came to school hungry. Here on this mountain, where the meagre soil occurred only in patches, and parents struggled to feed their families, the pupils had little equipment to work with in this makeshift school, but Hannah was now absolutely clear in her mind they had something valuable that had been sadly lacking in Dundrennan.

She felt herself grow thoughtful, as memories of happy times with her sisters when she came home from school continued to flood back. She remembered how they had encouraged her to paint, and embroider, to read aloud to them and write poems. How fortunate she had been.

As they sat together in the warm sunshine enjoying the last of their tea, Hannah decided it would be much more fitting to celebrate all that Marie and Daniel had achieved in this unlikely situation, than regret what might be missing.

She had so many questions she wanted to ask in the remaining minutes of playtime, she hardly knew where to begin, but when Marie came and sat down again after picking up and comforting the littlest girl who had fallen and cut her knee, Hannah told Daniel she had one question, not of an educational nature, that just wouldn't wait any longer, as she'd been puzzling about it all morning.

'And what would that be?' he demanded, turning towards her, his blue eyes twinkling in a way that seemed to suggest he 'saw' more than most sighted people.

'Well, you did ask me to come when I could spare the time,' she began, looking at him and smiling, 'but you greeted me this morning before I'd even said a single word. How *did* you know I was there?'

'Shall I tell her, Marie, or shall I keep it a secret?' he asked, leaning towards his niece with a conspiratorial whisper.

'Well, to tell you the truth, I was wonderin' about that myself?' Marie replied promptly, her large, dark eyes opening wide.

'Well then, if I have double my usual audience, my vanity will always get the better of my inherent modesty,' he said, smiling and turning from one to the other and then seeming to rest his gaze on Hannah.

'It is entirely a process of deduction,' he began. 'I heard footsteps and recognised Sam, and Rose, and Mary, as I would always do, when they walk towards me. But, I then observed that Sam was not talking to Rose in the way he usually does. Mary, however, had just finished making a comment that I did not hear properly, but I deduced from her tone that it had not been addressed to either Sam, or Rose, but probably to an older female companion. The most likely candidate was you, Hannah, my dear. You have a way of inspiring confidence in young people. And you are a very good listener. Don't you agree, Marie?'

'I do indeed, Uncle Daniel,' she said warmly. 'If I knew Hannah was going to come and help you here I could go off happy,' she went on, turning to Hannah herself. 'You see, Hannah, I think my Liam is really thinking of America when it comes to the bit, but he knows I don't want to leave Uncle Daniel and the scholars if there's no one to help him, so he's not admitting it,' she said, shaking her head.

Hannah looked away, touched by the real concern in her eyes. She knew, in that moment, that however much thought she should give to taking this new opportunity being offered to her, some part of her had already decided.

A handful of children in an out-of-the-way place in a remote westerly corner of Ireland, with few prospects of work, or betterment, and no one apart from their ill-provided parents concerned for them. How could she turn her back on them any more than Daniel had, if there was anything she could do to help?

At the end of playtime, when Marie rose to go back to work, Hannah decided she needed some time to herself. She had not intended to stay so long and had brought no piece to eat. If she went back home she could have a bite by the fireside, and come back in time for Daniel's story, which always ended the school day.

She was concerned that neither Marie nor Daniel had had anything to eat themselves, but when she mentioned it to Daniel he explained that he preferred his piece after playtime, while Marie was at work with the children. Marie, he explained, would have a cooked meal waiting for her at her mother's house as soon as school ended, so she only brought food when her mother was away staying with one of her sisters.

One thing was very clear to Hannah as she walked back home to Ardtur and stirred up the dying fire — and that was how well Daniel and Marie worked together. She tried to remember how long it was now since they had begun their work. She counted on her fingers. Rose had been six and Sam not quite five. Rose was now nine and Sam just eight, so it was three years ago.

Perhaps she had thought it was longer because the children going to school seemed such a permanent part of their life, like the visits of the draper from Creeslough who collected her needlework, or their walks up to see Patrick's Aunt Mary, 'over the hill' in Drumnalifferny, or her own visits to the much older couple she had met in Ramelton. The wife had once lived in Dundrennan, though that was long before Hannah was born.

It was when Hannah stood up to go and wash her mug and plate that she noticed the two envelopes on the table. One had been delivered by hand and she recognised the familiar brown envelope without needing to open it. It was the quarterly request for rent. The other envelope had a Scottish postmark and was addressed to Mr Patrick McGinley. The writing was just as familiar as the style and shape of the brown envelope had been. She picked it up and looked at it closely, her eyes filling with tears, staring at it as if there was something the envelope itself could tell her. But she already knew what the letter would say. It always said exactly the same thing.

Her father was sending the money for the boat fares to Scotland, a sum that would be repaid in weekly instalments from the wages of the team of labourers through the next six or seven months. Patrick would organise their departure within the week. He would not return until the autumn. She felt lonely already.

She washed her mug and plate, cut some slices of soda bread and wrapped them up for Daniel, then wandered round the room as if she had forgotten something. But it was nothing she could put a name to, just a feeling that she was soon to be alone and would have to make up her own mind what to do next.

Marie was not getting married till Easter, still

a few weeks away, but it would help both Marie and Daniel if she could decide what she was going to do before Patrick and his team had to make their way to Derry for the boat.

★ ★ ★

She walked slowly back along the familiar track, savouring the first truly spring-like day of the year. The birds were active, darting around in the bushes, taking off and landing in some random activity she could not explain. Somewhere a blackbird was singing. She was almost sure the hawthorns were greener than they'd been in the morning and the sun was now high in a completely blue sky. How often one could look back up at the mountain and see its rugged outline without even a wisp of cloud.

'A pet day' Aunt Mary would call today. A gift to be cherished but not to be expected, something that might not come again, or at least not for a few more weeks.

She gathered her thoughts. What had not been mentioned in any of their talks yet was the question of payment. Clearly Marie did receive a salary, but how much, and when, she did not know. She did know that Rose and Sam took their two pennies each week along with their pieces of turf for the fire every Friday morning, but she guessed that some of the other children would be irregular in their payments. They might indeed bring extra turf, or some potatoes, or meal, but actual money might not always be available. What she could be sure of was that

Daniel would not turn any pupil away because they hadn't brought their pennies.

There was no one sitting on the stone bench as she walked up the slope and all was silent as she approached the open door of the cottage. She paused and listened and after a few moments she heard Daniel's voice. It was a mere whisper, but within moments she found that it was the voice of a Fairy Queen coming to the aid of a princess locked up in a tower in a dark forest. Even here, outside the door, she could hear every word clearly for there was no sound whatever from any of the pupils.

At the end of the story there were cheers, then the scrape of feet on the floor, as the class stood up to recite a blessing, a protection for the dark hours of the night until the dawn came again. She heard the 'Goodbyes' to both Daniel and Marie, as they began to spill out into the dazzling sunshine, going off in both directions, up and down the rough track towards the scattered groups of cottages where they lived.

'Hello, Ma. Have you come back for *us*?' demanded Sam, the moment he set eyes on her.

'No, of course not,' replied Rose quickly. 'We can go home by ourselves, Sam. Haven't we been doing that for all of this year?' she said, looking at Hannah for agreement.

'Yes, of course you can go home by yourselves,' agreed Hannah, giving them each a hug, 'but that's when I'm at home waiting for you. Today, I'm here, because I need to talk a bit more to your teachers. We can all go home together. I'm sure Miss McGee would let you go and look at the books while I'm busy.'

Rose nodded promptly. Clearly, she thought that was a good idea. Sam was less enthusiastic, but at a nod and an encouraging smile from Hannah, he followed Rose back into the cottage, just as Daniel was coming out to greet her.

'Ah, Hannah, you've come back. I thought maybe you'd had enough of school for one day!'

'No, Daniel, not a bit of it. I needed a bite to eat and I knew the fire would need making up. I think I've a few more questions to ask.'

'Well, ask away, for you know you'll only get honest answers, even if it's not to my advantage,' he said, as he sat down at the far end of the stone bench to leave room for her.

Hannah couldn't bear the thought of Daniel being at any disadvantage after the splendid account she'd had of what they'd managed to do for this handful of children. But clearly, Daniel had already faced that possibility and what he said next restored her hope.

'When I first thought of running a school, you may remember a good friend of mine suggested I went round the local gentry and asked them if they could help out,' he said, looking at her directly.

She certainly remembered now that she had encouraged him but she'd forgotten that it was her who suggested he ask their local gentry for help. She'd written letters on his behalf to the charitable organisations active in the county, who might give some support. She'd also made a list of children in Ardtur and the adjoining townlands who might become his pupils, so that he could speak to the parents and see what help might be forthcoming from them.

'I was treated kindly enough but what I collected up wasn't a large sum. In the end it was only enough to get started. A few benches and desks and exercise books and such like. But all that money is gone now,' he went on matter-of-factly. 'When Marie first thought of helping me, we added up the pennies the children brought each week and to begin with, that made a salary for her.

'Not surprisingly,' he went on wryly, 'it proved to be irregular through no fault of the parents, so I had to add to it from some small savings I had,' he said, speaking in the same steady tone he'd used all day. 'Those savings are almost gone and the pension I've had for many years from my half-brother is now in some doubt. If that goes, I won't be able to pay my own rent, never mind find a salary for an assistant,' he went on quickly, with a short laugh. 'Probably, we did well to manage for as long as we did, but now I need an income for me, as well as for a teacher. There's nothing for it but to ask for a miracle,' he ended, throwing up his hands towards the blue sky, his voice grown solemn.

She'd certainly have to agree; if that were the case, the prospects looked bleak. She was surprised now that he and Marie had asked her to come and even more surprised that given the overall situation they had both talked with such enthusiasm about all they had done.

She looked closely at his face, now in shadow as the sun sank beyond the ridge of the mountain behind them. The brilliant blue sky remained, but the temperature had dropped suddenly and she shivered.

He took a deep breath and went on.

'You must be wondering why, in the circumstances, I asked you to come and kept you from your sewing and your work at home. I've been asking myself that too,' he added, laughing wryly. 'But I have thought long and hard and I still have this feeling that if anyone could see a way forward, it would be my friend Hannah. She's the girl from Galloway who gave up her comfortable home and left Scotland, left all her family and friends to marry the man she loved and to make a home and a family for him on an Irish mountainside. That's the kind of miracle that might save the school.'

4

'Daniel, I'll only be a moment or two,' said Hannah quickly, as she stood up. 'I'm just going to see what the children are up to now school's over. I expect Marie will be leaving soon to go to her mother's.'

She hurried across to the door of the cottage, preoccupied with what he had just said about needing a miracle. She was dazzled by the strong light reflecting off the whitewashed walls, her mind racing as she wondered what she could possibly say to him in reply.

She peered into the shadowy room. Marie was nowhere to be seen, but over by the back window where the light was best, Rose was sitting on a chair reading to her brother. Sam sat cross-legged on the floor, looking up at his sister with a solemn face. He was listening to every word.

'Well, are they reading?' asked Daniel, as she came and sat down again on his right side — the best position for catching the gleams of light from the lough and an occasional sight of the swans.

'Yes, they are,' she replied. 'And a very good advertisement for your school, they are too,' she added firmly. 'I'm quite amazed to see Sam listening so attentively and I did think Rose was reading rather well.'

'Well, like their mother, they're bright,' he

said. 'A pity this country of ours can't offer them somewhat more in the way of schooling,' he went on, an unusual note of bitterness creeping into his voice.

'I owe you some explanations, Hannah,' he said directly, before she had time to reply. 'When I told you of my plan to set up a school some years back, I said I had a pension from an estate where I once worked. That wasn't strictly true. It was my mother who worked for the estate. She was a servant, lovely to look at by all accounts and foolish enough not to resist the advances of a very affluent young man. He was my father, of whom we will not speak,' he said abruptly, pausing and staring away towards the far horizon.

'It was *his* father, and not him, who made some attempt at reparations to my mother's family when she died in childbirth and I lost what little sight I might ever have had. He provided for me in childhood, sending me first to school and later to live with my aunt, Marie's grandmother. It was he who set up a pension for my lifetime.'

Hannah realised suddenly that she did know something of Daniel's background but it had seemed such a long time since he'd told her that his mother had died at his birth and that he'd been brought up by her older sister. She cast her mind back, trying to remember details of what had not seemed all that important at the time.

'It was that pension and your encouragement that let me set up this school in the first place,' Daniel continued. 'Without his provision and

44

your good sense, the children you saw today would have no possibility of betterment. I do have hopes for them and whether my hopes succeed or fail, I'd still like to share them with you as I did in the first place.'

Hannah was about to say she had done very little to help him apart from listen and write a few letters on his behalf, but he did not even pause. Staring away across the rocky path that led down to the lake, he went on quickly, his voice softer.

'Do you remember the story you told me one of those afternoons when I came to see you, when I first talked about starting the school? You told me of your father's family being evicted from Strathnaver and the way your father and uncle travelled the length of Scotland on 'burn water and the kindness of the poor'.' He turned towards her and dropped his voice as he quoted her exact words.

For a moment, Hannah couldn't speak, tears jumping unbidden to her eyes. How could she ever forget that story, one her father had told over and over again?

Daniel was repeating the words 'burn water and the kindness of the poor' to himself, as if they had some special significance for him. When he spoke to her again, his tone was firmer.

'If I can somehow find the resources to go on with the school, I have a project in mind as ambitious as your father's wanting to own a farm,' he announced firmly. 'I want to teach these children English. Or Scotch, as they call it in these parts,' he added, laughing wryly, 'so that, whether they go, or stay, they'll have more possibilities open to them than they have at present.'

'But how would you do that, Daniel?' she asked, baffled at the very idea of it.

'Very easily, my friend, if I *still* had a school to teach in.' He hesitated and then went on: 'If I've had the foolishness to deny all knowledge of English, and indeed of having been educated, because of the nationalistic fervour of my youth, then I think it's time I found some way of reversing that limiting decision.'

Hannah was completely taken aback. He had switched to English, had spoken firmly, and fluently, when she'd never heard him speak anything other than a soft and eloquent Irish. To her amazement, he had moved completely away from the captivating, melodic voice so admired by all who gathered nightly to listen to his stories and poems. He was speaking just as fluently as he spoke in Irish, but his English was more formal in tone and had a much sharper edge than anything she had ever heard him say in Irish. But the real shock for Hannah was that she recognised an accent rarely to be heard in the hills of Donegal.

She thought how the villagers or even her own dear Patrick might react if he heard someone speak in this manner.

'Sure, he's gentry at the least and maybe some lord or other. I've only heard one man talk like that and he was a lord, some visitor or other from England to Stewart of Ards,' she imagined her husband saying.

'You can see there would be a problem for me,' Daniel went on quickly, before she had recovered herself. 'My change of approach to the language of our overlords could cause problems with people who have known me for a long time. They might find it hard to accommodate their view of me to my new way of speaking.'

'But would you feel you had to speak English outside the classroom?' she asked, now moving to English herself.

It would be a shock indeed for all the friends and neighbours who were just as unaware of this part of Daniel's history as she had been herself.

To her surprise, he did not answer her question directly. Instead, he began to explain how this state of affairs had come about.

'My pension comes from the estate of an English lord you'll probably never have heard of. His family once had land in Donegal, but sold it off at the turn of the last century to concentrate on their English lands. Some of the family are well known for their interest in agriculture and the improvements and innovations they've made and written about.

'Over the years of my life those estates have been divided up between a number of sons. Some flourished, some didn't. Last week, I had a letter telling me that as the pension I received was discretionary and in the gift of the title holder, now deceased, I would have to provide evidence 'of my right to continue receiving the aforementioned sum',' he said, the now familiar sharpness of his tone moving towards real bitterness.

47

'You know yourself, Hannah, that these days, between trying to improve their land and not always getting their rents, any more than the landlords here, English landlords are looking for savings on their outgoings just as much as the ones in Ireland are. I would imagine it's not even a personal thing. It's probably just some man of business looking to see where economies could be made for his employer.'

'So you could lose your pension?' she asked anxiously.

'To be strictly accurate, I've already lost it. It has been suspended for the moment, until I make an appeal. Meantime, I can afford a bite to eat, but I may not have enough to pay the quarter's rent and it's due at the end of the month.'

Hannah took a deep breath, utterly distressed at the thought of Daniel being without money.

'Don't distress yourself, my dear,' he said quickly, his voice softening, as he moved back to speaking Irish. 'Much worse things have been happening to my countrymen for several centuries now. If all else fails I would at least be eligible for the new workhouse in Dunfanaghy where I could continue speaking Irish and thereby keep hidden the secret of my unfortunate birth.'

Hannah worried about Daniel and the future of the school. It had been very discouraging to begin with, but they had persisted in their efforts and eventually one trader in Dunfanaghy produced a sum of money quite beyond their expectations. At the very same time, Marie

48

finished her training as a teacher and decided that instead of staying in Dublin as she had planned, she would come home to be near the young man with whom she'd fallen in love. At that point, Marie and Daniel had made their plans, had decided to travel hopefully, and things had gone rather well.

It was a very different situation now. Marie was going and without Daniel's pension there was not enough money to support a master, never mind an assistant. Keeping the school going looked almost impossible and the project of teaching English seemed highly doubtful, if not already condemned to failure.

★ ★ ★

Apart from Sam saying that he was hungry, and very thirsty, neither of the children said very much on the way home. The temperature was dropping rapidly as the sun fell yet lower behind the mountain, but the late afternoon was still bright.

Hannah knew she was preoccupied with all she and Daniel had talked about, but now as she picked her way along the rocky path overlooking the lough, she remembered she hadn't had time before school to fetch water from the well. There might be some left in the bucket but even if there was, there was only the remains of yesterday's bread and neither jam nor butter to put on it.

She felt suddenly tired as they turned off the broad track and began to make their way up the well-trodden path to the main group of cottages and outbuildings. The door of their own cottage was open and for a moment she was alarmed.

One of the many things she had to learn when she first arrived in Ardtur was that there were no locks on doors. Neither were there any thieves. Patrick's explanation was that there was nothing worth stealing, but her nearest neighbour, Sophie O'Donovan, had explained more fully that if there was no one at home a neighbour might come to leave something on the table, an item they had borrowed, or a jug of milk, or butter that had been asked for. As often as not, in a village of open doors, they did not close the door behind them unless it was raining hard or the wind had got up.

There was indeed something sitting on the table as they came in together. Three things, in fact. As the children hung up their schoolbags she lifted the lid on a familiar covered dish and found a large pat of butter.

'You're in luck, children,' she cried. 'Aunt Mary's sent us down our butter. Shall we make some toast with yesterday's bread?' she asked, as she peered at the other large item, her own baking bowl that contained chopped-up potatoes.

For a moment she was puzzled. The potatoes were not peeled but they had been cut in pieces.

'Of course,' she said to herself, smiling as she remembered the message Daniel had made the two boys memorise earlier in the day when they'd sat in the sun at playtime. She tried to recall it: *You've divided up a whole lot of numbers and planted some rows of words . . . if your potatoes do as well you'll have plenty to put aside for the winter* . . . Well, something like that, she decided, as Sam asked if he could fill the kettle for her and Rose began to fetch mugs from the dresser.

A moment later, Patrick appeared at the door, his face streaked with sweat, a second, slightly smaller baking bowl in his hands.

'Da, are ye plantin'?' cried Rose.

'Can I come and help you, Da? asked Sam. 'When we've had our tea and toast,' he added quickly.

Patrick kissed them all and then met Hannah's gaze.

'We got finished quicker than we thought and yer man let us go early,' he explained, 'an' I foun' yer father's letter waitin' on the table. Ye've not looked at it yet,' he went on, glancing at the brown envelope, sitting just where he had left it. 'He wants us at the end of next week.'

Hannah's heart sank. 'So soon?'

'Aye, well it's not far off the usual. The season's a wee bit earlier in your part of the world, but I thought I'd better make a start on the tatties, seein' we've a wee bit more groun' since old Hughie died.'

She nodded and took the water bucket from Sam who had fetched it from the cupboard. There was just about a kettle full left in the bottom. The seed potatoes and the plans for next week could all wait till they'd stirred up the fire, made the tea and sat round the table exchanging the news of the day from Casheltown and Tullygobegley, over toast and Aunt Mary's butter.

5

Cutting the seed potatoes to create an 'eye' in each portion was not a very skilled job, but Patrick, always cautious by nature, and knowing the children would want to help as soon as they came home, had made sure they were done properly by cutting the pieces himself and leaving them ready on the table.

Now, when he went back to the work of planting the main crop, Rose and Sam followed him, knowing exactly what they had to do. As he turned over the soil, they would place the cut portions, eye side up, where he pointed. Without their help the continuous bending would have made the job both painful and exhausting.

Hannah was grateful that the children were now old enough to help him with the planting. As she began to clear the table and think what needed doing next, she was equally grateful that she had an empty kitchen. There was quite enough to do to catch up on the day's tasks, but now she also had to give her mind to all the extra things that needed doing to get ready for Patrick's departure.

Part of her mind was indeed focused on what had to be done right now — making up the fire, fetching drinking water and washing water and making champ for their supper — but, try as she might, she could not stop thinking about the experiences of the morning.

She had been quite amazed at Daniel's capacity to teach so effectively despite his disability. She'd always assumed Marie had done most of the work and Daniel had confined himself to Irish history and storytelling. Then she thought of how amazed she'd been to find he had such a command of English. But, most of all, what simply would not leave her mind was the unbearable thought that should he not manage to get his pension reinstated, he'd not only have to give up the school, and his dream of teaching his pupils English, but he might have no option but to go into the workhouse.

And then her eyes fell on the napkins, still waiting to be hemmed.

The napkins were the least of her worries. It was true that the draper, expected tomorrow, would not pay for an incomplete dozen, but given the rest of her month's work, baled and wrapped ready in the dust and smoke-free safety of the bedroom, that was no cause for worry. She'd almost finished her full assignment. He would take all she had done, make a note of the missing four and pay her for that complete dozen when he came next time.

When he handed over the money for this month's work, she'd already have enough to pay for the meal and flour they bought regularly, the milk from her neighbour and the butter from Aunt Mary. The delayed income on the final dozen would not leave her short this month.

She took a deep breath and tried to collect herself. She reminded herself that it was not just a question of money. She always felt anxious and unsettled when Patrick was going away and this was the way it usually showed itself. She'd simply worry quite unnecessarily about something or other.

'Surely, after all these years, I should be used to it,' she said aloud in the empty kitchen.

Of the two of them, she was the more practical one. She was certainly better at ensuring they always had enough money for food and the essential clothing for Patrick she couldn't make herself, the heavy trousers and the underwear he needed till the weather got warmer, the boots that got such hard wear, the cap he wore both winter and summer.

Compared to most of their neighbours, especially those with five or six children, they were well off. She saved in the summer when Patrick sent home money every week and had it by her if there was no work for him over the winter. Of course, this last winter there had actually been some work on the roof of the farmhouse at Tullygobegley so she had not had to dip into so much of last summer's savings.

Sometimes too, her father sent her a gift of money after the harvest, but this she never used. The gold coins rested in a small fabric bag she'd made for them and were kept in a box that had a place in the hard earth under their bed.

Patrick had smiled and shaken his head some years back when she'd asked him to dig a hole to hide the old wooden box. Sometimes, since then, he would make her laugh by suggesting some extravagance like a new dress for her, or a waistcoat for himself. Then, knowing he was joking, she would say: '*But if I did that I'd have to get you to dig under the bed.*'

She smiled, feeling easier, as she peeled the last of the potatoes for supper and went outside for the handful of scallions to chop up and mix in with them when they were cooked and mashed with Aunt Mary's butter.

'Come on, Hannah,' she said to herself, as she waved to Patrick and the children at the far end of the garden. 'Why don't you just accept that you wish he didn't have to go, so you could share your bed every night and have the comfort of his arms?'

★ ★ ★

Supper was later than usual that evening and both children were so tired they could hardly keep their eyes open while they ate. They'd done very well, Patrick insisted. Sure, they were nearly half the way down one side and now they had the whole weekend ahead of them. There was no school and he would have his two helpers for both days. Sure, wasn't that just great?

Rose and Sam smiled at him wearily, looked pleased and made no protests whatever about going to bed.

'I don't think we'll be far behind them,' said Patrick, as she came back from tucking them in.

'You're right there, love. I don't think I could thread a needle this evening, never mind hem another napkin.'

'Aye, ye look tired. Did ye have a busy day?' he said gently. 'I wondered where ye were when the house was empty for ye said last night ye'd a batch to finish.'

She looked across at him. His face was still tanned even after the winter, his hair as dark as his eyes that looked straight at her, as they always did, with that gentleness she remembered from their very first meeting when she was only seventeen.

'I'm going to miss you so much, my love,' she said, suddenly, surprising herself.

'An' sure, d'ye not think I'm goin' to miss you just as much?' he replied briskly. 'It wou'dn't be much good, wou'd it, if it didn't matter all that much one way or another?'

She laughed and shook her head. 'You're quite right, but I'd love to have you home all the year round.'

'Aye, well. I'd need no persuadin', but sure what is there by way of work here? An' even if we were in Scotland an' me not an educated man, I'd still have to travel about the place,' he said, his voice dropping.

'Being educated is not the be all and end all of a man. There are other things just as important,' she said firmly.

He just looked at her as he bent down to the hearth to smoor the fire with turves, so it would stay alight all night.

She watched him placing the turves methodically with his habitual look of total concentration, then got to her feet and lit the small oil lamp to take them to bed.

* * *

56

In the end she told him the whole story of Daniel and the school and how he wanted to teach his pupils English. Sitting by the fire, on their few remaining evenings, she didn't even put out her hand for her sewing bag, but sat enjoying a mug of tea with him as she waited to see if he had yet more questions to ask.

'An' if he could get his pension back, wou'd he be able to pay an assistant to take the place o' Marie?'

'Well, it would be a start, but then the income from the children is very variable,' she said steadily. 'You know Rose and Sam have their two pennies each, every week, and the turf's not a problem, but there are other children who would be less regular and there must be some can only pay at certain times of the year when there's less flour and meal to buy.'

'Aye, it depends, doesn't it?' he said thoughtfully. 'An' if yer man were to put the rent up, sure that has to come first, or the family's out on the street! Have ye any idea what to do to help him? Sure, you're far better at these things than I am. I wou'dn't have any idea what to do.'

His face was a picture of distress and she longed to be able to tell him it was all going to be all right. But she couldn't do that. He'd been honest and she would try to do the same.

'Well, I can certainly write letters for him. But I'd need to know who to write to and what to say,' she began, laughing. 'It's not so much my command of Irish as having to use the right legal phrases and so on. I thought I'd ask our friends in Ramelton. Joseph and Catriona know all the

57

professional people, the doctor, and the land steward, and the minister. I'm sure there must be a solicitor they know as well who would be able to tell me how to go about it.'

'Ye might have to go under the bed for that,' he said promptly, a small smile flickering across his face. 'But it might be worth it. Wou'd ye like to go back to the teachin' yerself, like ye did afore I stole ye away?'

'I hadn't thought about it before,' she confessed. 'But like I told you Daniel hoped I might be able to help him out.'

'I know what yer father wou'd say,' he went on quickly. 'That money is meant for you, Hannah, to use in any way you want.' He looked at her, his usually mobile face almost stiff with concentration, his eyes sharply focused on her. 'Say the word and I'll dig it out fer you in the morning.'

'But, Patrick, we might need that money,' she protested. 'What would we do if one of the children needed a doctor? Or if you had an accident, heaven forbid, and couldn't work . . . '

'Hannah, you know I'm not a religious man an' I only go to Mass now an' again to keep Aunt Mary and the priest happy, but I think you always know what wou'd be the right thing. Just you send up a wee prayer and you'll not go far wrong. An' I'll do all I can to help, for Daniel's a good man and I know you're a great teacher yerself . . . sure, didn't you teach me an' those other young fellas who were with me then long years ago at the farm? Some o' them had never even held a pencil, or a pen, in their lives before.'

To her great distress, Hannah felt tears stream down her face. She wondered if perhaps, in the firelight, they might not show, but what Patrick did next was unambiguous. He came and put his arms round her, took out his large, crumpled handkerchief, wiped away her tears and held her close.

'Not a word now,' he said softly. 'We'll go and sleep on it and see what the light of day shows us in the mornin'. You do the lamp an' I'll see to the fire.'

★ ★ ★

The remaining days flew by. The potatoes were planted, the draper came and collected Hannah's consignment of napkins and left her a bale of new ones. Before she'd even counted them, she mended the older pair of Patrick's working trousers and reinforced the new pair he'd bought in Derry on his way home last autumn. She baked wheaten bread and oatcakes that would supplement what food the men could buy on the journey and threaded new shoelaces into well-polished boots.

Patrick himself went round the house looking for jobs that might need doing. He borrowed a ladder and replaced some worn straw rope on the thatch of the roof ridge just to be sure it would not suffer with summer storms, then he took the donkey and cart and collected turf from his piece of bog to replenish the stack by the gable and build it up as high as it would go in case of bad weather.

One morning he got up very early indeed. He needed to walk over to Churchill to look for the carrier he knew there and catch him before he set out on his day's work. For some years now, Keiran Murphy had brought his wagon over to the old churchyard by St Columbkille's tiny, ruined church at the head of Lough Gartan. There he waited till the men from round about who were bound for the Derry boat came with their families. It was the custom when the men were going off for many long months for the family to walk with them and keep them company as far as the church, join with them in asking a blessing and then say their goodbyes.

Now, Patrick paid Keiran a deposit out of the money his father-in-law had sent him and when the day and time were agreed, walked back to Ardtur knowing it would not be long before Hannah would be back there with him to say their farewells.

Hannah had always found both parting and the accompanying rituals hard to bear. She agreed bidding goodbye to the men bound for Scotland was not as sad as when families went to a place like The Bridge of Tears at the back of Muckish, to say what would probably be a final farewell to immigrants bound for America, but she still found the parting weighed heavy, surrounded by weeping women and distraught children.

Patrick had long ago agreed with her that the children should not come, but would go to school as usual, but she knew he needed her to be there with him, particularly so she could meet all his workmates, some of whom were going for the first time. These men and boys would be his constant companions for the next six or seven months. So she would go, she would try not to cry, but as the time grew shorter she longed for the parting to be safely over and Patrick's first letter to her, written on the Derry boat, secure in the pocket of her apron.

★ ★ ★

The April departure day was cloudy with the odd drifting shower, but there was no cold and the air was so still that the early evening crossing from Derry would probably be flat calm.

As Hannah walked back alone from the stone-built oratory where each man had laid a tiny item on the altar — a coin, or a woven cross, or a card with a prayer on it — she felt a dragging weariness. She blamed it on the early rise and the long walk, but a mile or so from the ancient churchyard she felt a familiar dampness between her legs.

She sighed and knew the first thing she had to do when she got home was to fold a pad of old, torn fabric from the supply she kept in the bedroom and put her stained knickers to soak in cold water before she tried to wash them.

She was glad the door was still closed when she walked wearily up the last rocky slope. No letter on the table, no offering from a neighbour, nothing to prevent her making herself comfortable and then sitting by the fire with a mug of tea.

She did what was necessary and sat down gratefully. Comfortable now, the pain in her back eased by a cushion carefully placed, she sat looking into the fire and found herself overwhelmed with sadness. For days now she'd been aware that her monthly bleeding was late. She'd had to keep reminding herself not to tell Patrick. If she had told him, he would have been so pleased, and so hopeful, for he had long wanted them to add to their small family. But it was not to be. At least she had not raised his hopes. There was no harm done.

Patrick's wish to add to their family was not the familiar pressure of a man wanting sons, like her father had, it was a longing for the family he himself had never had. His mother had died in childbirth and he had been brought up an only child, by his Aunt Mary, who had never married. He had longed for brothers and sisters then. It was some time after they were married before Rose and Sam appeared and he had been so delighted.

But their arrival had not happened easily. There were delays and difficulties. Hannah had miscarried several times. She had been reassured by friends and neighbours that miscarrying once, twice, or even three times, before a first child was not unusual. But when that happened to her, Patrick was beside himself with distress.

Sadly, even after the safe arrivals of Rose and Sam there were further miscarriages. That was why she'd been so hoping for this last week or more, that she might carry a third child while Patrick was in Scotland. That would have been such good news to share in their letters. But the stain had made it clear. She was simply late. There was no pregnancy to celebrate.

Suddenly, she felt overwhelmed with weariness and sadness, feeling the emptiness of the house and the long months ahead before Patrick's return. Whatever this year of 1845 might bring she could now be sure it would not bring the longed-for third child.

6

It was a mild, sunny morning a few days later when Hannah, hearing the sound of footsteps, looked up from her sewing and found a tall stranger standing at the open door clearly deciding whether to rap with his knuckles on the wood itself or to use the impressive knocker, the work of a local blacksmith and a gift brought as a welcome present from her Scots friend, Catriona, who lived in Ramelton.

'Good morning, do come in,' she said, standing up, immediately curious as to what such a well-dressed stranger could possibly want.

He returned her greeting so hesitantly, with so brief an apology for his inadequate Irish as he doffed his hat, that she laughed.

'Well, your lack of Irish will not stand between us,' she replied, switching to English, and observing the look of profound relief that crossed his rather angular but handsome face.

'Were you looking for someone?' she asked, unable to contain her curiosity any longer.

'Yes, I was. A Mister Patrick McGinley. I have some friends in Dunfanaghy and one of them mentioned that he spoke some 'Scotch' as they called it, and so would be able to tell me about the conditions here. Specifically, the work available — or lack of it — for those with very small acreages. I should explain,' he went on quickly, 'that I work part-time for a charitable organisation concerned with the economic difficulties you've been experiencing in Ireland, particularly since the famine year back in 1838. If we knew more about the causes of the problems we might be in a better position to help.'

'My goodness, how splendid,' replied Hannah, as she waved him to the other armchair. 'I'm afraid the bad news is that my husband is already in Scotland for the harvesting season, but the better news is that my English is much better than his and I may be able to help you. If I can't answer your questions then I'm sure I know someone who can.'

She smiled to herself when she saw an undisguised look of relief spread across his face. *Poor man*, she thought, *this is not exactly the sort of place he's familiar with.* In the way he spoke, there was more than a trace of an accent that spoke of formal education. She was already wondering what he and Daniel might make of each other.

'Now, please make yourself at home. I was about to make a mug of tea,' she began. 'I hope you'll eat a piece of cake before you ask your questions. How did you get here, by the way?' she asked, noticing for the first time his boots, highly polished but not exactly in keeping with his very well-cut tweed suit.

'I walked,' he said smiling and relaxing somewhat, 'But only from Churchill,' he added. 'My friends in Dunfanaghy lent me their pony and trap, but they said it was too rough going for the mare beyond the village. I think they envisaged me being 'cowped into the ditch' as we might say at home,' he ended, grinning.

'And home is?'

'Yorkshire. A big, old house outside Pickering. My family are clothing manufacturers, have been for a long time. I have three brothers working with me, so it's possible for me to be away at certain times of the year.'

He stood up again as she set her sewing aside and reached for the kettle. 'Forgive me for not introducing myself sooner. Jonathan Hancock, at your service, ma'am,' he said with a smile as he held out his hand. 'Would I be right in thinking you come from somewhat further north on that same island across the water? Across the border, perhaps?'

She laughed as she filled the kettle from the enamelled bucket and hung it over the fire, thinking as she did of the way in which people put together the clues to make a stranger less strange, exactly as they had both just done.

'Yes, I suppose I still have my Scots accent when I speak English,' she said, as the thought occurred to her. 'I lived near Dundrennan, in Galloway, and my husband is there right now working for my father.'

'And you are here on your own?' he asked, surprised.

She shook her head. 'No, I'm here because we have two children at school. They're still too young to make that long journey, even setting aside the expense,' she explained, as she brought mugs and a jug of milk to the table.

'And there is a school? I'd not heard about that.'

'That's not entirely surprising,' she replied, turning towards him as she took out the cake tin and cut him a generous slice. 'It's not a National School, not up here; it's what the Irish call a hedge school. Do you know about them?'

'No, I've never heard of a hedge school,' he said slowly. 'Surely they can't be in hedges!'

'Some were, apparently,' she replied, 'but, fairly, more were in abandoned houses, or sheep folds that had been given a sod roof, or a covering of layers of branches. Have you heard of the Penal Laws?' she asked gently, as she heated the teapot.

'Oh yes, I *do* know about those,' he said. 'They discriminated against Catholics in particular and everyone else in general, other than Anglicans, of course, so they couldn't have churches, or chapels, or priests, or meeting houses. There's a Mass rock in a field near where my cousins live, not far from Creeslough. I asked them if it was still in use and they said it was, but apparently, the law has either been removed or has simply faded away. Must have done, for there's now a chapel nearby,' he said, as she helped him to a slice of cake.

'I don't think they've been repealed,' she replied dubiously, 'but certainly there are chapels and priests, though some remote areas have no money for a building. That's mainly why Mass rocks are still being used. But the reason I asked,' she went on, 'is because the Penal Laws *also* discriminated against Catholic *education*. They weren't allowed to have schools even where there might have been the money to create one.

So people had to improvise. They're still doing it. Though I should say the 'authorities' whoever they might be, do now just turn a blind eye. There's a hedge school in the next townland run by a friend of mine and his niece in his own cottage,' she said. 'Or at least there is at this moment. They have financial problems and may have to close.'

She paused as she poured the tea and then turned towards him. 'I'll tell you anything I can that you want to know but if I'm defeated I'll find reinforcements for you. I think perhaps you've come just at the right moment.'

★ ★ ★

The more they talked, the more sure she was that Jonathan Hancock was going to be able to help. However different his life might be, he seemed to have a capacity to understand very different situations, and he quickly revealed that he knew perfectly well how much, or how little, land was needed to feed a family if there was no other source of income.

'Do you mind telling me how much land you have yourself?' he asked politely.

'No, of course not,' she said. 'I can see perfectly well why you need to know, but I do get confused with the Irish system of measurement, especially the roods and perches. At home, we had the five-acre field and the ten, or the twenty, so I can visualise those. But the small measures here are beyond me. But I do know that last year the landlord did transfer a piece of land from a cottage that became derelict when its elderly owner died. At least a rood, I was told. He put up the rent, of course, but it means we have an extra piece of potato garden. We can walk round it later if you like. My husband and the children planted the potatoes before he went to Scotland.'

Jonathan looked away and for some moments he didn't speak. She saw such a look of sadness pass across his face that she forgot what she was going to say about their nearest neighbours and the struggle they had to feed their much larger families on the smaller patches of garden they had.

She waited patiently as he produced a pencil and notebook. He put it down on the edge of the table but did not begin to write.

'I've read a good deal about Ireland from various travellers but I had no idea how difficult it might be,' he began. 'My relatives both in Creeslough and in Armagh are all landowners, and while they're kind-hearted people and generous in their own way, some of them just don't appreciate the situation many of their tenants are in,' he began, his body tight with tension. 'They can't see that only radical change will remove the risk that all these people live with.'

'If you mean political change, I'm afraid I'm not very well informed there,' Hannah came back at him. 'I've always felt that the lawmakers were too far away from the problems. I could never see how their deliberations could meet the situation if they'd never had experience of it for themselves.'

To her surprise, he laughed — a genuine, warm-hearted laugh.

'You would be so welcome at our local Meeting,' he said, enthusiastically. 'There are some wise people there and they insist that the first thing you must do, if you want to help people, is to go and look at the situation and try to see it from their perspective. That's what the Friends have tried to do; that's why I'm here.'

'So you're a Friend, are you?' she asked, beaming at him. She knew a little about the Quakers and their principles. 'I thought you might be. I have some cousins in Scotland who go to Meetings in Dumfries. I do know a little about your beliefs though my own family were Covenanters, good-hearted and kind, in my father's case, but usually very rigid and unbending.'

The talk moved on as they shared their very different lives and activities. It was quite some time before Jonathan paused and picked up his notebook.

'I think you've just answered a question for me I didn't know I needed to ask,' he said with a smile. 'Here I was, focused on information, like acreages, but what I really need to know is how the Central Committee could help improve matters. In this situation, in this place, at this time. What most needs doing right here? Now.'

'I think I *can* help you there,' she said, intrigued by the change in his mood, 'but might I suggest that first you begin making whatever notes you need to make, while I go and find some eggs to make us a bite of lunch.'

70

Jonathan had protested politely that he couldn't possibly impose upon her for lunch, but by that point in their conversation she was quite at ease with him. She remembered what she had once read about the Quaker view of life, their commitment to 'plain speaking' and to honesty in all their dealings. That had always seemed so appropriate to her.

Suddenly, as she searched in the outhouse for hidden eggs, she remembered her eldest sister explaining to her that Quakers would not swear oaths but only give their word. For a long time, she said, they had not been able to be Members of Parliament because of their unwillingness to swear. Her sister couldn't remember who was responsible for solving that problem, but 'affirmation' came to be accepted as the equivalent of 'swearing'. It was, of course, in keeping with the simple Quaker doctrine, that 'My Yea is my Yea, and my Nay is my Nay'. The first Quaker Members of Parliament, mostly Scottish, were then able to take their seats.

Jonathan was scribbling vigorously as she came back into the cottage by the back door, three brown eggs in one hand and a covered dish of butter in the other.

'I have to confess I was hungry,' he said later, as he wiped his plate with a piece of bread, but I had not the slightest expectation of anyone giving me such a nice lunch, or indeed any lunch at all. Thank you so much. I do hope there is something I might be able to do in return.'

71

She laughed and pointed to his notebook. 'I haven't got anything written down, *but* I do have a list in my head,' she said. 'Could I share your practice of plain speaking and tell you what is on my list?'

'I should be delighted,' he said firmly. 'I've only got two more days here and then I'm due to go to Armagh.' His voice dropped markedly. 'I'll probably get back in the autumn, but you can always write to me, care of my home address if there's something else I can do. My housekeeper will always know where I am. Now, tell me more.'

★　★　★

After lunch a heavy shower of sleet came sweeping down the valley. It cleared as quickly as it had come, but one look at the sky and Hannah knew she'd better warn her visitor that he stood to get thoroughly soaked if he didn't get off the mountain before rain settled in for the rest of the day.

'The children might just get home dry from school but with them I can at least change their clothes by the fire,' she said, looking him up and down as he stood up, put his notebook in his pocket, and nodded.

'I'd like to have met them, Hannah, but I might manage that another time. This area of Donegal and the area round the city of Armagh is my personal research territory because I have family connections there. I've been to both places often enough, but I haven't yet any contacts for this work in Armagh. Do you know Armagh at all?'

'No', she said, sadly. 'I came straight to Donegal on the Derry boat, so I've seen nothing of the rest of Ulster. I'd love to travel, but I haven't even travelled in Scotland, just from Dundrennan to Gretna Green and then along the coast north and west to a little place called Cairnryan. One of my brothers, Matthew, married into a boat-building family nearby. He gave us a bed for the night and wished us joy on our marriage. It was very good of him for I hadn't seen him for years. He's the youngest of the brothers, but still much older than I am,' she said, as she walked to the door with him and looked up again at the threatening sky.

'I don't know how to thank you,' he said. 'I've learnt more from you in one morning than I've learnt in most of my reading and all my efforts to study reports from the Central Committee. I shall write and tell you what I've been able to arrange. Please,' he said solemnly, 'will you keep me informed of anything you think I might be able to do. I do hope we'll meet again.' He held out his hand as a few large drops of melted sleet dripped from the thatch.

'Good luck,' she said. 'I'll do anything I possibly can to help.'

He raised a hand in salute and moved swiftly down the rocky track, which now glistened with moisture.

★ ★ ★

She moved around the kitchen, clearing the table, bringing out mugs for the children's expected tea. What an extraordinary thing to happen. Even before she had worked out exactly what needed to be done to resolve the problems of the school and Daniel's threatened income, help had appeared in the most unlikely guise.

He'd given her the name of an elderly Quaker who had been a solicitor and was still entirely capable of advising her what to say and what to write in order to see if there might be hope for restoring Daniel's pension. He'd also assured her that reading books, pencils and paper could be provided quite quickly for the school and that she would receive at the same time a list of educational aids, like maps and copybooks, from a Quaker-run organisation in Dublin who would provide them free of charge.

As she refilled the kettle and took up her sewing, she wondered what Patrick and her father would say when they heard her news. Patrick would probably say: 'Sure, haven't you the lucky touch an' always have had,' while her father would laugh and say: 'Sure, didn't you always get what you wanted but never let it spoil you.' As for Daniel, he might not say very much at all, but she would look forward to seeing the anxiety melt away when she shared with him all that had happened since a smartly dressed stranger had knocked at the door in the middle of the morning.

7

The children were unlucky. They were almost home when the next heavy shower caught them as they turned off the main track along the lakeside and hurried up the steep, rocky track towards the open door where their mother stood waiting.

'Come in. Come in,' she said, looking at their rain-spattered clothes, 'and take off your wet things.' She handed each of them a warm towel to dry their faces and hair. 'Are your shirts wet through?'

'No, that's why we ran,' said Rose, breathlessly, as Hannah looked them over.

'We have a message for you from Daniel,' Sam mumbled, his head now enveloped in his towel. 'He said we were to give it to you right away,' he added urgently, as he emerged, his damp red hair sticking out in tufts, his face even paler than usual from the final race up the track.

'Well, you can give it to me as soon as you've dried yourselves. Are your shoes wet?'

They agreed that they were, and took them off, placing them to dry well back from the fire so that the leather would not be damaged. The other children at school didn't have shoes, but Rose and Sam had shoes for wintertime. When the weather got warmer they would be put away and they would pick their steps gingerly down the track until their feet hardened again and they could run without having to look out for every piece of projecting stone.

'Well then, what about this message?' she asked, as they took it in turns to comb their damp hair.

She tried not to smile as Sam drew himself up to his full height and repeated exactly what Daniel had asked him to say. Rose then made her equally well-rehearsed addition.

'Well, then,' Hannah said, 'if you have some tea, I'll go and ask Sophie if you can stay with her till I come back. Could you take a book and read to her? You know she likes that.' She brought bread and butter to the table and poured their tea, her mind already fully occupied with what they had just said.

Sophie O'Donovan, her elderly neighbour, lived with her son a very short distance away. Jamsey was one of the younger men who had gone to Scotland with Patrick, and Hannah had assured him before he went that she would 'keep an eye' on the older woman. As she expected, Sophie was glad to have the prospect of company, though Hannah knew she'd have been even happier if instead of their storybooks, the children had been able to read the newspapers, which came to Sophie by various means. She loved reading the news and the fact that the newspapers were usually weeks, if not months old, troubled her not at all; it was only the smallness of the print that defeated her elderly eyes but had not dimmed her fascination with the doings in the wider world.

'I won't be long, Sophie, but Daniel says he

needs to speak to me. Can I send them over when they finish their tea?'

'Sure, don't hurry yerself, woman, I'm not goin' anywhere an' they're no trouble at all.'

Hannah threw a shawl over her everyday clothes and set off under a dark sky, the children safely settled with Sophie who had greeted them with smiles. Sophie had reared a large family herself and only Jamsey, the youngest, unmarried in his forties, still lived at home. All his brothers and sisters, except one, had emigrated to either America or Australia. The one still in Ireland, Sophie's youngest daughter, was now a nun in a closed order in Dublin, and permitted to visit for a week only, in summer, every second year.

★ ★ ★

Daniel's stone bench had a pool of water lying on it and Daniel was nowhere to be seen. Hannah peered into the dim interior of the cottage and saw him in the light of the fire as he stirred it up ready to add fresh turf. He turned towards her the moment he heard her foot on the door stone.

'Hannah, I was waiting for you. Will I light the lamp so you can see your way around the furniture?'

'Hello, Daniel. I came as soon as I could. Yes, it has got very dark with the rain but I can see you perfectly well in the firelight. Now come and tell me right away what has happened. The message you sent was word-perfect, as you knew it would be, but I'm sure you knew it didn't really tell me anything. Except that you needed to see me.'

'Well, it's been a very unusual day,' he began, sitting down heavily in his own chair. 'I had two visitors but no Marie. The first was her young man who came early to tell me she'd had a fall and has broken her leg. She's away with her mother to the hospital, but he says the doctor told them when she has it set, she'll not be able to put her foot to the ground for two or three months at best, never mind get here every morning from her mother's place.'

He knocked out his pipe into the fire and began to refill it methodically.

'Marie getting married was problem enough as you well know. Now this brings her going right forward from late June. Then, out of nowhere, I have this young man from Galway who appeared when we were reading. He'd come to see if I could give him a job. Apparently, he's thinking of becoming a priest but he's too young for the seminary, or perhaps, too immature. I'm not sure at all about him. However, it seems someone put him in touch with our local priest because he'd said to some of the brothers at the seminary that he wants to improve his Irish.'

Daniel raised his hands heavenwards, making sure he did not tip out the glowing embers in his pipe.

'So, what does he speak if not Irish? Surely not English if he comes from Galway,' asked Hannah, totally puzzled by this unusual situation. 'That was where you said, wasn't it?'

'Oh yes, he says he's from Galway all right.'

'Well, I know there are quite a few people who have some English here in Donegal,' began Hannah, 'but they're nearly all harvesters going to Scotland and England to work every year. Surely they don't do that down in Galway, do they?' she asked, thinking how much further the sailing would be than it was from Derry.

'Well, all I know is that the young man's father comes from County Down. He told me his father is a coastguard and served in Donaghadee and then in different parts of England and Scotland. It seems when he was posted to Galway town he married a local girl. Sometime later he was moved out to Kilkerrin where he was in charge of the station. Apparently, most of the other coastguards there were from across the water so everyone spoke English. I gathered his mother, who was a Cullen, learnt English herself, but his father didn't take to learning Irish at all. His father, he says, was a Protestant, so because the young man was the eldest son, he was sent to a Protestant school in Dublin.'

'And he wants to be a priest and come and work with you in the meantime?' she said, baffled by the details of the story.

'That's the general idea,' Daniel replied flatly, 'but there are a number of new problems, as well as the ones you know about. To begin with, he'd have to find lodgings and he'll have to have a salary. He had saved up some money, he says, but getting here took it all. Now, he hasn't a penny to his name.

'I think he's bright enough,' he went on, 'and now Marie has had to leave, he *might* be part of the solution to my wanting to teach the children English, but, as you know, Hannah, I have no money to pay him. As Marie is off work she'll not expect me to pay her any more, but I already owe her for the last month,' he said anxiously.

He paused and took a couple of deep pulls on his pipe.

'Even more of the children weren't able to bring their Friday pennies today,' he added wearily. 'I admit I am accumulating a fair pile of turf instead of the pennies, but if I have to close the school, I'll have neither turf, nor pennies, and now there's no pension either.'

He looked up at her as if he wanted to see her reaction.

Hannah thought, as she so often did, that it was not surprising people couldn't believe he was blind.

Despite the grim picture he had painted, there was not the remotest touch of self-pity in the look he gave her. He was simply waiting patiently to see what she would say.

'Daniel, you'll hardly believe this,' she began, 'but I had a visitor myself this morning. A Yorkshire man, a Quaker, with very little Irish. In fact, he had so little, he could hardly manage a polite good day, despite the fact he's a very well-mannered man. He'd been sent by the Quaker Central Committee in Dublin to do research. He said they want to find out how men like Patrick — labourers with no land beyond their patch of potato garden — support themselves and their families. But we talked about more than that, and when I told something of the difficulties we face, he wanted to know what the real problems are, here, in this part of the country, so that they can help in the most effective way possible. They clearly have funds and from all he said, I think, in fact I'm sure, that he's going to be able to help us.'

'Do you think so?' Daniel said, a small smile flickering across his face. 'Well, didn't I say a few days ago that *you* would be the one to create a miracle when all us so-called good Catholic believers were still on our knees praying for divine aid!'

'Oh, Daniel,' she protested, 'I've done nothing yet but give him a lot of information about potatoes, and flour, and meal, and feeding a family and explaining that the school has very little in the way of books and stationery. When I told him that neither the master, nor the assistant teacher's income was guaranteed, he made a note about it. And he gave me the address to send off an order for stationery. I said I'd send it together with a book order direct to Dublin when I'd talked it over with you.'

'And they have money for this?'

'Yes, they have,' she said firmly. 'He told me the Quakers in America are very generous, but as well as that, they get gifts from people they don't even know, from all over the place, because these people have heard by word of mouth about some project or other the Quakers have started. He told me about one scheme where they're trying to introduce other varieties of potato that might resist disease better than the Lumper. And they give away packets of seed, like turnips and

81

swedes. He said it had been clear for a long time that depending on potatoes alone was too risky.'

'They've done that, have they?' he asked, surprised. 'I know nothing at all about any other varieties of potato. They do seem to know what they're doing.'

'Yes, he knows that if there was another famine, like the one in '38, having other vegetables might at least bridge the gap until supplies could be provided or shipped in from other countries.'

'But you say he's thinking about more than just the food on our table. If there's funds he could provide, he's brought back the possibility of keeping going, if I could just somehow get my pension reinstated.'

'I did speak to him about that too and he gave me the address of a Quaker in Armagh I can write to. He's elderly and long retired but he was a solicitor and he still works for Richhill Meeting. Jonathan Hancock says he will advise anyone for free if it is for the benefit of those in need.'

Daniel shook his head slowly as if he simply could not believe his ears. 'I've heard about the Quakers, but I've never met one,' he began. 'How does he come to be in Donegal?'

'Apparently he has family connections in both Armagh and Donegal, not Quakers themselves from what he said, but willing to help him do his work. He's a cloth manufacturer in Yorkshire by trade. He noticed my napkins that I finish, or decorate, and he asked me too about home workers and sewing and things that women could do if they had any basic skills. He's very sharp and businesslike, but kind with it.'

Daniel sat silent for a little, turning over all she had said.

'Hannah dear, from dark to light in one short day. As they say: *The Lord works in mysterious ways*, but I still have one problem after all your good news.'

'What's that, Daniel?' she said gently, seeing a look of sadness cross his face.

'This young man who came this morning. I didn't know what to make of him. He's educated all right. He's been taught to think and he speaks Irish well enough. He even has Latin and a bit of Greek from what he told me, but there's something not right about him and I've no hope of working it out. I'll have to leave that to you, Hannah. Can he do the job Marie did, and can he teach English here without me having to declare myself and help him? In fact, can he teach with only me to help him? He's not very sure of himself . . . I need you to size him up,' he said, clearly coming to a conclusion. 'Can you do that for me, Hannah, after you've done so much already?'

'Well, I can certainly try,' she said. 'He must be serious about teaching to have come all this way. Where's he staying? With the priest?'

'Yes, but I don't know which one, or whereabouts. I did ask him to come and see me again tomorrow. Could I send him over to you then? I need to know what you see. You don't see just with your eyes, Hannah, you always see with your heart.'

Hannah had no idea when the young man would appear. Apart from insisting on punctuality at school, Daniel troubled himself little about what he called 'clock time'. As far as he was concerned, the day divided into morning, afternoon and evening. He was always at home, so beyond school hours, where punctuality was part of his discipline, there was no need to be more specific.

Nevertheless, as the morning passed, Hannah found herself wondering if perhaps the young man had changed his mind about working in this remote place, among complete strangers. As always, she collected herself, set aside her thoughts and concentrated on what had to be done. She was behind with some of her routine jobs and her allocation of napkins was barely started. Then, with it being Saturday the children wanted attention and the first letter from Patrick was newly arrived and just asking for a reply.

She was reading a story to Rose and Sam after their mid-day meal when they all heard the familiar scrape of boots on the track outside. Before the young man had even knocked at the door, both children had jumped up and said: 'Hello.'

Given she knew who it must be, Hannah admitted later that she was completely taken aback. The slightly built young man who smiled down at the children could have been Sam's elder brother. Red-haired with creamy skin and freckles, he waited politely at the door until

Hannah stood up and invited him in.

'Mrs McGinley,' he said, speaking softly in Irish, 'I'm John McCreedy and your friend, Mr McGee, said I should come and talk to you. I'm sorry if I'm interrupting a good story.'

'Don't worry, John, we can finish the story later,' she said, replacing the bookmark Rose had made in school and closing the book.

'Now, Rose and Sam, John and I need to talk about school. Would you like to see if there's anyone out to play, or visit Sophie, or go back to the jigsaw in the bedroom?'

Both children were eyeing the visitor with great interest, but Rose at least knew the rules.

'Ma, we told Sophie yesterday we'd come over sometime today.'

'Good. Then take that little bowl of eggs I've left on the dresser. Tell her they're for her and that mine have started to lay again.'

They went off promptly with Sam still looking over his shoulder, totally intrigued by this unfamiliar person who spoke Irish indoors when they always spoke English indoors, unless their father was present.

'Do sit down, John,' she said, waving him to the other armchair and stirring the fire to produce a cheering glow. 'I'm sure you'd like some tea and cake, but if you don't mind, I think we should talk 'school' for a bit and see if we can help each other,' she said easily. 'Now, if you were to become Daniel's assistant you'd need to be able to do all the things Marie did. Did Daniel explain how they worked together? You can imagine the limitations of Daniel being blind. Do you think you could manage to work with that?'

'Yes, I think I could. The little I saw of him with the children, I thought how very fortunate they were.'

Hannah was taken aback once again. There was no trace of lack of confidence whatever in his reply.

'Why was that, John?' she asked, genuinely interested in what he might say.

'Mr McGee is a native speaker and a story-teller. Clearly, he has a wealth of story and poetry at his fingertips. He can educate those twelve children in the things that are really important, the history and traditions of their own culture.'

'But, John, some might say that educating them thus would not prepare them for the harsh realities of the world out there. What happens if they have to leave Ireland as so many do? To emigrate, or travel to do seasonal work like my husband?'

'You're thinking about Mr McGee's wish to have them taught English, aren't you? He did ask me some questions about that. He seems to think that teaching his pupils English would help them in the future.'

'And don't you think it would help them?' asked gently.

She watched him closely. He was speaking Irish, clearly and without difficulty, but she detected a flatness in his tone she could not account for.

'English is the language of our oppressors,' he said bitterly.

For a moment, Hannah was surprised by the

vehemence of his reply. She paused, and decided the only thing to do was try to find out why he was so very hostile. Like with every other group of people, she knew speakers of English among the landed gentry who were hostile and others who were not. She thought of Jonathan Hancock and the trader in Dunfanaghy who had provided the initial funds for setting up the school in the first place.

'But English is also the language of Irish emigrants all over the world,' Hannah replied, 'and of travellers, and visitors, many of whom are sympathetic to our economic difficulties. Have you heard of the Quakers?'

'Yes, there are a lot of them in Dublin where I was at school,' he said, softening a little. 'I had a friend who attended Meetings, but he is an exception. The English are no friends to the Irish.'

Hannah paused and looked into the fire, wondering where this bitterness had come from. Clearly, although he had used all his money getting to Donegal, his family was not poor. How else could they have sent him to school in Dublin?

'Would it be against your principles to teach English?' she asked.

'Not if it meant I could stay here and improve my Irish,' he replied promptly.

'But it's such a long way from your parents and family,' she said. 'Will you not miss them? Do you have brothers and sisters?'

'I have sisters,' he said, 'and grandparents and lots of cousins. All Irish,' he added quickly. 'But my father doesn't like me being with them. That's why he sent me away to school. He didn't want me to be like them.'

'And what about your mother?' she asked softly.

So that's it, she thought to herself, as she saw the look of utter sadness that crossed his face.

'She does what my father wants. Always has done.'

Hannah was grateful that Rose and Sam arrived back at just that moment.

'Mrs O'Donnell came to see Sophie, Ma, and she had a pile of newspapers. I thought we ought to come home,' she said, looking from her mother to John and back again, clearly uneasy.

'Good girl yourself,' said Hannah quickly. 'You were quite right to come away for they don't see each other very often. Now you and Sam go and see if you can you finish that jigsaw while John and I talk a bit more. And then I'll make us all tea. Can you eat a piece of cake, Sam?'

Sam rolled his eyes and John McCreedy laughed, his face transformed.

Hannah saw a different person from the embittered young man who viewed 'the English' as his enemies. Then she noticed Sam was watching him, as he put down the empty egg bowl on the dresser. 'Sophie said thank you, Ma, and she said she hoped you'd come in tomorrow now she'd got a paper full of news.' He paused, as if considering something.

Suddenly he made up his mind. He turned towards their visitor. 'You've got red hair just like mine,' he said bluntly. 'Did your grandfather

88

have red hair too? Mine did.'

'Yes, Sam, he did,' John replied easily. 'He was from County Down, but his father had come from Scotland. He had a red beard as well.'

It was only at that moment Hannah realised that since the children appeared, she had been speaking English. Now, for the first time, John had replied to Sam in English.

There was much she had yet to find out about this troubled young man, but of two things she was sure. There was no hesitation in either his Irish, or his English and he responded well to children. Perhaps over tea and cake she would let the children ask their questions. She might learn a lot from his responses, but she'd already found out what Daniel needed to know. Whatever John's personal pain, he would not let it get in the way of his teaching.

8

The weekend when young John McCreedy visited Hannah in Ardtur turned out to be to be a busy one for both of them. With Marie out of action, Easter now passed and two months of the school year still to go, it certainly wasn't the right time for Daniel to declare a holiday to give Hannah and himself time to work out what to do next.

Obviously, Daniel couldn't manage the school by himself. Hannah was well aware of how concerned he must be about that, so later, on the Saturday morning, she left the children in the charge of their new friend, John, and went to see the schoolmaster. She wondered how he was coping when it seemed as if one problem was coming after another.

It had rained heavily in the night but the wind had dried the rocky path and the hawthorn bushes were no longer threshing in the breeze as Hannah set off. As she walked briskly over to Casheltown the sun appeared for the first time that day. When she arrived, she found Daniel sitting on the stone bench deep in thought.

'Hannah, is it you?' he asked, as she tramped the last few yards. 'I was thinking of you not five minutes ago.'

'Well, I'm here now and I think I've got some answers to our questions, which no doubt will lead to yet more questions, but we'll not let that trouble us, will we?' she said encouragingly, as she sat down beside him.

The sun was intermittent but the morning was now both calm and mild. They were able to stay outside and carry on with their talk and it wasn't long before they'd agreed there was everything still to hope for provided they could just keep the school going for the next month or so. But clearly the question of John's character troubled Daniel, as much as where they would get the money to pay him.

'Daniel, there's nothing wrong with his Irish,' she said reassuringly. 'I let him go on speaking Irish till the children came in. He's as fluent in Irish as he is in English. I do think he's got a personal problem with his attitude towards English, but I can tell you about that another time. Do you still want to keep quiet about your own command of English?' she asked.

'Well, you could probably say I was another one with a personal problem with my English,' he said wryly, 'so, yes, I'd prefer it if we could keep that piece of information between ourselves.'

'Why not?' said Hannah laughing. 'It might be a dreadful shock to your admirers up and down the valley if you, of all people, were to start speaking English, but I think John himself may need an English speaker to help him get started with teaching it. He may be absolutely fluent but he has never taught before. If you like, I could come two or three mornings in the week to help him get going. I haven't even asked him yet if he can deal with number work and writing, but I'm fairly hopeful. He is very quick on the uptake, as they say in my part of the world.'

Daniel beamed, delighted by the prospect.

'It's good of you to give up your time, Hannah, when you know I can't pay you, at least not yet. And indeed that's another task you've taken on for me, writing to the solicitor in Richhill, forby those orders for books and note-books to Dublin. And what about your sewing? Have you had any time for that at all?'

'No, to be honest I haven't, and I don't expect to have much in the near future, but it's only for month or two. We'll have to see where we are at the end of that time.'

The sun, which had been blotted out by sudden clouds, re-emerged. It beamed down on them so strongly they both closed their eyes and looked upwards, feeling the unexpected warmth on their faces. Through the gap in the windblown trees and hawthorn bushes, her eyes still half-closed, Hannah saw the sparkle on the waters of Lough Gartan.

Suddenly, she felt her heart lift. She was sure it would be all right. John would find his way in teaching and the school would survive. But there was now the small matter of finding him lodgings and the fact that the poor soul hadn't a penny to his name, though after what her new Quaker friend had said, she was sure payment for his teaching would eventually appear, even if it were delayed for some weeks. Now, it was just Daniel himself who was left with the anxiety of the school's debt to Marie and his own penury. She wondered just how he had managed to feed himself when he hadn't even the produce of a potato garden to help him.

She fell silent as she began to think what could be done. She still had all of her napkin money from last month and Patrick had given her most of what he'd earned in Tullygobegley. There were now only three of them to feed and the early potatoes would soon be ready to dig. She did a quick calculation, did it again, then laughed at herself.

She was almost sure Daniel's pension would eventually be restored. This situation would not create an unforeseen expense. This was merely a loan. Even if the money held in reserve in the cracked teapot on the dresser was not enough, she was quite prepared to go under the bed and bring out one of the sovereigns her father had sent as a gift to her and the children.

'I take it you're having a think,' Daniel said, turning towards her.

'And how did you know that?' she asked lightly.

'I think you could say it was the dense quality of the silence, heavy with moment. I hope your deliberations were satisfactory,' he said.

She laughed and put her hand on his. 'Yes, I think you'll be pleased with the outcome, but I ought to be getting back shortly to the children. I'm thinking about John. Sam was in his questioning mode, which, as you know, can be taxing,' she said wryly, 'and you and I haven't discussed the books yet for that order.'

'Well, there is still tomorrow, not even started yet,' he said philosophically.

'There is indeed, but I think we should do the books if we can before I go. We're certainly a bit further on today. I've worked out that I can lend you the money to pay Marie and get back to normal yourself for a month or two, at least till the pension is restored.'

'And what if it isn't?'

'We'll meet that when we come to it,' she said. 'I feel sure it will be restored, but if it isn't, we can apply to the Quakers for a salary for you as master. They would think that only fair. It might even be more than your original pension was. You never know.'

'Well, with your luck it probably would be. As long as it's enough to pay you back, that's all I would ask.'

★ ★ ★

Hannah walked slowly on the way back, needing the space to think what she would do about John, but by the time she arrived in Ardtur and met Sophie's visitor just leaving, she had a plan.

She turned aside and stopped at Sophie's open door.

'Hannah, come in, come in. I heard all about your visitor from Sam. Is he keeping an eye on the childer for you?'

'He is, Sophie. It will be good practice for him. That young man is going to be Daniel's assistant at the school.'

'Ach, sure good. Poor Marie will be so relieved. I heard she was more cut up about letting Daniel down than about breaking her leg.'

94

'That doesn't surprise me,' said Hannah, shaking her head. 'She's very good-hearted and the children were fond of her, but, of course, she'd have been leaving anyway and there would still be the problem of replacing her. It would be a shame if we lost the school for want of a teacher, wouldn't it?'

'Aye, it would that,' agreed Sophie vigorously. 'Sure, I never went to school m'self and I'd give anythin' to be able to write. I can read a bit, an' I can listen to the news being read to me till the cows come home, as the sayin' is, but I can barely write my name. An' it takes me a good couple o' minutes.' A smile crinkled her lined and weather-beaten face.

Hannah beamed at her, delighted by her easy manner. Sophie may not have been educated, but she paid attention to everything going on around her and had an incredible memory for people and places she had visited, or even simply heard about.

'I've come to ask a favour, Sophie,' Hannah began hesitantly.

'Ah, sure, ask away. If I can I will, that's for sure.'

'I think our young visitor is going to need somewhere to stay. He's with the priest over at Churchill, but that's too far away for school at nine o'clock in the morning, even if the priest would think of having him permanently. Do you think maybe, Sophie, he could have Jamsey's room while he's away? You'd get paid, of course, but it might take a wee while to come through. I thought if you don't want the bother of a meal in

95

the evening, he could come to me for that. So long as he has his breakfast with you while I'm getting Rose and Sam off, oh and a piece for lunchtime. I'd be surprised if he couldn't make it himself for he seems very down to earth for all he's been so well educated.'

'An' sure, why not?' she replied promptly. 'He might even read me a bit from the paper in the evening,' she went on cheerfully. 'Though, mind you, I'd not talk to him if he had exercises to correct at the table. I could just do my bit of sewing over by the fire an' he could have the lamp.'

Hannah breathed a sigh of relief. That was half the problem solved. She would go home now and make a meal for them all and then consult John about his lodgings when the children went to bed. If he could come and stay with Sophie, then working out how they were to teach English together would be so much easier.

* * *

It was long past mid-day when she walked across to her own front door and heard John reading to them. He stopped the minute she appeared, stood up and asked her if all was well.

'Yes, John it is. I hope you'll be pleased, but I take it you've not had a bite to eat?'

'We did have glasses of milk, Ma, but there was no bread,' said Rose. 'I knew we should have offered,' she added, looking uneasy.

'You did quite right, and it's not your fault. Could you all eat a plate of champ if I made one

96

for us? We can have some bread to our supper if I bake later . . . '

Sam rolled his eyes and rubbed his tummy. 'I'm so hungry, Ma,' he said, so vigorously that they all laughed.

'It will take another half hour, I'm afraid,' she said, taking her potato knife from the drawer. 'Would you like to take John down to the lake and see if there are any new cygnets? Would you mind a walk, John?' she asked.

'It would be a great pleasure,' he said promptly. 'I'm used to the sea and the city, but mountainy countryside like this is totally new to me. I'd be so happy if I could stay,' he added, a slight hesitance in his voice that spoke to Hannah of anxiety.

'Well, I think I have good news about that, but we can talk later,' she said, selecting potatoes from the creel by the door. 'Enjoy your walk.'

★   ★   ★

'So you think it's a good idea, John?' Hannah asked, as they came back from a brief visit to Sophie, leaving the children reading to her. John had tired them out searching the lake for cygnets, so they seemed happy to sit quietly reading the papers to their neighbour.

John nodded vigorously. 'Sophie's a very thoughtful lady,' he replied, 'and there's nothing wrong with her memory, is there? I'd enjoy listening to her and reading the newspaper to her. May I ask where she gets them from?'

'You may indeed, John, but I've never found

97

out myself for sure,' Hannah replied, laughing. 'My best guess is from one of her many nieces who works in a hotel in Ballybofey — rather a posh place that gets a lot of English visitors. I think that must be how we come by *The Times* and the *Illustrated London News*. Often they're months old, so they've probably been passed round long before they get here, but I suspect they originally get left behind in the hotel bedrooms.

'Now, John dear,' she continued, 'you are looking tired and you have a long walk back to your lodging tonight. It's been a busy day and you've clearly made a big impression on Sam and Rose. Can you manage if I ask you some questions about teaching before you go?'

He nodded and smiled shyly. 'I do so want to teach Irish children. I'm even more keen now I've seen how much they can learn from a man like Mr McGee. I'd learn so much myself from just listening to him.'

'Have you always wanted to teach, John?'

'I don't know,' he said suddenly. 'My father wanted me to go into the Coastguard Service; that's why he sent me away to school. And I tried to want what he wanted for me. I really did try, but I just couldn't. I didn't want to leave my home and family and go off to England, or Scotland, and live among strangers. I just couldn't bear the thought,' he said, looking distraught.

'But, John,' she protested gently, 'we are all strangers here, in this valley, on a mountainside in Donegal.'

'Yes, but you are my own people. You speak Irish and you help each other and you don't always think about getting rich and having big estates and driving poor people out of their homes. I can't bear what the English have done to our country. I hate them all, every last one of them.'

'And the Quakers who are going to give us books and paper and pay you a salary? Aren't they English?'

'Yes, of course they are,' he said, 'but they are an exception to the rule.'

'And what about the Scots?'

'I've never met any till I met you, and you speak Irish.'

'John dear, I can see you've not been very fortunate in your experience of the English,' she said slowly. 'Would you believe me if I said there are many good, kind English people who would do so much to help us here if only they could? You could ask Sophie — she's far better informed than I am about matters political.'

'Yes, I could, but I don't see why it matters. I'm here and I know I'll be happy here.'

'It matters, John, because Daniel has a project. He would understand completely how you feel, but he wants his pupils to learn English. He sees it as something that will help them earn a living, if they work seasonally in England, or Scotland, like my husband, or if they emigrate, or if they are apprenticed to merchants. You can see how committed he is to all things Irish, but he needs you and me to teach English.'

'You and me?' he asked, his face brightening.

'Yes, John. I used to teach in my own old school in Galloway, and English, or Scotch, as the haymakers call it, is my first language. I learnt Irish from my husband and I taught him to read and write and speak English. Many, many people in Donegal speak Scotch, like all those who take the boat from Derry every springtime.'

She paused, suddenly feeling weary, and waited to see what he would say.

'If it's what you and Mr McGee think best for the school then I'll do all I can. But you'll have to help me,' he said firmly. 'I'm well used to children. I have five sisters and dozens of cousins and I get on fine with most of them. Teaching English was the last thing I could ever have imagined doing. But then, that was back in Galway and I'm in Donegal now.'

9

Hannah slept badly on the Sunday night following young John McCreedy's second visit to Ardtur, her dreams haunted by a red-headed man with a beard, who refused to speak any Irish, even when his wife and all his many relatives spoke little or no English. She wondered if John's father came from a Covenanter background, as firm in his convictions as her own father had once been in his.

Her own father had softened with age and her sisters had told her that he was a different man by the time she knew him, kinder and less rigid in his beliefs, able at last to appreciate the men who had been coming to work for him for years, though they were of a different religion and spoke a different language.

As she woke up on Monday morning, she found herself thinking of her father, and her brothers and sisters, none of whom she had now seen for the ten years of her marriage. It was bad enough to feel so far away from all of them, but at times she felt that their loss made it even harder to bear the absence of her own dear Patrick for at least half the months of the year.

She and Patrick had spoken often enough of how he might find work that would let them be together all year, either here in Donegal, or together in Scotland, but as Patrick so often said himself, he was not an educated man. The only jobs he could find would be labouring work and he would be hard put to find better than what he already had with her father. Providing a home for her and the children in another part of the British Isles would be more than the modest income from his work could sustain.

Waking so early, she had time to reread Patrick's recent letter before the children woke up. She realised as she unfolded the small blue sheets that she already knew it by heart. But it was all she had. At times like this, she felt so lonely. No father, no mother, no sisters, no brothers. Just letters that were sometimes infrequent. She had never regretted marrying Patrick but she had not realised how solitary she would feel when there was no one there to share the problems, when there was only herself to care for Rose and Sam.

As she got out of bed, she reminded herself that the first weeks of Patrick's absence were always the worst. Things should be easier now that some of the problems over the school had been solved. She realised that she was actually looking forward to teaching again, something she had so enjoyed in the schoolroom back in Galloway and indeed in the kitchen of her home, where her father's harvesters had spread out their exercise books on the well-scrubbed kitchen table they normally had their meals at.

She gathered herself for the morning routine. Today, Monday, she would send Rose and Sam off to school with John. He had now brought his meagre bag of possessions over from the priest's house in Churchill and had taken possession of

Jamsey's empty bed, a very short distance away in Sophie's house.

Having John nearby would give her a little extra time this morning, but given she had offered to work with him three mornings in school, she had a lot to do within it. She was going to have to bake an extra day's bread, do the weekly washing, make a start on that letter to the solicitor in Richhill, and copy out neatly the list of books and stationery that Jonathan Hancock had said she should send to the Quaker Central Committee in Dublin. They would forward it to the Committee that dealt with books and education for which they provided money.

It did look as if there would be no time left for sewing napkins and she began to wonder if she might lose her distribution if she fell behind with her quota. At that point she stopped herself sharply. There was no point thinking about that today. The draper would not be here for a month at least. Many things could change in that time.

Sam and Rose sat quiet over breakfast but were clearly pleased when they heard John's foot on the doorstep.

Hannah exchanged glances with John and could see he was in the best of spirits.

'I'm afraid you and I will have homework to do tonight, John, after supper. Did you tell Sophie that we were both going to work tomorrow?'

'Oh yes, I did and she's pleased to hear it,' he said cheerfully. 'But she hopes that some nights I'll be able to read to her if I don't go up to

Daniel's to listen to his stories.'

She checked that John had been given his piece as she tucked Rose and Sam's into their satchels. She kissed them both, wished John good luck and walked out with them into the bright April morning to see them off.

When they all turned back at the foot of the hill to see if she was still watching, she waved to them, thinking yet again how extraordinary it was that John and Sam could look so like brothers and what a happy thing it was that Rose had now begun to treat him as if he really was.

There was even more to do than Hannah had noted on her mental list and she was already beginning to think longingly of taking a basin of warm water into the bedroom and changing out of her working clothes when she heard a step outside and a shadow fell across the table where she was preparing the first of two batches of dough.

'Shemmie,' she said, surprised and pleased. 'It's a long time since you've been. Has the fishing not been good?'

He lowered his heavy bag by the open door and came gratefully to sit by the fire, holding out his wrinkled hands to the warm glow. The morning was bright and there was no wind. Hannah was perspiring with heat and effort, but Shemmie looked half frozen.

'Wou'd ye have a wee crust o' bread, missus dear? Fer I got no breakfast. The carrier was passin' and it was that or walk all the way and it's a brave way from Dunfanaghy.'

'It is indeed, Shemmie. You look frozen.'

104

'Aye well, the fish is cold and the cold gets inta me.'

'Now there's no bread baked yet, so I haven't a bite to give you, but would you eat a bowl of porridge? It wouldn't take long if I stirred up the fire.'

'Boys, that would go down well,' he said, his voice full of relief. 'An' I'll make sure you get the biggest fish in the bag,' he went on, his usually expressionless face producing the beginnings of a smile.

She covered the dough with a clean cloth, moved the griddle from the chain over the hearth where it was heating and replaced it with a small black pot. Once she'd measured the oats and water and mixed them thoroughly, she poured them into the pot, stirring the fire beneath so that the flames licked round the sooty bottom. Within minutes the water began to steam very gently.

'There's not much wind this morning, Shemmie, so it'll take a wee while. Do you often have to walk the whole way?' she asked, as she dusted her hands and came to sit down opposite him.'

'T'tell you the truth, missus, I'm not fit now to walk the whole way, so I have to keep lookin' out for lifts. Sure, the men that knows me is good enough about that but they can't always tell where the job is goin to be till the mornin' itself. They might be for Letterkenny, or Derry, or Gortahork. They mightn't know, no more than I do, if I'm goin' t' have fish. Alls for it is I get up if I hear a cart. But sure, maybe it's not goin' anywhere I'm known. People don' like buyin' fish from a man they don't know. Aye, an' there's fewer boats about. Sure, there's only coracles down on this part of the coast and the slightest bit of wind and they're up an' over. They're really only a summer thing. That's why I've not bin here for a while. There's no shortage of fish.'

'Oh, I didn't know that. I thought you just hadn't any to sell.'

'Na, na, the few old men that had proper fishin' boats say the waters be teemin' in these parts, but they're too old to haul in the sails, an' pull up the nets, an' their sons is away foreign, so they've had to give up. So now there's only the coracles left.'

Hannah leaned forward and stirred the porridge. She wondered how Shemmie managed to make enough money to buy oats and turf.

'To tell you the truth, missus,' he said, his face resuming its sombre look, 'if it weren't for one of m' sons away over in London who sends me the odd postal order I'd hafta to go to the work-house. God forbid,' he added, hastily crossing himself.

Hannah wondered how she could possibly help him. Yes, she could buy his fish but only what she could cook for tonight and tomorrow. Then she thought of Aunt Mary.

'Will you go up as far as Warrenstown today, Shemmie?' she asked, as she fetched a bowl and a jug of milk.

'Not if I can help it,' he said promptly. 'It's a brave steep climb.'

'Yes, it is, but if I buy fish for Patrick's Aunt

Mary, I can send the children up to deliver it.'

'Ah, good luck to you for a kind lady,' he said, as she handed him his bowl of porridge and left the jug of milk within reach. 'Sure every fish is another meal between me an' poverty.' He stirred his bowl and added some milk.

She watched him as he ate his porridge, savouring every mouthful. How fortunate she was to have a good husband who sent her all he earned and a father who sent her gifts of money at Christmas time. Unlike so many of her neighbours she was not short of money. Most of them had only the bit of bog and the potato garden that went with the house, but if they had a large family to feed and could get no other work, it simply wasn't enough. There was always the next lot of rent to pay, extra meal and flour when the potatoes were all used up, clothes for the children. Only the better-off families could think of finding the pennies to send their children to school. Those were the families that had money coming in from America, or Australia, or England.

That was what Daniel had said so firmly when he first admitted he wanted his pupils to learn English but couldn't see how he might go about it.

'A child that has English can travel,' he'd said to her, his tone sombre. 'He, or she, can earn far more in a week than their brothers and sisters can earn in a month, left behind to labour on the family's bit of land.'

Tomorrow, she and John would begin the English lessons, though how they would begin,

107

and what they would do, she had no idea. That was something else she had to give her mind to when she'd chosen her fish, counted out her pennies and sent Shemmie on his way.

★ ★ ★

Fish was a rare treat for Rose and Sam and they tucked in energetically when suppertime came, but for John, who politely said how nice it was, he admitted it was a regular meal, one they had often at home in Kilkerrin.

Some of the coastguards on the station went fishing when they were off duty, he explained, both on the bay and on some of the nearby rivers. Fish was always available. Sometimes, he added honestly, the catch from the bay was so good that everyone got tired of pickled fish and would start thinking quite longingly about the familiar bowl of champ.

After their meal, Rose and Sam heard the sounds of laughter and asked if they could go out to play. They could, Hannah agreed, but only for an hour. It was clear they had both forgotten they had homework to do.

'Well then, John, how did things go today?' Hannah asked, well aware that they had only the hour before the children came back and they had as yet no plan at all for how they might introduce the first English lesson.

'It went well,' he replied soberly, 'but the children are at such a disadvantage by not having enough proper seating. I asked Mr McGee if he would mind if I organised something temporary until we saw what the Dublin people could offer us.'

'And what did he say?' Hannah asked, wondering what Daniel had made of the unexpected request.

John smiled happily, his eyes bright. 'He said, 'Good man yourself. If you see something that you can improve, just go right ahead. I'll not be standing in your way.''

10

The pleasant weather of late April that had brought greenness to the hawthorns and tiny blooms to the first wildflowers in the grass took a sudden dip towards the end of the month and into the beginning of May. Rain swept across the mountain in grey curtains, blocking out the view of the lake, making the rocky paths look like streams, while the wind swirled around the cottages, blew down the chimneys and on occasion filled the schoolroom with smoke.

Bad weather always made more work for Hannah. School clothes had to be dried overnight, the floor had to be washed more often, and now that she was teaching three mornings a week she seldom had time to sit by the fire. If she did find a quiet space to sit and reflect, she was already far too tired to think of sewing. At times, she even had to press herself to write the daily instalments of her letter to Patrick.

But despite the problems of fitting in everything she had to do, she could not help feeling a surge of delight when first one, and then another, large box was delivered to Daniel's cottage in Casheltown. The boxes had come from Dublin, as promised, by Jonathan Hancock. The first one contained stationery: pencils, pens and ink, rubbers and blotting paper, drawing paper and both crayons and coloured pencils.

She would never forget the look on Daniel's

face as the pupils clustered around him and she and John opened that first box, passing over the items, which came out one by one, for him to inspect. She watched him stroke the covers of exercise books, sniff the unfamiliar odour of crayons and feel the sharp points of pencils and pens.

Later, when the second box came, he clutched the shiny copies and asked first one pupil and then another to open at random and read him a paragraph. It was difficult to tell whether it was the pupils or the teachers who were most excited.

By the time the weather improved enough to sit again on the stone bench and look out at the snow-like dusting of blossom on the hawthorns, a great deal had happened to secure the future of the school.

To begin with, the elderly Quaker in Richhill to whom Hannah had written, was able to assure her that it was just a matter of time before Daniel's pension was restored. He explained, as simply as he could, that a trust had been set up soon after Daniel's birth when it was clear that he was blind. As he was *still* blind, and as the source of the funds from which his pension came was in such good heart, there could be no reason for his pension being withdrawn. It might take a little time to have it restored, but even if this were so, she could be assured that all the missing payments would be refunded.

Daniel, relieved and delighted, worked out that he could pay Marie from what he proceeded to call his 'back pay' and would be able to make

111

John a small allowance until his promised salary from the Quaker Charitable Society had been arranged.

It really did feel as if the sun was shining on all their efforts — from John's attempts to beg, or borrow, benches to seat their pupils properly, or the first endeavours at 'teaching Scotch', something they had delayed because of an outbreak of flu, which kept many pupils at home just when the bad weather began.

Neither Daniel, nor John, nor Hannah, had had any idea as to how their pupils would react to learning English. They did agree that handing out the grammar books and proceeding formally might not be the best way. Daniel and Hannah talked about it when they took a short break mid-morning, and John and Hannah shared their thoughts after their evening meal on the fine evenings when Rose and Sam went out to play.

Daniel suspected that some of the children did, in fact, hear English spoken by people like the rent collector, or the land agent. Much would depend on the nature of those people. There might be some hostility or there might be acceptance.

That was when John suggested taking a light-hearted attitude to begin with, then see if they could engage their interest by trying to make use of any small familiarity with English the children might discover they already had.

Daniel thought it worth a try and Hannah, though not entirely easy about the part she was to play, was more than willing to see how John's plans might work out. And so they began.

In the small space at the front of the class, after their usual morning lessons, John produced an old and very battered hat, put it on, and stood looking around him, rocking on his heels and whistling. From time to time, he looked down anxiously at something on the ground beside him. Then Hannah stood up, picked up a basket she had brought to school with her and came to look critically at the space behind John's legs.

'How much are you wanting for the chickens?' she asked, speaking slowly in English, and looking him straight in the eye.

'Ah, they're great chickens,' he replied, shaking his arms as if they were wings, and looking down at them. 'They'll be great layers. Eggs galore,' he went on, cupping his hands round a large imaginary bowl. Say ten shillings for the box, and cheap at the price.'

'I'll give you five,' said Hannah sharply.

For the first time, the class, who had been unsure what to make of the ongoing scene, laughed aloud. They listened, fascinated, as John and Hannah continued to bargain and after much haggling Hannah finally got her imaginary chickens, which she carried off and deposited with her basket beside the chair where she sometimes sat.

'So do you think perhaps learning English might not be too bad?' John asked, addressing the class now in Irish.

'Did you understand any of the words?' he went on, looking round the class who were still smiling.

From a variety of children, words were offered. 'Chicken' and 'shilling' and 'egg'. They were repeated and written on the blackboard.

And then Daniel repeated the new words. They were the first words his pupils had ever heard him speak that were not Irish. He agreed with them that Scotch wasn't that difficult after all. 'A few words every day,' he said, 'and in a wee while you could go anywhere and talk to anyone.'

⋆ ⋆ ⋆

Sitting together on the stone bench while John finished the morning's lessons, Hannah knew that Daniel was delighted with the success of John's plan.

'Yes,' he said, 'I once had a friend, a teacher himself, who used to say, 'The secret with children is to work from the known to the unknown. Find a link to the child's own experience. If you can make a connection, however slight, it's like a beam of light to their path and you're halfway there.''

'I wasn't too sure when John suggested our dialogue,' began Hannah honestly, 'but I'm impressed. They're all so excited and they thought it was wonderful when *you* said the words too. Was it difficult for you?' she asked, breaking off, remembering his own unhappy relationship with the language that he'd once admitted to her.

'No more than it was for young John,' he said promptly. 'If you hadn't told me his father was from County Down and didn't think to learn any Irish, even when he took an Irish wife, I might not have understood him so well. Knowing his background, I'll do everything I can to back him up. He deserves all the help he can get. What would I do without you both?' he added, rather sadly.

'And who was it started the school in the first place?' she came back at him. 'Who was it tramped around trying to find enough money for a blackboard and a few books, and now look what we've got.'

He smiled. Hannah always gave credit where credit was due, whether it was the children, or anyone else. If he could have had a daughter, he would have wanted one like Hannah.

★ ★ ★

Later that day, when Rose and Sam were playing in the sunshine with some of the other children in Ardtur and John was reading newspapers to Sophie, Hannah cleared up after their evening meal and took out Patrick's last letter from the drawer in the kitchen table.

He apologised, as he so often did, for having no 'news' of any kind and then went on to tell her of the work they were doing, the state of the crops, the kindness of the weather and the good-heartedness of her father's new house-keeper, who had been so caring to the youngest member of the team, away from home for the first time and clearly feeling homesick.

She smiled, picked up her pen, scanned what she'd already written to him earlier in the week and continued.

You would have been so proud of Rose and Sam today when we had the first English class. I had explained to them that the other children might have no English at all and they must be careful not to speak up just because it was easy for them. So they said not a word until John began writing on the board, and then they just joined in when the class practised the first words and some simple sentences.

Do you remember, my love, how you used to sit at the kitchen table in the farm and I had to coax you to speak? You seemed to be so shy. It was only three years later you confessed it was not the English that was the problem, you were afraid if you said anything you'd give away your love for me. Three whole years, you kept me waiting! But in that time my father came to know you better. In the end your thoughtfulness was rewarded when he gave us his blessing. You were right indeed, for I was only just seventeen when you first arrived.

She put her pen down and stretched her aching shoulders. Between carrying turf and water for the house and writing on the blackboard in school, she often had a pain in her neck by the end of the day, but she had no complaints to make. Sometimes she saw Sophie, or Aunt Mary, struggle to lift a bucket less than half full. It meant they had to go to the well two or three times every day and all their everyday tasks took longer.

She tried not to think about growing old, or about losing her dear Patrick. She wondered if all women had such fears, or whether it was only because she was so happy in her love for Patrick, that she was so aware of just how much she had to lose.

She wrote a little more, decided that she must post the letter tomorrow before it got any longer and took out the shiny, new English book that they would use in the morning. It was as she opened it that she thought of Jonathan Hancock who had told her where to write and what to ask for. Without that visit of his so much would be different.

'I wonder does he know about coracles?' she said quietly to herself.

The children would be back soon and bedtime was close, but when she had tucked them up, she'd make the effort to write and tell him all she'd learnt from Shemmie the fish man. He'd helped her and many people would benefit from his help; perhaps there was something she could do to help him in return.

★ ★ ★

In the seven weeks that remained of the school year, all the pupils in Daniel's school made good progress, not only in the new venture into English, but also in all the other subjects Daniel and Marie had introduced to them. It was as if the new books, now carried home at night with such pride, had encouraged even the most reluctant of pupils. Confidence had grown and it seemed as if new discoveries were being made all the time.

Hannah's greatest joy came one morning

unexpectedly. She was looking at sketches and drawings of 'My home', done for homework, when she found that Johnny Donnelly, a large, awkward boy who spoke only when spoken to, had produced a sketch Hannah herself would have been proud to have made.

She stared at it and found herself near to tears. While all the other children had drawn houses, some like their own, some copied from picture books, Johnny had produced a landscape. Using the crayons, which none of the children had ever seen before, he had created a picture of Lough Gartan and the mountain slopes beyond with sunlight falling on the water from a sky piled with clouds.

John agreed with her. It was an amazingly perceptive drawing from a boy who had never had a coloured pencil, or crayon, in his hand before. Hannah found a place for it, and for some others, on the whitewashed wall of the schoolroom where all Daniel's visitors in the evening could see it when they came to talk, and play their fiddles, and listen to his stories. She then went and told Daniel what had happened.

Daniel was delighted. At the end of morning school, before Hannah went home, he went round the class asking each pupil what they thought of Johnny's picture. 'Did you hear that, Johnny?' he asked at regular intervals, while Johnny blushed with pleasure and said nothing.

At the end of his inquisition, Daniel announced to the whole class that Johnny had just won a prize. It might take a little while to arrive, he warned, but Johnny would be receiving a box of watercolour paints and brushes, as well as a sketch pad, for his own use only. They would be arriving from Dublin, with only one condition: that he kept drawing and sketching.

Hannah and John both smiled to themselves as they listened to Daniel addressing the class. They knew that Daniel had just received his 'back pay'. At times in the course of the last few months, from Marie's accident and the loss of his pension, Daniel had almost despaired of keeping up the school. Now, with all the help they'd had thanks to Jonathan Hancock, the school had been saved. Johnny's prize was one way in which Daniel was going to celebrate.

11

It had taken Hannah a long time to adjust to the 'summer' months in Donegal. Unlike the long, sunlit days, a feature of the same months in her old home in Scotland where the farmhouse was built on a south-facing site, close to the Solway coast, the low stone cottage on the mountainside overlooking Lough Gartan was a quite different matter.

Often chilly and windswept, even at the height of summer, rain came suddenly, sweeping down the valley, so that clothes hung out to dry had to stay out overnight, or be watched for the moment when it was worth catching them up and bringing them to air indoors before the next deluge.

Sometimes, as she came and went, doing her morning tasks, she looked sadly at the handful of bright flowers she had planted in old or leaking cooking pots. It was true the plants had unfailingly survived the winters, but often they were so wind-battered they were slow to bloom in the summer. She longed for the bright faces of the geraniums or wallflowers she had once tended so carefully, year after year, in what had been her mother's garden.

To her own surprise, as July moved onwards, she began to miss her mornings at school quite badly and with it came missing Patrick even more than usual. While Rose and Sam had the company of the other children in Ardtur, only a few of whom went to school with them, she had neither Daniel nor John to talk to, her only companion the intimidating pile of napkins accumulated in the last six weeks of school, together with occasional visits from Sophie, who felt similarly deprived of John's presence and came regularly to ask if Hannah had any news of him, more recent than she had herself.

John, to Hannah's surprise, proved to be a vigorous correspondent. She had not really expected to hear from him when he went back to his family in Galway, but his letters began to arrive regularly, clearly labelled with his address, and she found she enjoyed responding to his questions and requests for news.

He seemed to be keeping busy by helping his mother to whitewash their coastguard house at Kilkerrin, looking after his younger sisters and visiting both grandparents and cousins. He spoke warmly of his grandparents, still robust and running a large farm. He also mentioned visiting old men known as storytellers in the district.

John explained to her how he had talked to the storytellers and told them about Daniel's stories. He said, he'd found that some of Daniel's stories were entirely familiar to them, but others he'd mentioned were quite unknown.

In a subsequent letter, he then told her he'd once asked Daniel if he knew a story called *The Two Bottles*, which he'd heard when staying with his Cullen grandparents somewhat north of Galway town itself. Daniel had listened carefully to his account of it, but said he'd never heard the story himself. He'd said that he found some aspects of it quite unusual.

It was obvious to Hannah that John was intrigued by the whole topic, so she was not surprised when his next letter revealed that he'd been looking for other storytellers in the Galway area who also knew the tale of *The Two Bottles*. He said he proposed to write down all the versions of it that he could find, to see what differences there might be between them.

Hannah found she was increasingly looking forward to his reports. To begin with, she had been touched that he took the trouble to tell her what he was doing, but then, as the letters arrived with such regularity, she reflected that perhaps she was the only person he knew who took any interest whatever in what he thought or did.

She had always tried to encourage him if he seemed unsure of some new plan he had for the classroom and in her first replies she had done the same over the storytellers.

Sitting by the glowing embers of the fire on an overcast afternoon at the end of a period of miserable dampness at the beginning of August, she put down his most recent letter and reflected that there were different kinds of loneliness.

Despite the fact that John had a large and lively family, that didn't mean he could share his thoughts with any of them, never mind his hopes or dreams. His mother appeared to be a gentle and kindly person, but so far in his regular letters he had never once mentioned his father.

She thought back to her own childhood, to her

122

three sisters who always had time to listen to her, and her father, who was a man of few words, but had a way of asking her if she was 'all right'. Often enough, when he thought she was not her usual self, he would summon up one of her sisters and then suddenly disappear to attend to some urgent task.

Perhaps she hadn't appreciated how fortunate she had been that even the loss of her mother at such a young age had not impinged upon her because she had so much love and care all around her.

To her own surprise, she found tears welled up and dripped unheeded onto the close-written sheets she still held in her lap. She wiped them with the back of her hand, made sure there was no sign of the children returning from their play, and returned to reading John's letter.

★ ★ ★

He'd begun by saying that as far as he could see, the old stories were being forgotten and more would disappear if and when some of these elderly storytellers died. He continued:

Just imagine, Hannah, how much we would lose, if Daniel were no longer with us. When school starts again, I'm going to begin writing down all Daniel's stories. I'm wondering if I made a collection of them, together with the ones I'm finding here in Galway, if we could get them printed in a pamphlet, or a book. I know nothing about printing and I suspect it would cost a lot of money, which I haven't got, but perhaps we could find a way. What do you think?

The pages that followed were on different paper and clearly had been written in haste. He'd included for her the beginning of the story he'd mentioned — *The Two Bottles* — and instead of getting up and starting to prepare the evening meal, she sat reading it, the flow of words and phrases calling up a man, not unlike Daniel, sitting by his fireside addressing friends and neighbours, telling it with all the gestures and flourishes she had so often observed.

There was a man, a right sort of a man, with a farm of land and four or five cows. But he had bad luck and a wife and a big family, and one by one he had to sell the cows.

Finally, one evening he says to his wife: 'There's a fair in the town tomorrow and I think I'll sell the cow an' get us a bit of money for we've no food.'

'Oh well,' says the wife, 'if you do that then we'll have no milk for the children.'

But the man said that one was as bad as the other and he'd sell the cow.

Anyway, that night he set out after the family had gone to bed, and he was coming along to where there was a cutting in the road, like between two hills, when the cow took fright.

'Oh, what ails you, woman dear?' says he . . . and he looks up and there against the moon he sees the outline of a man.

And the man slides down the slope to the road beside him.

'Good day, Mick,' says he, calling him by his name.

'Good day,' says the other.

'Are you going to the fair to sell the cow?' says the man.

'I am,' says Mick.

'How much would you be looking for her?'

'Well, to tell you the truth,' says Mick, 'I'd be lookin' a good price for her,' and he tells him the truth: that it was the last cow and the family were hungry.

Families being hungry was a new experience for Hannah when she came to Ardtur, but she'd been married only three years, when, in 1838, the potatoes failed. After two miscarriages there were still only two of them, so she'd used more bread and porridge to feed Patrick and herself, and only bought potatoes when they were a reasonable price. There were plenty of potatoes available in the markets, imported from various countries, but some traders were charging prices that only the gentry could afford.

She'd been so thankful that Patrick had work that winter. A road was being built some miles away under a new scheme for improvements that had recently been agreed by Parliament. Patrick was young and fit, but there were others in Ardtur notable for the heavy work involved. Sadly pressed, some had to go to the new workhouse in Dunfanaghy. There, the families were split up at the entrance. Husbands and wives were parted, the men set to work breaking stones. The children too were parted, brothers from sisters, and sent to their separate quarters.

When her only cow became ill, Patrick's Aunt Mary lived in fear that she too would have to go into the workhouse. Without her milk money she could not pay the rent or buy food for herself. Hannah and Patrick had been able to help her out. Mercifully, the cow recovered and a nephew sent her some dollars from Boston.

Hannah pushed away the memories of that failed harvest as they pressed back into her mind and took up John's story once more.

'Well,' says the man, 'I've no money on me, but I tell you what I'll do. I've two bottles here, and I'll give you those, and as long as you keep them whole and intact you'll never want for anything.'

'Ach now, my dear man,' says Mick, 'what good would your bottles be to me, when I've a family to feed?'

'Well now,' says the man, 'if you sit yourself down I'll give you a sample of what they can do.'

So Mick sits down, and the man puts the two bottles down and says, 'Come on now, bottles, do your duty,' and out come two waiters, one out of each bottle, and they lay a cloth and spread dishes and crockery and all that was needed for the grandest feast Mick has ever had.

Mick is afraid that there is some enchantment, and that this luck might not hold, but the man says it will be the same every time, so Mick gives him the cow and goes home.

When he goes home it still isn't day and his wife is in bed, for she isn't expecting him.

When she gets up she says, 'Well, did you sell the cow?'

'I did,' says Mick.

'Well, what did you get for her?'

'Well, I don't rightly know yet,' says he, 'but I'll show you. Call up the children, and set them round the table, for they went to bed hungry.'

So she wakens the children and sets them down at the table half-asleep, and Mick sets down the two bottles and says: 'Now, bottles, do your duty,' and out pop the two waiters who set the table, and spread a feast such as the poor woman has never seen.

Afterwards when all is cleared away the woman says: 'There's some enchantment in it. Sure, you might wake up in the morning and find no trace of the bottles at all.'

But Mick says the money from the cow would have run done anyway so they were just as well off.

Hannah turned over the page and found that the hasty scribble was now replaced by John's usual, clear handwriting.

This is what we might call Act 1. I'm afraid I haven't time to copy out Act 2 and Act 3 just now, but I promise I will. What I wondered was whether we could get the children to turn this into a play, perform it in Irish and then work on it so they could perform it in English. What do you think, Hannah?

But what Hannah thought was not to emerge for quite some time. As she turned over the last sheet to see if there was anything more written above his habitual neat signature, she heard a step outside the door.

To her surprise, she saw it was Sophie whom she had visited earlier in the day. She held a rolled-up magazine in her hand and dropped down gratefully into the armchair by the fire when Hannah welcomed her.

'I think I'm the bringer of bad news, but I'm not sure, for my eyes have been giving me trouble an' the print is so small,' she began, unrolling the magazine and pointing to an item on the front page.

'Is it what I think it is?' she asked anxiously, as Hannah scanned the minute print.

'I'm afraid so, Sophie. They say it's right across England and spreading fast. No sign of it here yet, but they seem to think it's almost sure to come. It looks like we're going to have the potato blight back again sometime in the next few weeks.'

12

The weeks of a humid summer passed slowly. Hannah felt oppressed by the low cloud and the general dampness of the air. The weather had a strange feel about it, as if somehow everything was suspended, the clouds not moving, the clothes not drying, the fire itself sulking. Even the children, her own and the children who lived nearby, seemed burdened by the lack of movement, arriving back from their play for meals, or an afternoon mug of tea with little of their usual liveliness.

As time passed, Hannah admitted she was grateful for the chance to catch up on her consignment of napkins. She'd persuaded the draper to leave a second month's supply for hemming, even though she'd done so little on the previous consignment, but she was in no doubt at all that if she defaulted at the end of August, the draper had plenty of women who badly needed the work she had done now for many years.

How she'd manage to make the time for her sewing when she went back to three mornings a week at school, she had no idea whatever.

She wasn't the only one to feel oppressed by the weather. Sophie, the most equable of women, began complaining about a variety of pains and aches she had never mentioned before on her frequent visits and even the younger women with children in the nearby cottages spent more time in each other's houses.

But, most surprising of all, Daniel, whom she visited one or two afternoons in the week, admitted to 'feeling low'. He actually confessed to Hannah that he was finding it a struggle to keep up his storytelling in the evenings, even though he was surprised to find he was receiving more callers than usual.

It was the draper himself, arriving close to the end of the month and accepting her offer of tea and a piece of cake, who made the comment that led Hannah to ask herself if Daniel had sensed something that was affecting everyone.

'Sure, ask any of the old people an' they'll tell you it's this weather brings the blight,' he said, stirring his tea vigorously. 'An' then once it starts, you'd need a long, dry spell, or hot weather, to put a stop to it, an' sure what chance is there of that kinda weather in these parts? Did you never have it like this where you come from? Galloway, isn't it?'

This clinging humidity was not something she'd met on the farm, but then they were near the sea there and sheltered from the north and west. She remembered only golden summers and green fields. But perhaps distance lent enchantment and she was not being very accurate.

'I certainly don't remember it ever being like this for more than a day or two,' she replied. 'But then, my father reared sheep and cattle. He did grow some vegetables, but that was only for the family; it wasn't to pay the rent.'

'Unlike the poor folk in this godforsaken

place,' he said sharply. 'Have ye heard there's blight now over in Antrim and Down? They say it came in on ships, but once it's in, it can spread in the air. The next thing it'll be in Tyrone and Fermanagh,' he said, as he gathered up the crumbs of his cake with a wet finger and finished them off. 'Will I leave you the full quota or are you still teaching at the school?' he asked, throwing on the cap he'd dropped to the floor when he pulled his chair up to the table.

'Yes, I'll see you get the full bale,' she said, making up her mind immediately. 'Some other things will just have to wait. If things are bad with the blight round here, then my husband probably won't find any work when he comes back from Scotland.'

'Aye. Ye've a head on your shoulders. He's a lucky man,' he added.

He laid two small brown envelopes on the table, picked up the two heavy bales of napkins as if they were small parcels and turned towards the door. 'That was a great mug o' tea. I'm beholden to ye,' he said, as he raised a hand in farewell and disappeared down the steep slope to where he'd left the donkey and trap tethered to a bush on the edge of the main track.

★   ★   ★

Later that day, the children settled with their storybooks, reading to Sophie. She walked up to see Daniel. He greeted her warmly and then fell silent. His mood seemed even lower than it had been a couple of days earlier.

It came as a surprise to her to see Daniel, the most articulate of men, sit silent, even for a few minutes. She felt quite unsure what to do.

'I'm afraid I'm but poor company this afternoon, Hannah,' he said slowly, while she was still looking at him. 'I've had some bad news about Johnny Donnelly.'

'Oh dear, I *am* sorry. What's wrong? Is the poor boy ill?'

'No. Thank God, he's well enough. It's his father is the problem. It's only a smallholding and they have five children,' he began matter-of-factly. 'He says he has no money for Johnny to be painting pictures and learning a foreign language, now he's big enough to go to work! And very bitter he was too, despite the fact the school's had no money from him in months and I've not pressed him.'

'But where would he find work for Johnny?' Hannah protested. 'Yes, he's a strong lad, but if the work isn't there, why take him from school?'

'I did actually say something of the sort myself, but Dermot Donnelly was in no mood to listen. All he said was that there were plenty of gentry about the place and they all needed servants. He was on the lookout, but, in the meantime, Johnny wouldn't be back at school come September.'

'Oh, Daniel, no wonder you're annoyed,' Hannah burst out. 'What are we going to do?'

'I haven't any idea,' he said sadly. 'But what I would guess is that there'll be others like Dermot, anxious about what may happen and striking out where they can, regardless of the real situation. So, after all the hard work, mostly yours, Hannah, the school that you saved will once again be at risk.'

'Daniel, we can't let it go now after how well it's been doing. I could write to Jonathan Hancock again. And what about John McCreedy? He'll be heartbroken if the school goes, never mind his job going with it. He's worked so hard.'

'Aye, and so have you. And you've not had a penny piece.'

'Well, we thought I'd just be temporary, but it does look as if you do need someone to at least some of Marie's tasks. Should I go and see Johnny's mother? She might be able to do something.'

'She might be able to stop her husband suggesting to all and sundry that the school ought to close if we're going to have blight again,' he replied sharply.

'Oh, Daniel, and what help would that be to take away possibility for the future?'

'Hannah dear, it is not in your nature to see the worst side of people. Johnny's father is just thinking of himself and no one else. He'll strike out at anyone he thinks is in his way, right or wrong. But maybe the mother has some say. She might have, and she might not, like John McCreedy's mother.'

At the thought of John's mother, Hannah sighed. A woman could only do her best if she had someone to help her. Someone like Patrick, who would always listen, even if he didn't agree. They had never fallen out over the children, or over money, or even over not having enough money. They had always done their best and given thanks for having each other and enough to eat and having the strength to do their daily work.

'Daniel dear, I can only try. I'll go now and come up again tomorrow for I don't want to leave the children too long with Sophie. She's very good to them, but she gets tired. Now don't worry, we'll manage somehow,' she said, taking his hand and squeezing it.

'Well, good luck to you. I'll say a prayer for you, though I used not to be a praying man,' he said, as she stood up.

★   ★   ★

Johnny's home was in Staghall, not far away, but up an even steeper slope than the one to either Ardtur or Casheltown. The low, thatched house was at the highest point of the scattered settlement and by the time she got there Hannah was tiring and out of breath.

'Missus Donnelly,' she said smiling, as she knocked the open door.

'Aye.'

'My name is Hannah McGinley. I help at the school.'

The younger woman's face dropped something of its hostility, but she was immediately distracted by a crying child. She turned away without a word, leaving Hannah leaning wearily against the doorpost.

'Are ye not comin' in?' she asked crossly, when she returned some minutes later.

'Thank you,' said Hannah, taking in at a glance the untidy kitchen where three younger children stared at her and the baby still whimpered uneasily.

'Daniel McGee told me your husband was hoping to find a job for Johnny. Do you not think maybe he would do better if he had another while at school?'

The wooden chair was hard and squeaked on the uneven floor if she moved as much as a muscle and her back already ached. She was beginning to feel she'd made a dreadful mistake thinking she could do something to help Johnny, whose work had improved by leaps and bounds as he started using his watercolours.

Barely able to write his name before the crayons arrived from Dublin, he could now write stories and accounts of happenings at home or at school, which were a part of every day's work. He was quick at figures, and to everyone's surprise had only to be told a word, or phrase in English once, for him to repeat it accurately.

She wasn't sure whether the woman sitting watching her across a smoking fire was hostile, or just very awkward. She had no idea what to say to her. She was very thin, her lank hair falling round her pale face, her heavy skirt stained with spilt milk.

'Has Johnny been painting any more pictures in the holidays?' Hannah asked, as the silence grew more awkward.

'No,' she replied abruptly. 'His da thinks it's a waste of time. Sure, when did playing with crayons put food on the table!'

'Well, it might, if he had a bit more practice and some encouragement,' Hannah said, shocked at her own sudden response.

'Sure, who'd want pictures of this place? Would you give money for his scribbles?'

'I would indeed, if I were a visitor from England, or home from America and had money. There are people who would treasure Johnny's pictures if they could see them.'

'Are ye jokin'?'

'No, I'm not.'

'An' can ye get us money from what he's done?'

'No, he needs more practice, and the pictures need to be mounted, or framed. Then they'd need to go to a gallery, or a hotel, where people could see them. It would take time and he'd need more time at school.'

'Sure, we haven't got two pence to spare every week,' she came back at her sharply.

'Do you have any turf?'

'Aye, a bit.'

'Well perhaps a bit extra turf would make up for the two pennies.'

'I'll have to tell his father.'

'Yes, of course,' Hannah said quickly, now somewhat anxious that the creaky wooden chair was about to collapse. 'I'm afraid I must go. My children are with a neighbour.'

'How many have you?

'Just two, Rose and Sam.'

'You're lucky. I have five and one on the way . . . '

★ ★ ★

136

Hannah was so exhausted by the time she'd walked back to Ardtur that she just about managed to make up the fire before it went out. She sat, waiting for the kettle to boil, hoping that Sophie had not seen her arrive and would therefore keep the children just a little longer.

She had her wish. It was only after she had drained a second mug of tea and begun to reflect in amazement at what she had said to Johnny's mother, when she heard their excited chatter.

'Look, Ma. John's come back early. Isn't that great?' Sam shouted, despite the fact he was now standing beside her.

'And he's brought the other two parts of that story you read to us. *The Two Bottles.* D'you remember?' added Rose, full of excitement.

Above their heads, John beamed at her and raised his eyes heavenwards.

'Oh yes, I remember,' Hannah said, her spirits lifting, as she kissed the children and gave John a hug.

Suddenly, the day looked brighter.

★ ★ ★

By the time Hannah had made supper and they had all had second helpings, it was obvious that both children were tired out. John exchanged glances with her and asked: 'What about a bedtime story?'

'Oh yes, please. Pleeease will you tell us what happens next,' they chorused.

Hannah smiled as she saw John take his manuscript from the satchel he had brought with him. To her surprise, he did not begin to read. He started asking them questions, clearly testing to see if they remembered what had happened so far.

She listened, fascinated, as John used exactly the same technique she had heard Daniel deploy night after night when people gathered in his home to listen to his stories.

The children certainly passed muster, she thought, as they described how the man, 'a right sort of man' called Mick, had set off for market in the middle of the night to sell his last cow because his wife and children were hungry and there was no food in the house.

Satisfied at last, after they had described the magic feast provided by 'the two waiters', John took up his closely written sheets, paused for seconds only, till he had their total attention, and began:

Anyway, all went well and Mick and his family were well fed, although there wasn't a cow about the place . . . One day Mick met the landlord who lived near. Now the landlord used to see a couple of Mick's young lads hanging about the place, and he had given orders for someone to give them a meal. But he hadn't seen the young lads lately and he was curious.

'*Good morning, Mick,*' *says the landlord.*

'*Good morning, yer honour,*' *says Mick.*

'*Tell me, Mick,*' *says he,* '*where are the young lads? I gave orders for them to be fed if they came up and I haven't seen them about. Where are they?*'

'*That was very good of yer honour,*' *says*

Mick, 'but they don't need meals any more.' And he tells him the story of the bottles.

The landlord can hardly believe it, but Mick brings out the bottles and gives him a great surprise.

'Mick,' says the landlord, 'that's great altogether. I'll buy them off you.'

'Indeed,' says Mick, 'I wouldn't part with them for any money. Sure, they're all we have.'

'Well, Mick,' says the landlord. 'You used to have a right farm of land here, before your luck went. What if I were to restock the land for you with five or six cows and gave you £100 as well?'

Anyway, Mick said he'd think about it, and he went and asked his wife what he would do. So she said that he should take the cows and the money, for what would they do if the enchantment wore off?

So Mick sold the bottles and got the cows and the £100, but he never had good luck with them. One by one they went and so did the money until eventually one night he was sitting with his wife and they were down to the last cow.

The children were fascinated. Sam was sitting so still Hannah could hardly believe her eyes. Normally, some part of Sam was in motion whether he was sitting or standing, and for both of them to refrain from interruption, when they seldom ever stopped talking, was a new experience indeed.

She couldn't help but admire John's technique, his significant pauses, his warning eye movements that told them something was about to happen.

139

So Mick says to her: 'We've no food and there's a fair in the town tomorrow. I think I'll go and sell the cow.'

'Well, if you do there'll be no milk for the children.'

'Ah,' says Mick, 'sure, you know what happened the last time, and you never know, the same might happen again.'

So, off Mike went . . . and he came to the same spot, and he was casting his eye up to the spot where he had seen the man and sure enough the man appeared.

'Good morning, Mick,' says he. 'Are you going to the fair again?'

'I am,' says Mick.

'I thought I told you not to part with the bottles . . . '

Well, finally Mick tells him he would settle for the same again, so the man produces the two bottles.

'There's no use testing them,' says the man, 'for they're the same as I gave you before, but don't abuse them and only use them when you need them.'

So Mick puts the bottles in his pocket and goes off home.

Anyway, the wife is waiting up for him for she is expecting him. 'Did you see him?' says she.

'I did,' says he.

'And did he give you two more bottles?'

'He did,' says Mick.

So they get the children out of bed and sit down round the table and Mick says: 'Now, bottles, do your duty.' And out pop two black *devils and hit them all over the head with mallets till they are all black and blue and calling for mercy.*

Afterwards, when they have finished, the wife says to Mick: 'What'll we do now?'

'Ah, wait a while,' says Mick, 'an I'll be meeting the landlord,' says he.

John looked from one child to the other and folded the small sheets neatly to fit into his breast pocket. It was a moment or two before it dawned on them that he had stopped reading for the night. Before they could protest, John raised a finger.

'Now I want you to go away and think what's going to happen next and you can tell me tomorrow.'

They opened their mouths to object, but John was quietly relaxing and Hannah, taking her opportunity, said that it was time they were in bed.

She had just tucked them in and kissed them goodnight when she heard John speak to someone. She couldn't hear the other voice, so she wasn't prepared for the sight of young Martin Brady, a tall lad who stood awkwardly in the open doorway, though John had clearly invited him to come in.

'Missus McGinley, me ma sent me up to tell ye an' all the neighbours at this end o' the track . . . Look!'

The daylight still lingered but the kitchen had grown shadowy and the lamp was not yet lit. It was as he held his hand out towards her that she caught the hint of an unpleasant smell.

It was John who spoke first.

'Where did you get that?' he asked calmly.

'In our piece,' Martin replied, 'down at the low end where the spuds are usually the best. Can ye smell it?'

They both nodded.

'An' the stalks are all black,' he went on, wrinkling his nose. 'They were as right as rain yesterday when I dug them for the dinner but they're just a mess the day. It's the blight, isn't it?'

13

Ardtur,
Gartan, Co. Donegal
Thursday, 28 August, 1845
My dearest Patrick,

I do apologise, my love, for the delay. The last few days have been so busy that even when I had a moment to myself I hadn't the energy to pick up my pen and write your daily bulletin. So I am sitting here with all the morning chores still to do, pen in hand, to make up for lost time! The only thing I've done towards the day's work is put the last of yesterday's turf on the fire to keep it in while I write.

Thank you for your letter and all your news. I'm so glad everything is going well and that young Paddy from Tullygobegley has settled in so well. He certainly seems to have lost his shyness from what you tell me of the tricks he's been playing. Not often you get my father laughing out loud, though he does always appreciate a joke.

There hasn't been much to laugh about here, though the children and I are perfectly all right and in good spirits, so you mustn't worry about us. It is good of Seamus's wife to send the Derry paper so Seamus can share it with all of you. Probably you heard the news of the blight before we did. Not all *of our potatoes have gone. Apparently, they say, the poorer the soil, the better for the spuds . . . certainly the ones at the top end of the garden where the soil is so very poor are still perfectly all right.*

You mustn't worry about the blight. As well as your postal order I have had two months' napkin money and there's no need at all for me to 'go under the bed' if I have to buy meal and flour instead.

Hannah smiled to herself and blotted what she had just written. She was pleased that she could reassure him and make him smile at their private joke. For the moment, no one in Ardtur seemed to be short of food. It would be another matter when the surviving potatoes ran out.

She took up her pen again.

Young John McCreedy returned yesterday, though school doesn't reopen till next week. We were all delighted to see him and he brought the rest of that story of The Two Bottles I told you about. But I was shocked by his news when we got some time alone while the children went down to play at the Friels'.

Apparently, his father had spoken to someone high up in the Coastguard Service who offered a place for John to be trained up. He just assumed John would be pleased and take it. But when John said no, he had found a job as a teacher, his father lost his temper and told him to 'away back to it then and don't come here again.' So the poor young man has no home to go to, though happily now his salary has been agreed and backdated, just like Daniel's pension.

I feel so sorry for John's mother. She doesn't seem to have any say in the matter. She writes to him often, but she accepts that he is totally committed to the school. He says that he will not go 'home' but adds that he knows he is sure of a welcome with his mother's people, the Cullens. Meantime, he seems to have been writing a lot and I haven't had a chance yet to ask him what he's up to.

As you know, he has his evening meal here because Sophie doesn't cook much any more, but he makes his own 'thank you', by helping with the jobs. It's John who digs the potatoes and carries round the turf. He's a great hand, as they say, at finding the eggs of that hen who always lays away.

I am sending this to the post today, my love, but I shall start another letter in instalments tomorrow. Take care of your dear self and tell my father I said he's not to work too hard!

With all my love,
Hannah

Hannah closed up the letter and left it ready on the table waiting for any neighbour, or visitor, who might be going 'down the mountain' today. She couldn't go herself with the children still at home for Rose had never been a good walker, tiring easily and getting distressed and fractious — unlike Sam, who seemed to have unlimited energy. She then looked around the big kitchen where the empty porridge bowls still sat at the far end of the table and the fire was sulking because it hadn't been raked. She needed to bake bread and think about tonight's meal, especially as John would now be joining them and he had a good appetite.

Still she didn't move, feeling oppressed by something. There was plenty to think about with school starting again on Monday, which would be the first day of September, but whatever was teasing at the back of her mind, it wasn't school. Then she remembered Johnny and his drawings, and the poor bedraggled woman she had spoken to after Daniel had told her about his father taking him away from school to be a servant for 'the gentry'.

She could hardly believe now what she had said to her about Johnny's drawings. Fairly, she'd had no time to plan and consider what she was going to say. Now she sat, her hands folded in her lap, waves of anxiety flowing over her. She thought she'd been foolish. How could she know Johnny's pictures were good, just because she liked them? Though, on the positive side, John had agreed with her and he did have some experience of painting, having been able to go to exhibitions of paintings while he was at school in Dublin.

She sat for a few more minutes and then, as if the sight of the unswept hearth was too much for her, she jumped to her feet and began to clear the table.

'Wise or foolish, you've made your bed now,' she said, to herself, 'and you'll just have to make the best of it. Otherwise there's nothing whatever to change Johnny's situation.'

★ ★ ★

It was mid-afternoon by the time she had caught up on herself and baked both soda bread and wheaten. She thought of several more things she ought to do, but as her back was already aching, she took her sewing box to the fire and collected the next napkin from the bundle.

Sometime soon, the children, who had made some new friends at the low end of the track overlooking the lough, would arrive back for their afternoon mug of tea, but meantime she'd enjoy the quiet and try not to think of the mountain of napkins she'd committed herself to do.

She had barely begun stitching and was concentrating hard when she heard a step on the door stone. She looked up and saw a large man she had never seen before.

'You Missus McGinley, works at the school?' he demanded shortly.

'Do come in,' she replied, standing up and offering him the other seat by the fire.

'I'm not stoppin',' he replied, taking only a few steps into the room. 'The wife tells me that ye think ye can sell our Johnny's pictures, if that's what ye call them. D'ye know what yer talkin' about? What sort of money would that be? For we're in a bad way an' I'm afraid yer man will throw us out if we can't pay the rent, an' it's near due.'

The tone was just as unfortunate as his original question, but the look of distress that crossed his face was a different matter. Before she had time to reply, he pulled a cardboard packet from below his jacket and started spreading a jumble of sketches, drawings, and watercolours on the well-scrubbed kitchen table.

Hannah came to the table immediately and started sorting them, laying them out in groups from the least finished to the most complete.

'I used to do watercolour when I was a girl,' she said slowly. 'I had three sisters who encouraged me, but I never produced anything as good as this one,' she said, picking up a watercolour that used the same perspective as Johnny's first sketch, the one he had made with the crayons that had been sent from Dublin.

'I told him to experiment with laying a wash,' she went on, deliberately not looking at Mr Donnelly. 'Look at this sky with the blue and patches of grey cloud,' she said, not troubling to conceal her enthusiasm. 'It's beautifully done.' She finally turned to look him full in the face.

'I doubt there's many in this place cou'd do the like of that,' he admitted. 'Were your people gentry?' he asked cautiously.

'No, my father and brother were evicted from Strathnaver and came south to Galloway looking for work. He always wanted to farm, so he did fifteen years in a draper's shop in Dumfries and saved the money to buy a few acres. And he was good at it,' she added firmly. 'Raised cattle and sheep mostly. My husband is one of his harvesters.'

'Wish I'd bin raised on a farm,' he replied, looking downcast. 'But my father was a fisherman. The old man who owned the boat sold it during the last bad time, an' sure there's no fishin' left aroun' here now. All I can get is odd jobs . . .'

He broke off as they both heard a step outside the door.

'John, come in,' said Hannah turning towards him. 'This is Johnny's father,' she went on. 'Look, he brought these pictures. Mister Donnelly, this is John McCreedy from Galway. He works full-time with Daniel McGee at the school.'

To Hannah's great surprise, Donnelly held out his hand to John.

'Dermot Donnelly, pleased t' meet ye,' he said. 'Our Johnny talks about the both of ye,' he said, as he saw John's eyes immediately move to scan the pictures laid out on the table.

'I don't want to take him from the school fer I didn't get any schoolin' m'self,' he went on quickly, 'but things are very bad with us. I don't know what I'm goin' t' do,' he said, pressing his lips together.

'Well, maybe if we had a mug of tea, we'd get a bit further,' Hannah said, hooking the kettle over the fire. She tried to remember if she still had any cake. She had no idea. But nor had she any idea what could be done for the Donnelly

149

family. What she *was* now sure off was that with help and some kind of outlet, Johnny's work would sell. But it might take time and the problem was they had none.

She moved around the kitchen making tea and opening the cake tin, grateful when she found she could manage to cut three slices, even if they were small. As she came back into the kitchen from the small chilly outshot where she kept the milk and the pails of water, she was pleased to hear Dermot Donnelly talking away quite easily to John.

They were talking about fishing in Galway Bay and in the local rivers. John had been allowed to go out on the coastguard boats when they were off-duty and had permission to fish, but what he preferred was fishing with his grandfather in a small lake near their home where there were both salmon and trout.

It was when John asked Dermot what the fishing was like in North Donegal that Hannah remembered Jonathan Hancock's latest letter. When she relayed to him all she'd learnt from Shemmie, the fish man, he'd written back immediately. He knew there were very few fishing boats left, just curraghs and coracles, which were only fair-weather craft; but he had never before heard that 'the coast was teeming with fish'.

She poured tea and passed round the cake, her mind fully occupied trying to remember exactly what he'd said in his reply. She remembered how surprised she'd been when he said buying boats was only a question of money, which was available, but it looked as if there would be a shortage of fishermen, and worse still, no local source of either boat building, or repair. He'd also said that it looked as if fishermen from some nearby region in the north, or even west of Ireland, or from a similar coastal area in Scotland, would be needed to literally teach a new generation of young men how to fish. He'd started work on it and would let her know when he made any progress.

It wasn't going to solve the immediate problem for the Donnellys, but if there was at least a prospect of employment for Dermot himself, it might perhaps take away some of the anxiety here and now.

She made up her mind, waited for a break in the conversation and said: 'Dermot, if you were offered a job teaching lads to fish, would you be able to take it?'

She would never forget the way he looked at her, amazement and relief alternating as he tried to grasp what she was saying.

'I can't tell you when yet, or where, but there's a plan being made to bring back the fishing here on the north coast. Now that the blight has come, it may well speed things up. We'll just have to see what we can do in the meantime, but it would be a proper paid job and I'm sure you'd be given a share of the fish as well.'

'Sure, wou'dn't that be great?' he said, looking from one to the other. 'We can hol' on a bit longer if we have a bit of hope, an' sure you wou'dn't tell me what wasn't right.'

'No, she wouldn't,' said John firmly, 'and in

the meantime I'm going to see if I can order card through school to mount John's pictures. Then, until we can get someone to frame them, we can at least display them in some of the hotels. I've no doubt at all but they'll sell.'

For one awkward moment Hannah thought Dermot was going to cry, but instead he jumped to his feet.

'I wasn't planning to stop and the wife'll be worried that I'm not back to dig the spuds for the supper,' he said awkwardly. 'I don't know how to thank yez,' he added, as he gathered himself. 'Ye'll see Johnny at school on Monday with a few more of them watercolours that ye liked.' He nodded to the little pile of work that now sat on the dresser.

'Do you still have potatoes?' asked Hannah.

'We do. No sign of the rot, thank God, but some o' the neighbours down below us has lost some.'

'Let us know if they run out and we'll see if the Quaker man who came here can help us,' Hannah said firmly, making up her mind to write to Jonathan right away.

She stood up herself, then eyed the two cakes of bread she'd set to cool in the back window.

'Here,' she said, picking the bigger one. 'That might help out till you get your potatoes dug. I'm sorry I have no paper to wrap it in.'

14

The first weeks of September 1845 were very busy indeed for Hannah. As well as teaching three mornings a week and keeping John and the children properly fed, she had to make time to work on her consignment of napkins, look after the cottage, write letters to both Patrick and her father, and, yet more urgently, since the visit from Dermot Donnelly, write to Jonathan Hancock who was now planning to come again later in the autumn.

The more she thought about the news coming from neighbours along the length of Lough Gartan, the less hopeful she was that there would be enough sound potatoes to put in the clamps that would carry them through the winter until the new crop in May, or June, of next year, depending on the weather, of course.

Prices of flour and meal had already gone up. There were certainly potatoes to be had in the markets but their price also rose from week to week. Meantime, Sophie provided not only news of the rising admission figures for the new Dunfanaghy workhouse, but also from the rest of Ireland. She even brought a copy of the *Illustrated London News* with a drawing of a woman and two ragged children 'hoking' in an empty field, for any potatoes that might have survived and not been found by the 'tattie hokers' when they harvested the crop early, to try to save it.

It was an image Hannah could not get out of her mind.

Meantime, to her great relief and surprise, the school flourished. Thanks to John and Daniel and a woman called Bridget Delaney living nearby, they used a small grant from Dublin to provide a piece for every child at mid-day. With the arrival of the grant, nothing need now be said when only turf was brought on a Friday and no pennies were forthcoming.

'I can't believe how well they've done with their English,' said John, lingering by Hannah's fireside one evening after Rose and Sam had gone to bed.

'Daniel is so delighted I'm afraid he's going to get enthusiastic enough to break his vow and end up replying to someone in English,' replied Hannah, smiling as she took out her sewing.

'No, I don't think he will,' John said, shaking his head. 'He has his place as a storyteller in this valley and it means so much to him. But I sometimes do wonder why he is so against speaking English himself.'

Hannah raised her eyebrows. 'I used to know someone else like that,' she said cautiously, looking up from her work.

She was pleased when he laughed. She had not forgotten how bitter he was when he first arrived, incensed by his father's refusal to learn Irish, apart from the bare minimum he needed for doing his job as a coastguard.

'I'm afraid that was between me and my father,' he said honestly. 'He hasn't changed any, but I have. If we want to keep up the Irish language and our culture and traditions, we also need to move with the times. English is indeed the language of those who oppress us, but it is also the language of good people who are trying to help us, like your friend Jonathan Hancock and all those Americans who are sending money home to Donegal.'

'Are you still not in touch with your father?' Hannah asked gently.

'No,' he said. 'I write to my mother every week, but she says he never mentions me and if *she* should mention my name he just ignores her. I don't know what I can do. What would you do?'

'It is hard for me to imagine what it must be like,' she admitted. 'I was close to my father when I was a child. Indeed, I still am. But I do remember when I was leaving home to marry Patrick, my father said he'd give me some advice. And I can still remember exactly what he said. He said that grief and heartache come to us all, but the greatest danger of all is bitterness. He told me when I was sad, or grieved, always to ask for comfort from God, or from my friends, because if you give in to bitterness you'll never live life fully even if you go beyond your three score years and ten.'

'So I must try not to be bitter.'

'I'm sure it is easier said than done,' she replied.

He nodded and looked thoughtful, staring into the glowing embers of the fire. It was a couple of minutes before he spoke again.

'Perhaps, like Johnny's father,' he began,

'something had hurt him and he just didn't know what to do when I said no to being a coastguard. D'you think I was wrong?' he asked suddenly.

'No, I don't,' she said firmly. 'You're a very good teacher. It would have been such a pity if you hadn't followed what prompted you.'

'Thanks, Hannah. I'm so grateful I have you to talk to. I should go now and read to Sophie. She'll be waiting for me and wondering what's keeping me. I'll see you in the morning,' he added, standing up. 'Are you sure you have all you need? Turf? Water? Just say the word.'

She smiled and took up her napkin again. 'It's amazing the way the bucket and the creel just fill up by themselves, these days,' she said lightly. 'They never seem to run empty.'

To her surprise, he bent down as he passed her chair and kissed her cheek.

★ ★ ★

Although there was little good news from neighbours either in Ardtur or beyond in the length of the valley, Hannah could hardly believe how much good fortune seemed to focus on the school. Attendance was better than it had ever been and a gift of dollars from another niece of Daniel's in America meant they were able to buy another sack of oats to share out. Any child who said, when asked in the morning, that they'd had no breakfast, was given a piece of bread and jam to keep them going. Then, at the end of the school day, they collected a large bowlful of oats to take home to provide an evening meal for their family.

The first sack didn't last long. Just as it was about to run out, a postal order arrived from Jonathan Hancock who said his mill workers were going to collect a penny a week for them. In the hasty note that came with it, he also wanted to know if Hannah could use serviceable, but flawed fabric for clothing.

It was only when Jonathan arrived in person that she found out just how many people were employed in the family mills. Even before she had done the calculation, she breathed a sigh of relief. No family who had a child at school, or who lived nearby, would go hungry this side of Christmas.

* * *

Jonathan appeared at the kitchen door one Friday morning at the end of October when she was already watching out for the letter that would tell her exactly when Patrick and the harvesters would be leaving Dundrennan and heading home. To her surprise, he immediately began to tell her enthusiastically about his work in Armagh and how he had met and been welcomed by Sir George Molyneux at Castledillon.

It was perfectly clear from what he said that Sir George was one of those landlords who was fully committed to helping his tenants in bad times. He was Chairman of the Armagh Workhouse Committee and he had shared with

157

him a good deal about how the system worked, who could go for help, and what conditions in the workhouse were like.

'I'm afraid I now understand why people would rather starve than go there,' Jonathan said sadly, as he sat down at the kitchen table and accepted a large mug of tea.

'And why is that?' she asked, as she offered him a very modest slice of cake.

'All the new Irish workhouses are built to the same pattern,' he began. 'When a family is allowed in, the men and women are separated from each other immediately. So are the children. There's a men's yard and a women's yard, a girls' yard and a boys' yard. The woman who works as a secretary for Sir George and sends me copies of the workhouse minutes told me when I last spoke to her that children are punished for trying to climb the walls to see their parents. When they go in, however weak they may be from lack of food, the men are set to work breaking stones and the women to do all the washing and cleaning for the whole workhouse. There are teachers for the children but they have classrooms at opposite sides of the building. The girls and boys never see each other. The secretary Sarah Hamilton says that Sir George has protested, but the rules are literally set in stone. The workhouse, apparently, was built to be discouraging. And it certainly is, the absolute last resort except for those already starving.'

For a moment Hannah could not speak. She thought of the twelve children in Daniel's cottage and the way they so often sat on the floor, squashed up together, so as to leave a space at one end of Daniel's kitchen for putting on a play they had written. Even when they gathered for the story with which Daniel always ended the school day, they sat down together, the only division between them being the tallest at the back and the smallest at the front.

The children simply took it for granted that they helped each other. The bigger boys and the older girls collected the pieces for mid-day and made sure every child had its full portion; they picked them up when they fell at playtime and read to them when it was time to choose a library book.

A single thought came into Hannah's mind: how could she bear it if she and her children were ever separated? The thought appalled her. Or how would she cope if she was forced to live without Patrick? It was one thing to endure the pain of the necessary parting to get work, but at least through that time they could write to each other as often as they wanted, could think about each other and count the weeks till they'd be together again. And they knew that come late October, Patrick and all his colleagues would be on the way to Stranraer for the Derry boat.

'Oh, Jonathan, how awful. I didn't know that. I couldn't bear to be parted from Patrick and the children, no matter how bad things were.'

He looked at her and smiled sadly. She saw an expression of such distress on his face that she asked the question that had suddenly come to her mind.

159

'Jonathan, are you married?'

'Yes, I am, but my wife is being cared for in The Retreat, which is outside Armagh,' he said steadily. 'She doesn't know now who I am.'

'Oh, Jonathan, I *am* sorry,' she said, not at all surprised to find that he was married, but left wondering why his wife should be so far away from their home in Yorkshire.

'Olivia's family are landowners in the Richhill area,' he said. 'It seemed kinder to place her where her own family could visit her more easily,' he went on. 'But she doesn't know any of them now either.'

'And you still come to see her?'

'Of course,' he said. 'Several times a year. But I admit it helps me that I now have my work for the Yearly Meeting to do both here in Donegal, where I have cousins, and in Armagh where most of my in-laws live. One feels so helpless. You'd understand about that.'

'Yes, I so hate not being able to help people when I see them in need.'

'So I have observed,' he said, smiling and relaxing visibly. 'And I do have some good news for you,' he went on, looking pleased.

'And I have some for you too,' she replied, grateful that his distress over his wife seemed to have been forgotten for now.

'Well, I hope you'll be as pleased as I am. I contacted your brother, as you suggested in your letter, the boat builder, through the local Meeting in Stranraer and he's sent me an estimate for the first boat, which I've passed on to the Committee in Dublin. There's already a plan to have three of them made and sent here, regardless of the course or severity of the famine. Fish would definitely improve the diet and reduce the dependence on potatoes. As soon as the first one is seaworthy there's a job for Dermot Donnelly. He will, in fact, have to come over to Scotland to bring her back to Dunfanaghy. Presumably, he is familiar with the nearest parts of the Scottish coast as well as with this stretch of the Donegal coast. Do you think he might still have any colleagues in the area who could come with him?' he asked, as if the thought had just occurred to him.

'I'm afraid I'm a complete landlubber,' he went on, 'but even I know it would take several men to sail a boat, especially in bad weather on this coastline.'

'Oh, Jonathan, that is good news,' she said, beaming at him. 'You can be sure, if there are any fishermen still around, Dermot will find them. He walks miles looking for work, but as you know there's even less work now than a few months ago. Even the landlords are cutting back, especially where they're not getting their rents.'

'Have you had any evictions?'

'No, not that I've heard off, but Sophie tells us that it's a different matter further south.'

'Sophie?' he asked, puzzled.

Hannah laughed.

'Sophie is my nearest neighbour. John McCreedy, my teaching colleague, is her lodger at present and he reads to her in the evenings, which she just loves. She manages to acquire newspapers and magazines collected up from a

161

couple of hotels where her nieces work and she has a fantastic memory. She remembers everything John reads and passes it on. We even get items from the *Illustrated London News*, though mostly the reports are a couple of weeks old, or even more, when we do.'

'So you'll have you heard then about the £14,000 collected in Calcutta?'

'Good heavens, no, I hadn't. How did that happen?'

'Well, it appears that over forty per cent of the Indian army are Irish and when someone appealed to a high-ranking soldier, Sir Hugh Gough, who was Irish-born, they were most generous. Then there were Indian princes and wealthy Hindus who gave to the collection as well. So far there's been £14,000 sent to Dublin. The Anglican Archbishop has organised a team for distributing it. You probably know how bad things are in Connaught,' he ended, his voice dropping.

'Yes, even the local papers have been reporting that,' she said, nodding. 'But how wonderful about India. Isn't it encouraging to see such generosity?'

'It is indeed,' he said. 'I sometimes can't believe the kindness of people who donate, even from what little they have. I just wish I could do more.'

'But, Jonathan, you do so much. That money from your mill workers could keep this whole valley from starving if the crop fails again next year. Pray to God it doesn't, but it has happened before.'

'Well, with more people like you and what you're doing through the school, and what Sir George and his people are doing from Castledillon, it's a start. We must live in hope,' he said, a hint of sadness creeping into his voice.

Hannah was only too aware of the change in his mood, but she didn't know what to say. What had happened to the girl he married was just beyond her imaginings. All she could do was pretend she hadn't seen the look on his face and try to distract him.

She stood up and took a linen envelope from the dresser. She had made a document case from some flawed napkins the draper had said she could keep. Now, she drew out from it the little pile of Johnny's recent drawings and watercolours and began to spread them in front of him.

They were still unframed, but John had mounted the artwork on firm card he'd made by sticking sheets of drawing paper together and flattening them overnight under a pile of books.

'My goodness,' he said, as he focused on the gaiety of the crayon drawings and the increasing delicacy of the watercolours in front of him. 'And this is the fisherman's son?' he asked, amazed and delighted as he noted the neat signature, *Johnny Donnelly*, in black ink in each bottom right-hand corner.

'The problem is how we sell them and how much we should ask,' she said anxiously. 'The family do need money for food though we've been keeping them going with the meal and flour we bought from the money you sent.'

To her great surprise, he looked up and

beamed at her, his sadness disappearing.

'Oh no, we'll not sell them,' he said cheerfully. 'If I 'give' them to the right people and then ask for a donation for school and your flour and meal supply, I think you'll be surprised at how much we raise. Johnny, of course, must have a small fee from each one. Enough to feed them properly till there's a boat ready to sail. But that will be only a token, if I'm right. Make no mistake, Hannah, these pictures will raise a great deal of money when I put them in front of the right people.'

15

'Ma, Ma, he's coming! He's coming!'

Sam burst into the kitchen well ahead of his sister and came to a sudden halt by the kitchen table. 'They've just stopped at the foot of the slope saying cheerio to some friends.'

Hannah, who was sewing and totally absorbed in thinking about the play her pupils had been performing in English that morning, jumped to her feet and hurried to the door, just as Rose arrived, red in the face and breathless.

There had, of course, been a letter telling her that the harvesters were leaving Mackay's farm on the thirty-first, the last Friday in October, but which boat they came on depended on whether or not they got any lifts with carriers going in the direction of Stranraer. It might take two days; often enough it had taken three.

There were still a couple of men shaking hands at the foot of the slope, neighbours from Casheltown and Staghall, but the moment they went their ways, Hannah saw Patrick turn and move slowly towards home, speeding up and waving when he caught sight of them standing at the door.

Instantly, Sam was on his way down again and Hannah saw Patrick smile as he stopped where he was and watched the flying figure approaching him at breakneck speed over the rough track.

Despite his sudden warm smile, Hannah could

see from the droop of his shoulders and his pale face that he was exhausted. He hugged Sam and kissed him and waved again, as Rose made her way down to him more slowly, much less indifferent to the roughness of the track.

For a moment, Hannah felt tears well up in her eyes, but she wiped them surreptitiously with the back of her hand, knowing he was still watching her, as she stood smiling, leaning against the doorpost.

'You look tired, love,' she said, when he had kissed her and held her briefly. 'Are you all right?' she asked as lightly as she could manage, knowing how much he hated what he always thought of as 'a fuss'.

'As right as rain,' he said, as she drew him in front of the fire and he dropped down gratefully in his usual seat. 'We had a bit of a storm the first night and all of us were sick. The boat had to run for shelter, a wee place called Donaghadee, in County Down, way south of where we were goin' and we had to lie up till the north-westerly blew itself out. Even then we were desperate slow roun' by Ballycastle, though when we did get to Derry we were lucky with a lift to Creeslough. If we hadn't had that we wou'dn't have got here till the morra.'

To her surprise, even Sam was silent as they held his hands, one on each side of him, leaning over the robust arms of the elderly wooden armchairs, as close as they could get to him. They soon recovered themselves and began to ply him with questions.

'Now, Rose and Sam, I have a question I must

166

ask Da first,' Hannah said, holding up her hand. 'Could you eat a bowl of champ?'

'Ach now, sure wasn't I thinkin' about your bowl of champ all the way up from Churchill. That's what kep' me goin' on the last bit, for none of us cou'd eat a bite after thon' storm. An' all we've had the day was a bowl o' porridge.'

★ ★ ★

An hour later, by which time Patrick had inspected the potato garden and Sam and Rose had finally run out of questions, they came back into the house to find John McCreedy laying the table while Hannah chopped scallions with fine scissors and added lumps of butter to a large baking bowl full of steaming potatoes.

'Patrick, this is John,' she said lightly, as she began to pound the potatoes with a wooden beatle.

'Pleased t' meet you, John. I've heerd a lot about you,' said Patrick warmly. 'It's great you and Hannah are able to keep the school goin'. Sure Donegal is desperate backward in schooling, so Hannah tells me.'

'Indeed it is,' John replied, coming round the table and shaking hands with the older man. 'Did I tell you, Hannah,' he asked, turning towards her, 'that Sophie found a report from Dublin that said Donegal had only nineteen per cent literacy?'

'What's literacy, Ma?' demanded Sam, who was still clutching one of his father's hands.

'I'll tell you that when you and Rose have

washed your hands,' Hannah replied, laughing.

'It's what I didn't have,' Patrick said, looking directly at John, 'until Hannah met me a few years ago in another place.' He looked round the big kitchen, as if he wanted to check that every detail was exactly as he had left it back in April.

Supper was lively and much enjoyed, though Hannah was aware how slowly Patrick was eating. The lines in his face had deepened and when John lit the lamp he looked quite haggard. John exchanged glances with her and immediately straightened up, ready to go.

To Hannah's great surprise, Patrick protested. 'Sit yer ground, man. Sure, the evenin' is only young an' I've a feelin' this pair is not ready for bed yet.'

There were vigorous shakings of heads.

Hannah looked across at the children, her own tiredness catching up with her at the end of the long day as she made mugs of tea and poured glasses of milk for Rose and Sam.

'Perhaps, Hannah and Patrick, I could read a bedtime story before I go,' John suggested tentatively.

Patrick nodded easily and Hannah sat down gratefully, her fingers wound round her mug, her eyes moving from Patrick to the children and back again. She settled back in her chair and relaxed as John brought a kitchen chair over to the fire and moved stools for Rose and Sam so they could sit, one on either side of their father.

'I wondered if you would like to hear the last part of the story of *The Two Bottles*,' he added, looking round at them all.

He was not surprised at the instant response from Sam and Rose, but when Patrick also nodded and smiled, he immediately took the neatly written sheets from his pocket.

'Well now, we must go back to . . . what was his name?' began John.

'Mick. An' he was a right sort of man,' shouted Sam.

'The man down to his last cow with nothing for his family to eat,' added Rose.

Patrick sat back in his chair, drew a deep breath and closed his eyes, as John proceeded to get the two children to reconstruct the story. Patrick himself remembered reading the first two parts in one of Hannah's letters and sharing it with his fellow workers one evening when they were sitting in the last of the sunshine outside what they all called their 'summer residence' in Mackay's barn.

'And why did Mick go and sell the two bottles when the magic waiters had been feeding the family?' John asked.

'Because his wife said the enchantment might wear off and what would they do then,' said Rose promptly.

Then John asked: 'And when Mick took home the new bottles what happened then?'

'They put the children round the table and Mick put the bottles down and said: 'Come on, bottles, do your duty' . . . and two black devils jumped out and hit them all over their heads with mallets till they were black and blue,' gabbled Sam, tripping over himself in his enthusiasm.

'And calling for mercy,' added Rose.

Finally satisfied, John found his place in the neatly written sheets, glanced at Patrick and Hannah, and made a pretence of checking that Rose and Sam were listening.

Then he began.

Afterwards, when they had finished the wife says to Mick: 'What'll we do now?'

'Ah, wait a while,' says Mick, 'an' I'll be meeting the landlord,' says he.

A couple of days later Mick met the landlord.

'Good morning, Mick, how are you?'

'Poorly,' says Mick.

'Did you sell the cow?'

'I did.'

'And what did you get?'

'I got two more bottles.'

The landlord was very interested then, and Mick told him that the bottles were different and only to be used on special occasions.

'Oh,' says the landlord. 'Well, I'm expecting English visitors in a day or two and I was going to show them the bottles I got off you before, but if you've got something better, well, I'll buy them off you.'

Mick said no at first, and then the landlord offered him ten cows and £200 and then he made the bargain.

So Mick gave him the bottles and told him to be sure and not to put them to work till they were needed.

Well, the landlord waited, and the day came that the friends arrived, so the landlord took out the first bottles and told them to do their duty, and they did, and all the guests were amazed at the great service.

'Then,' says the landlord, 'but wait till you see what I have here.' So he set the second two bottles out and told them to do their duty and out popped the two black devils with their mallets and beat them all until they were black and blue. And the guests were in great consternation.

So, afterwards the landlord's wife was at him to get rid of the bottles, so he went to meet Mick.

'Mick, that was a dirty trick you played on me,' says he.

'That was the way I got them, yer honour,' says Mick.

'Well, will you take them away now?' says the landlord.

'I will not,' says Mick, 'unless you give me the other bottles as well.'

So the landlord agreed, and Mick took the second bottles and broke them and took the others home, and they laid the table and the bottles did their duty as before, so they had the ten cows, the £200 and the bottles and all was ended happily.

Hannah and Patrick clapped and Rose and Sam beamed in satisfaction as John rose and wished them all goodnight, and disappeared without further ado.

'I think perhaps now it really is bedtime,' said Hannah firmly.

'Yes, indeed,' Patrick agreed, just as firmly. 'It has been a long day.' He kissed them both. 'Yer ma and I won't be far behind you,' he said, looking across at Hannah, with a gentle smile that told her exactly what he was thinking.

★ ★ ★

Hannah insisted that Patrick did not go off first thing next morning to look for work. In the event, she need not have been concerned about him overtaxing himself. He quickly found that there was no work available in the length of the valley, and none whatever on the farm where he had helped with the new roof at the beginning of the year.

Hannah tried to reassure him that she had enough money saved from the summer to carry them through the winter, especially if he could help with some of her jobs, so that she could catch up with her sewing on the days when she wasn't doing her three mornings at school.

But she knew Patrick was uneasy and although he began looking for jobs in the house and in the potato garden she could see that he was not happy with the situation.

Sadly, neither could she see any way forward. It felt as if the joy of being home again was completely spoilt for him by having no work in prospect. When she asked him if he missed the company of the other men in the group, some of whom lived nearby, he shook his head. 'Sure what wou'd I want with them now I have you?'

★ ★ ★

November came and went, the weather unusually mild for the time of year. It was at the beginning of December that Hannah arrived home late one morning to find Patrick drinking tea with Jonathan Hancock.

'Hannah, how good to see you,' he said, jumping to his feet. 'Your good man has been telling me about his work in Scotland and how things are here in the valley. I've got some news for you and I think now I've met Patrick I may actually have even more good news than I thought!'

'Sit down, love, you've likely been on your feet all morning,' said Patrick gently. 'There's still tea in the pot.' He got to his feet and fetched a clean mug from the dresser. 'Do you want me to make us all a piece while you have a sit?'

'I'd rather hear the news first with my tea, unless you are both very hungry,' she said happily, looking from one to the other.

They both insisted that there was no hurry at all for a bite of lunch so she settled gratefully in Patrick's chair by the fire, amazed and pleased at how easy the two men appeared to be with each other.

'Well, to begin with,' Jonathan began, with a small smile, 'the Dublin Education Committee have approved a salary for you, Hannah, dating from when you first began back in the summer. The secretary said I was to apologise to you most sincerely. He says he missed the September Meeting through illness and that's why there has been such a long delay. I took the liberty of asking him for a postal order that I could cash

173

myself to save you the trouble of going down to Dunfanaghy,' he added, handing over a small bag of coins. 'I hope that was all right.'

'Oh, Jonathan, how thoughtful,' she said, delighted by the welcome sound of sovereigns that might make Patrick feel easier. 'That is very good news, Jonathan,' she said quickly. 'Patrick has been upset that there's no work to find, but this more than makes up for it, doesn't it, my love?'

'Well, it does take away a worry,' he said, nodding vigorously, 'but I'd still like to turn m' hand to something. I'm not used to bein' idle.'

'As it happens, Patrick, there is actually a job going, and I can't think of a better person to tackle it,' said Jonathan, looking pleased with himself. 'I've been given quite a lot of money for meal and flour, to bridge the gap till the new crop is ready, but I need someone to buy it locally and distribute it along the whole length of this valley. It would mean buying a cart, albeit a small one, and a robust donkey to pull it. There are funds for that, of course. Might you be interested, Patrick?'

Hannah watched Patrick's face light up as Jonathan explained exactly what was needed, finding those in need, repacking bulk bags into manageable sacks and delivering on a regular basis.

'Jonathan, may I ask where the money has come from?' Hannah asked, not bothering to conceal her delight.

'A certain young man whom I'm sure you both know started with crayons and moved on to

174

watercolour. Hannah gave me a packet of work when last I came,' he explained to Patrick. 'I hoped I could use his paintings as 'gifts' to contacts I have both here and in Armagh and then ask for a donation. I've managed to place three of them and have received £250!'

Patrick shook his head in disbelief and Hannah clapped her hands together in delight.

'I hope you'll both help me work out an appropriate small fee for Johnny,' Jonathan went on, 'and a larger payment, enough to keep his family going till the first of the boats is ready. I'm afraid there's been a delay there, but I've no doubt at all it will get funding when some Friends can visit Dunfanaghy and find out for themselves just how important it might be.'

'An' why's that? If I'm not asking out of turn?' Patrick asked hesitantly.

'No, not a bit of it,' replied Jonathan. 'There is no need to keep plans secret; it's just that we don't want people being disappointed. I didn't realise how few Quakers there are in Ireland, outside Dublin. Apparently there are only 4,000 and some areas have none. So if there isn't a local Meeting, plans have to go to the nearest one, or up the line to the Yearly Meeting, or the Relief Committee. At the moment funds are flowing in, but the problem is getting proper information about where it's most needed and then getting it out to people who can be trusted to make it go as far as possible.

'Which reminds me,' added Jonathan, smiling, 'speaking of getting things to where they are needed, I wonder if you might be able to find where best to buy a donkey, Patrick. The cart, I hear, is probably easy enough. A turf cart will certainly do, but I've no idea where one might find a donkey.'

Patrick smiled. 'I hafta admit, I know the very place,' he said. 'There's a field in Tullygobegley full o' them. I useta to look down on them when I was up on the roof o' th' house I worked on this time last year. 'An I saw yer man come out regular an' go roun' them, feedin' them carrots from a satchel and callin' them, each by name. I heerd he sells twice a year at some of the big markets nearby an' makes a good living from it.'

'My goodness, that is great news. I wish it were always as good,' said Jonathan, as Hannah, her tiredness forgotten, stood up to see if they still had butter for the bread she'd baked the previous day.

She'd forgotten that Patrick had been up to visit his Aunt Mary, so there was both butter and milk, and blackberry jam as well, pots and pots of it, her share of the rich harvest when she and John took the whole school out one sunny afternoon to visit all the well-known bramble patches.

That was when Sam had distinguished himself by filling his bowls faster than even Johnny Donnelly or any of the older pupils.

16

The arrival of Neddy, the name chosen by Sam, who insisted that all the donkeys in books were called Neddy, was much celebrated in the McGinley cottage in Ardtur.

Patrick took on the new task agreed with Jonathan with enthusiasm, not only delivering the flour and meal provided by money donated to the Quaker charities, but keeping his eyes open and talking to those he met, finding out if they knew any others in need. And there were many.

By November, families had already used up their diminished potato crop and so had none available to sell to help them pay the half-yearly rent, now due in late December. Quite a few of them, reluctant to admit their difficulties, had sold all their winter clothes and household tools so they could buy enough food to tide them over till the new crop was ready in late May or June.

Patrick quickly learnt to watch for children playing outside cottages, ill-clothed even for the unusual mildness of the winter weather, and then to make further tactful enquiries.

It had taken him only a couple of days to do a deal on the donkey from Tullygobegley and to find, in a nearby market, a good, robust cart built for pulling heavy loads of turf from the bog.

'Sure, isn't everythin' easy if ye've money in yer pocket,' he said, unsmiling, when he arrived

177

back home, late and tired, driving instead of walking.

It was only some days later, as Hannah waved him goodbye when he set off for Dunfanaghy to collect flour, brought in by boat from Derry, that she realised she too had received a gift with the arrival of the donkey and cart. Another day, Patrick might well be picking up supplies in Ramelton and if it were a day when she was not teaching, she could visit her friends, the Rosses, whom she'd seen only seldom since the arrival of Rose and Sam.

Catriona Ross was a good deal older than Hannah, but she'd been brought up in Dundrennan and knew Hannah's father and mother and her older sisters, when they were still at school. She'd never revisited Scotland after her marriage to Joseph, the grandson of some distant cousins, who had come to Donegal, bought a small hotel and never went back. Catriona enjoyed sharing her memories of the fathers and mothers of children Hannah had been to school with, or even the grandparents of the children Hannah herself had taught when she became a monitor.

As for Rose and Sam, the good-natured little donkey was their greatest friend. Patrick reckoned he was the best-groomed donkey in Donegal and Hannah agreed with him. She said she never had to be concerned as to where they were and what was keeping them for so long, when they disappeared 'to look after Neddy'.

Now that Patrick was helping with the household tasks and John well settled in his teaching duties, she had more time to herself. She was able not only to keep up with her sewing, but also to write letters to her father and sisters, as well as making her regular reports to Jonathan Hancock.

Jonathan always replied promptly, sharing his news from Armagh, telling her a little about other Quaker projects in which he knew she would be interested, as well as forwarding both ideas and donations. It seemed to her, looking back at the shy and uneasy man who had arrived at her door in April, that something had changed in his life. He was certainly increasingly happy and confident in the work he was doing.

He did say in one of his letters that he'd made a number of useful contacts in and around Armagh and one or two friendships as well, on his visits to Castledillon. He'd then given her a vivid description of Sir George's newly built, thirty-one-room mansion, overlooking a small lake, hidden in all directions from the roads to Portadown and Loughgall and set in gardens that were still being laid out.

He made her smile when he told her how Sir George appeared to live in fear of his housekeeper and how he sometimes just abandoned the disorder of the house, where workmen were still wheeling away barrows of rubble. Apparently, when the gardeners then started arriving with barrow-loads of topsoil and the housekeeper was heard to issue threats about spilt soil and dirty feet, he was seen disappearing at speed to hide in a summer house, already complete, down by the side of the lake.

Jonathan had been quite delighted by how quickly Patrick had managed to acquire the donkey and cart. He now requested him to treat the whole valley as his responsibility until the springtime when, hopefully, the new potato crop would not be affected and other Quaker projects for improving the food supply would come into effect.

Meantime, the winter months of early 1846 proceeded with unaccustomed mildness. Sophie announced regularly that, 'Sure, there's been no cold.'

When Hannah began to hear the same comment made frequently, particularly by older people, she found herself wondering if she detected a note of anxiety in their voices. She'd thought that the older people would welcome the savings in turf, at a time when cold weather always created the danger of the turf stacks running low, or even, in a really severe winter, of running out.

She herself was grateful for the mildness, which always made life easier. Her only sadness was the way in which the weeks seemed to pass so quickly. While one part of her rejoiced in the early signs of spring, another part was already aware that once the early potato crop was planted in April, the next event would be Patrick's departure for Scotland.

★　★　★

Meantime, the school flourished and all fifteen children now on the roll attended more often than before. As Patrick pointed out, it meant fewer mouths to feed at home if the parents knew there would be bread and jam provided when the children had not had breakfast before they left, and there would be a proper piece at lunchtime. Daniel was delighted with the extra provision. Now that his pension had been restored and small donations were arriving regularly for the school from American emigrants to whom the children had written, he was only too willing to 'forget' about the pennies due on a Friday. The misfortune of the crop failure had given an opportunity for education to fifteen young people who would now be better equipped for the future than most young people in the rest of the county.

Johnny Donnelly continued to produce both pen sketches and watercolours, and John McCreedy continued to mount them, now on high quality card, newly arrived from Dublin. Hannah cleared a drawer in the dresser so that she knew they would be safe till Jonathan's next visit. There was now a new baby in Johnny's family, but although, thanks to Johnny's pictures, they did have enough to eat, Hannah still wished that the Quaker fishing boats would materialise. She knew only work would satisfy Dermot's frustration, in the way Patrick's had been resolved with the arrival of Neddy and the turf cart and his responsibility for seeing that no one in the valley was short of food.

By now, the deep winter months had passed and on a soft, early spring day Hannah was able to go to Ramelton with Patrick and visit her friend Catriona while he collected supplies of meal and flour. She took a couple of napkins with her, knowing well that Catriona's hands were never idle when they talked. It was when she settled herself by a welcoming log fire in Catriona's sitting room, she remembered what Jonathan had said about the useable but slightly flawed fabric that he could provide, both from the Hancock mills and from others nearby, if only Hannah could find an appropriate use and outlet for it.

Hannah had indeed given the possibilities much thought, but she'd had to confess that none of the women she knew in and around Ardtur had either the time, or the skill, to make clothing. That seemed the only appropriate thing to make with what she knew was relatively heavy fabric. As they sat down together Hannah saw Catriona take up an Aran sweater she was knitting.

'Lovely pattern, Catriona. Is it for one of the boys?'

Hannah listened hard as Catriona brought her up to date on not just the recipient of the Aran sweater in Peterborough, Ontario, but all the rest of the family, in both Canada, Boston and Edinburgh. It was perfectly clear from all she said that, exactly as Hannah thought, Catriona had indeed no need of extra income by knitting, sewing, or anything else. Her husband, Joseph, had been a successful hotel keeper and trader all his working life and now, having reassured herself that all was well with them in their retirement, Hannah considered how she might ask for her friend's help.

'Have you had any distress in the town, Catriona? The shops seem to be all right, but there must be people with no work.'

'Oh, indeed aye,' she replied, her Scots accent still obvious even after a lifetime in Donegal. 'The hotel has had to let staff go and the gentry are makin' do with less in the way of servants. The Presbyterian kirk we go to in Dunfanaghy, is doin' all it can to help folk, but we're a vairy small number an' we can hardly go beyond our own members.

'Joseph is their treasurer,' she went on, her needles still flying, though she was looking straight at Hannah, as she always did. 'An' sure there's very few can fill the Freewill envelopes. Some families haven't even a penny to put on the plate. To tell ye the truth, the men who collect the offerin' these days just offer the plate at the end of the row and don't look down till it comes back t' their han'. An' between ye and me, as they say, I know Joseph puts a few pence on himself forby his weekly envelope so no one knows who hasn't got even a penny t' give, never mine an offerin' in an envelope. Sure ye know well enough they print the figures of the giving at the end of the year in the Year Book, but our man has had to ask the Elders to set that aside this year, so as to avoid embarrassment.'

'Oh dear, that must be very hard on some,' Hannah replied, knowing how meticulous both Catriona and Joseph were with the small square envelopes that bore a printed reminder about filling up the envelopes for the missed Sundays should they ever be unable to attend.

'Doesn't your minister's stipend get paid from the envelopes?' Hannah asked, an idea half forming in her mind.

'Ach, yes. In theory he does. The collection money goes to the Presbytery but everybody knows that's mostly what the Presbytery uses to pay the ministers. But if they haven't got enough coming in, I don't know what they'll do. There's no use my asking Joseph. Sure, he's the treasurer, but he's very secretive about kirk affairs, though I suppose you could say that's only proper when it's kirk business.'

Hannah told her then about the offer of fabric and asked her if she knew anyone who could make use of it. She explained that the workers would get paid for their work on the free fabric, just as she did for her napkins, but that the clothes made would then be sold very cheaply to those who had a little money and some given away without charge to those who were in need in the local area.

Catriona put her knitting down, asked question after question and then beamed at her. 'Have ye ever heard of the PWC, Hannah?' she asked slowly.

'No, I'm afraid not,' Hannah admitted, shaking her head.

'Well, it's a group of Presbyterian women. Every church has one, and they try to raise funds for various charities. I'm a member of ours, of course. And what you're saying sounds as if it's the answer to our prayers. We're committed to working for those in need but, to be honest, most of the women can't afford to knit, or sew, or bake cakes these days. That fabric would be a god-send. Where did you say it was coming from?'

The women were still talking and outlining both people and possibilities when Patrick arrived with Neddy and a heavily loaded cart. Catriona hurried out ahead of Hannah, greeted him warmly and told him the 'good news'.

Hannah could see that Patrick was both amused and delighted at Catriona's enthusiasm. He beamed at her.

'There ye are, Neddy. There's another job for you and me,' he said, turning and stroking Neddy's ears. 'Mind you, Catriona, you'll be kept busy, for there's women up our way have 'neither in them, nor on them', as the sayin' is. What decent skirt they might have had, they've sold for food and sure if we have any cold weather they'll be foundered in the rags they've left.'

'Well, we'll not let that happen, Patrick, not if we can get a hold of that fabric Hannah was talking about.'

'Oh, ye'll get it all right,' Patrick assured her. 'Yer man is as good as his word. I can see me maybe havin' to go to Derry to collect it, but sure we can manage that if we hafta. Right now, I must take this lady here away, for we'll have to walk a brave bit of the way. Neddy here has a heavy load an' there's a good few steep bits where we'll have to give him a han'.'

They parted from Catriona with kisses and handshakes, the journey back home no burden at all, with the pleasure of having found a purpose for the cloth and the knowledge that Jonathan too would be delighted with the outcome of the morning's activity.

17

The exceptional mildness of the last months of 1845 continued through the early months of the new year in Ardtur, as indeed it continued through most of Ireland, making the signs of spring so visible that all along the west coast, and certainly in Donegal, men began preparing to plant their first crop of potatoes several weeks earlier than usual.

Patrick McGinley could see no reason to wait and he too began to turn over the soil early in March and dig in the seaweed he'd been able to collect from the shore, as well as the small amount of manure accumulated in the barn where Neddy had his stall, alongside the turf cart and the tools used in both the potato garden and out on the piece of bog that came as part of his holding of 'dwelling house and garden'.

Hannah, who had remained busy all winter, actively engaged with both her teaching, her sewing, and all the things she did to support Patrick's work for their neighbours along the length of the valley, found herself strangely uneasy at the visible signs of growth, the small sprays of unfurling leaves on the hawthorns, the very first wildflowers in sheltered corners and even the odd garden flower in the collection of old pots under the south-facing windows.

On the evening when Patrick and the children settled at the kitchen table to prepare seed potatoes for planting the next day, she sat silently by the fire, sewing, and thinking of the letter she soon expected from Galloway. She was dreading it coming. It seemed that parting from Patrick would never get easier. She did appreciate that it was indeed the price they paid for their closeness, but somehow, just now, it seemed harder to bear than ever.

Her father, at least, was in very good spirits, pleased that, as he put it, 'there had been no winter'. In his most recent letter he'd reported an above average crop of both lambs and calves. From everything he said it was clear 'the season' was just as early in Galloway as it was in Donegal. That made perfect sense, when even here in Ardtur, further north and more exposed to the elements than the south-facing fields sloping down to the beaches on the Solway Firth, growth had already begun. It would be only a matter of days, rather than weeks now, before Patrick would be preparing to leave.

There were many other people equally concerned about Patrick's departure, but their reason was very different from Hannah's. There had been no easement whatever in the demand for the meal and flour he had been distributing since last October. Now, everyone in the valley knew that Patrick would soon be leaving with the other harvesters. Without his regular deliveries there would be no food till the new crop of potatoes were big enough to dig.

Jonathan Hancock had done his utmost to set up a plan to care for the whole valley with the resources he'd been able to gather from his own mill workers, from the donations he'd raised with the help of Johnny's pictures and the distribution of funds he'd had from the Friends Yearly Meeting. But he, like Hannah and Patrick, had thought things might improve in 1846. There had been talk of Public Works providing paid work, at least until the new crop was ready. But, so far in this area, nothing had happened. From what Sophie and John had gleaned from the wide variety of newspapers and magazines, English and Irish, they had access to, it looked as if nothing of a public nature had actually happened after all. No employment schemes. No relief. Apart from irregular donations from American emigrants directed to the school, or to individual families, nothing new was coming to support Jonathan's scheme, while the need of most families remained unchanged — and with the threat of the situation getting worse still if the new potato crop failed.

What indeed would happen when Patrick left for Galloway?

Hannah kept Jonathan informed and he was quite clear in his answer. If there was no change in the need then, of course, the work must go on, exactly as it had been doing. Could Hannah find someone to take over from Patrick until sometime in June, when the new potato crop was harvested? He would try to find the funds.

It was fortunate that in the same letter asking her to find someone to replace Patrick when he left for Galloway, Jonathan also gave Hannah an update on the fishing boat being built by her brother's small boatyard in Port William. Good progress, he said, had been made on the keel and an interim payment had been made to the builders, but the official visit of the Quaker researchers to Dunfanaghy and the North Coast of Donegal, planned for the early summer, had been unavoidably delayed. As yet there was no new date for the visit, which he felt sure would result in an order for further boats.

It was when Jonathan commented on what they would do if the crop failed that Hannah realised what a burden they had shouldered. She wondered if that was why Jonathan sometimes now sounded uneasy, or even burdened, in his letters, though he continued to answer her reports fully and promptly. Usually he managed to end with some piece of good news he thought she might not have heard via what he called 'her spies' — Sophie and her lodger, John McCreedy.

But at least the immediate problem could be resolved easily. Patrick went to see Dermot Donnelly and found that although he had managed to find some irregular work by his own efforts, he was only too happy to take over Patrick's task as soon as he left, to keep him busy until the hoped-for boat was ready.

The fact that Dermot had no barn attached to his cottage was solved very simply and to the great delight of Rose and Sam. Neddy would continue to live in Ardtur, fed and looked after by Dermot, but groomed, as Dermot promptly agreed, clearly amused, by Rose and Sam.

'Sure, it's no trouble at all to walk back and forward from home,' he insisted, to Patrick and Hannah as they shared mugs of tea, a few days before Patrick's departure. 'Haven't I walked miles in the last months in the hope of a few hours work, an' just to get me out of the house? We've had enough to eat, thanks to Johnny's wee pictures and that friend of yours, the Quaker man, but sure I can't bear being idle.'

Dermot was delighted at the prospect of a proper job for at least the next few months. With that confirmed and the promise of the first fishing boat ready to launch by the end of the year, the man Hannah had found so bitter and anxious at their first meeting was so transformed that he'd now become a welcome visitor.

★ ★ ★

Patrick's departure came and went.

Hannah shed silent tears in her empty bed and then kept herself busy till she judged, the weather being calm, that he was probably safely in Scotland, albeit with the journey still to make from Stranraer to the hamlet of Rewick. Then, next day, she took out her writing pad as soon as she'd finished morning jobs.

One of the first things she was able to tell him was that Dermot had called just when he was ready to set off with Neddy. She was touched when she found he had stopped to ask her if there were any jobs Patrick had usually done for her when he was down the mountain, for he'd be glad to do them for her.

Dermot was as good as his word. Some days later, when Catriona replied to a note he had delivered to her, she announced that a first batch of skirts and shifts was ready for sale or distribution. When Dermot asked if there was anything she needed him to do, Hannah promptly told him what was in the note.

'Well,' he replied, without the slightest hesitation, 'd'ye want to come out with me on one of the mornings ye're not at school, or can ye tell me what's needed an' I'll do it fer ye? Ye did tell me once what the plan was. Some gets the stuff for free; some pay a wee bit for it. Was that the right way of it?'

Hannah nodded and explained why it wasn't all for free. She watched him as he nodded his agreement.

'How would you know who had no money and was entitled to a free one?' she asked quietly.

'Sure, isn't that easy,' he said. 'Don't I remember what my poor wife wore afore ye came t' the door an' tole us about Johnny's wee pictures an' that Quaker man took a hand in helpin' us. I don't forget those times, nor shou'd I, just because I've m' hopes to go back to fishin' again. I was a right hand at that,' he added quietly.

The wistfulness in the way he said it brought tears to Hannah's eyes. She blinked them away quickly, smiled and said: 'What about size?'

'Ah, sure what about it? Women always know by the look o' the thing whether it'll fit them or not, an' sure if I know anythin' at all, some of them'll be that glad to get somethin' decent, they'll find a way of makin' it fit,' he added, with an easy laugh.

'An' don't be worryin' about the money,' he

said. 'I can tell them the more I gets from people that has a wee bit, the more garments we can get t' give away t' them that has nothin'. I'm a fair judge of honesty, even wi' the women who sometimes think men are stupid.'

Hannah laughed aloud and wished she had both the time and the energy to give a full account of his practical approach to both Patrick and Jonathan.

Meantime, as he said goodbye and she wished him well for the day's work, she reminded herself she now had two mornings' work to do, for tomorrow was a school morning and Daniel had asked her to organise a spelling quiz, which would also let him judge how successful, or otherwise, their pupils' command of English vocabulary had become.

About Dermot's capacity for the new job, she had no doubts at all.

★ ★ ★

There were now fifteen pupils packed in to Daniel's big kitchen. It had always been a problem when they all needed to write at once, for the few desks they had were only suited to the oldest boys and girls and they not only took up a lot of room but also had to be moved outside at the end of the day to leave room for those who gathered in the evenings to share the day's news and listen to stories and poems.

That meant, of course, the desks were often too wet to move back inside in the late evening, or next morning. When that happened all the pupils had to use slates, or pieces of board laid across their knees. As Hannah and John agreed, it didn't give them a fair chance at improving their handwriting. Worse still, now that copy-books were available, there was little opportunity to use them.

'Good news, Hannah,' John said, smiling, as he stepped out of Sophie's house and fell into step with her and Rose and Sam at school time next morning. 'I forgot to tell you last night when I was so hungry for my supper!' he said laughing.

'Well, what is it?' she replied, encouraged by his smile.

'We had a visit from Joseph Ross yesterday, your friend from Ramelton,' he added. 'Apparently, you told his wife we had no proper furniture for the school, so he came up before Easter and asked Daniel about the children, their ages and sizes. He came back yesterday after school and brought us two folding tables that will take three or four each. He says he's got a man making two more the same size but with shorter legs that would take three or four of the wee ones.'

'My goodness,' Hannah said, 'they never mentioned it to me when I last saw them.'

'He told me that too,' John replied, happily. 'He said you'd done a great favour for their PWC and this was to be a wee surprise and a thank you. There'll be benches to match coming in a week or so, and the whole lot can be folded up whenever we want to put on a play!'

Hannah was glad of John's presence at the evening meal now that Patrick was in Scotland, especially on 'teaching days' when she found herself weary and preoccupied as she made supper. She appreciated his appearing and passing on what news there might be that he could share with Rose and Sam present.

To her surprise, he seldom stayed beyond their bedtime when they could have talked more freely, so she spent many hours alone with her sewing, often too tired to write, even though she had letters both personal and otherwise that were on her mind.

As the days lengthened and the skies were still pale gold at eleven o'clock, she thought more and more of Patrick and her father working away in the fields, the long, long summer dusk full of the sound of the gentle splash of waves on the nearby beach, the bark of a dog, far away, carrying on the still air, the call of an owl hunting along the hedgerow of the biggest field.

The world of her childhood seemed such a very happy and secure place, unlike this island of Ireland, now her home, where in places people were waiting desperately for the new potato crop, their only hope of both paying the rent and keeping their home and having food to see them through the long months when the nights darkened earlier and earlier, and winter came.

★　★　★

The bad news came in dribs and drabs to begin with, the first news brought by Dermot himself. Collecting meal and flour in Derry, he had met some sailors from the Glens of Antrim. Over a week earlier, they had found the first bent stalks on the well-sprouted plants in their potato patches. By the time they sailed for Derry, the smell of decay was on the air and the few spadefuls of potatoes they'd dug revealed tiny tubers already blotched and beginning to rot.

Days later, John relayed some news from Fermanagh from the *Impartial Reporter*, a local newspaper sent to Sophie by her niece. The blight had just arrived there. This year there was no point trying to dig the potatoes to save them as they were still so small.

As the days passed there was no end to the reports. This time the failure was total in every part of Ireland, and Donegal was soon as badly hit as the areas where the blight had first been found.

'What are we goin' to do, Hannah?' Dermot said, when he found her kneading bread at the kitchen table on a Saturday morning while Rose and Sam were out 'looking after Neddy'.

'I don't know, Dermot. I just don't know,' she said, dusting flour off her hands. 'Jonathan Hancock is due sometime soon. We may just need to put on our thinking caps, as my sister used to say. We've managed so far. We'll think of something.'

18

Summer came early and with it, blue skies and breezes so light they merely ruffled the waters of Lough Gartan and gently stirred the long grasses that grew so prolifically by the waterside.

Sometimes, opening her door first thing in the morning, even before she'd hung the pot over the fire to cook their porridge, Hannah paused to look around, unable to resolve in her heart the enormity of what was happening in every county in Ireland and the relative peacefulness of this remote valley, where people still had enough to eat. Just enough, indeed, and hunger was familiar enough, but through the length of the valley no one was yet at risk of starvation. That was more than you could now say about the country as a whole.

Other parts of Donegal itself were not so fortunate. The island of Aranmore and the valley of Glencolumbkille had both been mentioned even in the Dublin papers. The workhouse in Dunfanaghy was already struggling to cope with the increasing numbers seeking help, and the 'public works' talked about so vigorously by the newly formed Relief Committees were emerging only slowly, against the hostility of powerful people in Dublin who insisted that 'feeding the idle Irish would go on forever if they were encouraged further'.

There was no good news that John could find

197

in Sophie's assorted collection of magazines and local papers; indeed, from more than one locality came reports of gangs of starving men armed with cudgels threatening food stores or trying to prevent cargos of grain being carried on to ships bound for England to pay the rents of absentee landlords.

Try as she would, Hannah could think of no new ways to earn money to supplement the funds supplied by Jonathan Hancock. More than once now, seeing the supply of meal and flour provided by school about to run out, she'd waited till a morning when she'd seen the children off to school and had then extracted a sovereign from the very small bag kept in the box under the bed. Now there were more memories than money under the bed, and though she looked at her treasures — a few precious objects, some documents, a brooch, a china teacup and saucer and a Gaelic Bible that had once belonged to her grandmother — she knew she couldn't feed the valley on stories and heirlooms. She tucked the box back under the bed, hoping she'd find another answer before her savings ran out.

She knew she could ask Dermot to exchange the precious coin for smaller money at the bank in Dunfanaghy. If he guessed what she needed it for, then he certainly never asked. She was then able to top up the dwindling sum in the school's cash box and hope that the next postal order from England, or Canada, or the USA would not be too long delayed.

She tried to focus on the good things that still

happened, and not let the need to find money dominate her thinking, when she knew that the reserves were dwindling once again. After all he had done already, only as a last resort would she tell Jonathan Hancock about their difficulties.

He had worked so hard last year, making contacts and finding sources of food, and now this year he continued to send regular postal orders from donations he'd managed from those contacts in Ireland, as well as from the workers in his mills and the relevant committees in Dublin. She did also suspect that sometimes some of the money came out of his own pocket, though she would never dream of mentioning it.

'Good morning, Hannah, and how are you today?'

'I'm well, Daniel. And how about yourself?'

'Ah sure, don't even weeds thrive in this sunshine,' he replied, looking up at her, a smile on his face.

She laughed and pressed his hand as she sat down beside him and he greeted Rose, and then John, and Sam, before they went indoors to make sure the room was set up properly before the other children arrived.

'Did John tell you he told a story here last night?' he asked, a twinkle in his eye.

'No, he didn't,' she said, amused. 'Perhaps he wanted to tell me when the children aren't with me. I don't often see him often on his own these days.'

'Do ye not now?' he asked more sharply. 'I wonder now why that might be, for he thinks so well of you. He often says how good you've been to him and how much he likes talking to you. He thinks he's very lucky to have someone like you when he's so far away from his own family. And indeed, I see his point,' he added, breaking off to greet each of the small group of pupils arriving together from further up the valley.

'Have you all had a bite to eat?' he asked.

Hannah saw the look of concentration as he listened for a 'no' or a missing response. Daniel's hearing was very sharp.

'And what about you, Sean?'

The reply was muffled. Daniel was not satisfied.

'Now then, Sean. I may be blind, but I am not deaf. Did you say 'not much'?'

Sean nodded and then realised that was no use to Daniel either.

'There was only a crust left and no milk, except for the baby,' he said slowly.

'Anyone else?' Daniel asked, looking severe.

Hannah watched the faces as they chorused, 'No, sir.'

'Now then, Sean,' he said more gently, 'go over to Missus Delaney and tell her I sent you for a bite to eat. Take your time. We'll not start anything new in class without you.'

Hannah watched Sean run off and waited till the other children dispersed.

'Is that a new one, Daniel, or has it happened before?'

'It's happened before,' he replied, nodding. 'Not often, but it *has* happened. Would you take a walk over to Bridget Delaney at lunchtime and ask her if she knows anything I don't know. The family may need more help,' he said, getting to his feet. 'Glad you're here this morning, Hannah; she'll tell you more than she'll ever tell me.'

While Rose and Sam sat in the sun eating their piece with the other children, Hannah went over to Bridget, a kind-hearted woman, who, like herself, sewed napkins to supplement the postal orders her husband sent from London where he worked on building sites for most of the year.

'Indeed, Hannah, the poor chile was hungry indeed. I'd say lookin' at him eatin' that slice of bread and jam I give him, he maybe hadn't had anythin' last night either. I haven't had time to go over to see Teresa for a day or two, but I did hear tell there's lay-offs even in London, forby Liverpool and Glasgow. Maybe she's had nothin' in the post this week. More's the pity of her.'

'Oh dear,' sad Hannah slowly. 'You're probably right. Can you manage to give him a bowl, or a bagful, to take home? Is the sack holding out?'

'It is. There's corn in Egypt yet, as the sayin' is, but it'll not go much further. Maybe just another week, if I'm any judge of it. Are we due yet for another one?' Bridget asked, her face failing to conceal her anxiety.

'Not sure, Bridget dear,' Hannah said, not wanting to worry her unless she had to. 'I'll check with Daniel and let you know on Friday. It's John who organises these things, but Daniel has it all in his head. He always knows exactly where we're up to on deliveries, even if John and I have both forgotten,' she said easily, trying to

201

reassure the older woman, even if she was fairly unsure herself.

The afternoon classes were underway and the buzz of voices flowed out on the still and warm air. Daniel was sitting in the sun where she had left him, just finishing his piece.

'Well, Hannah,' he said, as she approached. 'Have we another family in need?'

'Looks like it,' she said, dropping down beside him. 'Apparently there are lay-offs even on building sites in London. Did you know that?'

'Yes, I did,' he said soberly. 'These days, there's so much Irish labour around that men can walk miles in a day looking for jobs they've heard about and then find they've gone by the time they get there.'

'I didn't know that, Daniel,' she said sadly. 'Bridget has meal for tonight for Sean to take home, but she said the sack is low. Are we about due for a new one?'

'Not till August, I'm afraid. I know it's school holidays but we were still planning to carry on with the pieces. Are you telling me we're likely to run out of meal and flour?'

'I think it does look likely,' she said sadly, the weariness of her busy morning working with the children catching up on her, as she remembered the washing and cleaning awaiting her at home.

'Now don't you worry yourself, Hannah,' Daniel said firmly. 'You sound tired. Away home now like a good woman and sit down and sew a couple of napkins till you've rested yourself. I can worry about this one till I see you again on Friday. Then you can take over and worry for us both,' he said, making a gesture of shooing her away.

She laughed, as she stood up and looked down the rocky path, catching the sparkle of the lough behind the hawthorns, their snow of blossoms now gone, clusters of green berries already beginning to change colour. 'That's a fair deal, Daniel. I'll give it a try,' she replied, as cheerfully as she could manage, before she set off down the rocky track.

★ ★ ★

She was thinking of a large mug of tea and hoping that the neglected fire might still have a few bright embers, when coming up to her own front door she caught sight of something that scattered her thoughts completely. There, in an old black pot full of mint was a small red geranium with one floret wide open and a number of surrounding buds showing colour, prior to opening themselves. It was a rich, strong red, enhanced by the background, the textured, fresh green leaves of common mint.

'Oh, you little beauty,' she said aloud, as she bent to touch the dappled cream and green leaves of the cutting she had planted the previous year and forgotten all about.

Now, she looked down at the bright eye and remembered the broken fragment she'd found on the path after a night of wind that had toppled a large pot and rolled it up against the wall of the potato garden. The main plant was battered, but still in its pot, even if much of the soil had spilled out. This broken fragment had been too healthy to throw away, so she had simply made a hole with her finger in the space at the front of the small, undisturbed mint pot, pressed it into the moist earth and completely forgotten about it.

She straightened up as her back began to protest, immediately thought of painting it, then laughed at herself. Not only did she not have any paints of her own, but she hadn't touched water-colour for years, except to show Johnny how to lay a wash when he won his prize. She stopped, looked again at the vigorous bloom and wondered about Johnny. Would he give flower painting a try if she asked him to, or would he think that painting flowers was only something girls did?

Well, she said to herself, no need to speculate. Dermot would be here in a couple of hours' time. She might find the small, black pot heavy to carry up the hill, but he wouldn't. He could take it under his arm and judge for himself what it was best to say when he got there.

She went in and caught the fire just before it went out. She was still just as thirsty and longing for that mug of tea, but feeling much better than she had felt walking back from school. A flower blooming in spite of all that surrounded it.

★ ★ ★

It was only after she'd had her tea, sewn a couple of napkins and was about to begin making bread for their supper, that she noticed the envelope on the table. She picked it up hastily, turned it over and saw a familiar Scottish postmark. Waves of anxiety hit her when she studied the handwriting. It was neither her father's, nor Patrick's.

Something must be wrong. Her father must be ill, or perhaps it was Patrick who was ill and one of the other men from the valley was writing to tell her. Certainly, it was handwriting she had never seen before. Panic-stricken, she tore the envelope open so fiercely that a slip of paper fell from it unnoticed as she unfolded the single, large sheet of writing paper she pulled out.

She was somewhat surprised that the letter was written in English.

Dear Mrs McGinley,

I am requested to write to you by some men that you will know as they are colleagues of your husband, Patrick.

There is a slight problem with what I need to say next. Something happened last week that they do not wish me to speak about. Your father, Mister Mackay, would be angry if he knew, but the men tell me that you would not give them away and get them into trouble. Sadly, a number of them went drinking and got involved in some betting. You will understand if I do not give you the details of this enterprise. It took place some distance away from their work on their weekly half-day holiday.

Thanks to a kind man who saw how drunk they were and offered to let them sleep in his barn, they were able to sober up

205

and arrive back early next morning so that Mr Mackay did not know the details of the outing. They offered a generous amount of money to their host who had also provided them with breakfast. When he enquired about the money they were offering they confessed about a wager, which they had won. He asked them what they were going to do with the money.

It seems that they didn't know what to do and were somewhat at a loss as to how to dispose of so large a sum without owning up to what would most certainly cause difficulties, if not actual dismissal. The kind man, whom I think may have been a minister, suggested sending the money to someone they could trust who would use it well and not give them away. He also suggested that they ask me to write a letter on their behalf.

I hope I have adequately explained the awkwardness of the situation and I enclose the money order provided for them by the gentleman in question.

I am, madam,
Your faithful servant,
Andrew Campbell (Teacher)

For a moment, Hannah was panic-stricken.

'What money order?' she said aloud, as she stepped back from the table. She saw it flutter to the floor from the folds of her skirt, caught it up, looked at it in total disbelief, and burst into tears.

The money order would not only provide for the needs of the school, but also keep up the supply of meal and flour for the valley, for months and months to come.

19

There was much less sunshine as the days lengthened, though the grasses and trees still flourished along with drifts of buttercups and bright-eyed daisies and the fresh new growth on the heather. But increasingly the weather became damp and muggy with little sunlight managing to break through the low cloud.

With the downturn in the weather disappeared all hopes for the few remaining potato crops that hadn't already showed signs of blight. Except in a very few counties in the north-east of the country, workhouses began to fill and newspapers were reporting scenes of appalling distress as people queued for food, anywhere it was known to exist, or where it had recently been made available.

Hannah, whose own anxieties about the food supply for the school and their neighbours had been mercifully quieted by the extraordinary intervention of an unknown man in Galloway and the behaviour of a small group of drunken harvesters, listened as calmly as she could to the occasional outbursts of her young colleague, John McCreedy.

John had always seemed to Hannah to be a kind and gentle young man, and he most certainly showed no change in his dealings with Rose and Sam and the other pupils in the school, but in the last few months, on the now rare occasions when they were alone together, he relayed the news from Sophie's papers with an anger bordering on fury.

Unlike Hannah, who found the arguments of politicians and the Westminster Parliament utterly depressing, John studied the speeches and letters in all the newspapers he had access to, taking to heart the material and quoting accurately from what he had he read.

Hannah listened, as he condemned the things said by politicians. They were, he insisted, a weak and divided government and were doing as little as they could to help the situation. Some of them had even been heard to say that the famine was '*God's judgement on the idle Irish*'.

'How can you call a man idle,' he said, his voice rising to a quite unaccustomed pitch, 'when his labour is so utterly limited by the small amount of land he has? How can he be other than 'idle' when there is no other work he can turn to, no matter how much he might try?' he demanded bitterly. 'Could Westminster not at least stop both Irish and British merchants from profiteering?' he demanded. 'They just use the shortages to increase their prices week by week and no one can lift a finger to stop them!'

Hannah couldn't disagree with what he was reporting, as much of it was already being said by other friends, some who spoke in sorrow rather than in anger, but she grew increasingly anxious at the bitterness with which he spoke. It reminded her of the way he had once spoken about 'the English' when she had first known him. She wondered what could have happened to bring back the particular bitterness he was now expressing.

Since his return from his visit to his grandparents in Galway the previous year, he had been sharing the evening meal with her and the children as had been agreed when he became Sophie's lodger, but for months now, he had not lingered to talk afterwards as he had previously done.

At first, she assumed that it was out of good manners, or his kindly commitment to Sophie who so enjoyed being read to, or even his own obvious commitment to his work at school. Anything they ever decided to do in school always had John's full backing. He regularly prepared plays, and readings, quizzes and spelling competitions.

Of course, that all took time, as she herself well knew, but as the weeks passed and he still hurried away after saying a polite 'thank you,' and making sure, once Patrick had gone in April, that there was nothing she needed, like pails of water or creels of turf, she decided at last she must find some opportunity to ask him if there was anything wrong.

Time seemed to pass so quickly. She herself always had a list of things to do for school, another list of letters she wanted to write, a pile of napkins to sew, as well as all the household tasks. Then, to her surprise, on a lovely summer evening, the light just beginning to fade into a golden dusk, the children in bed hours ago, she looked up from her sewing to find John at the open door, poised as if he weren't sure whether to knock or not.

'John, I thought perhaps you had work to do this evening,' she said easily. 'Could you drink a mug of tea? I was just thinking of making one.'

He nodded and watched her put down the kettle and stir the fire.

'Hannah, I've had some news,' he began hesitantly. 'It was waiting for me after supper, but Sophie put the envelope on the mantelpiece and then forgot about it until I noticed it myself, just a little while ago,' he said awkwardly.

To her surprise, he pulled out a single, large sheet of stiff, good quality paper from his pocket and handed it to her. The heading was embellished with a design of shamrocks and Irish wolfhounds and the Dublin address laid out below was in embossed letters. She had to read it twice before she began to grasp what it was saying.

'So, they actually want to publish what you've written?' she gasped, staring at him open-mouthed.

'Well, they say it won't be for at least a couple of months,' he said sheepishly. 'There was also a note apologising for the delay in replying to me, but, as far as I could find out, this publisher is a very small concern and has to rely on grants and subsidies. If they'd had funding they could have let me know sooner about my submission. When I didn't get any reply, I just thought they didn't want to be bothered and hadn't the decency to return my manuscript.'

'And all those long weeks you were waiting, they were passing your work round folklorists and established researchers, it says here.'

'Yes,' he said, looking yet more awkward. 'I got very upset about the delay. I know now I should have told you — you'd have understood how I felt, but I couldn't face it when I was so angry. Please forgive me, Hannah. I can't think why I was so silly.'

'Now, John, there's nothing to forgive,' she said firmly, as she finally realised why he'd gone on disappearing so promptly after supper even in recent months. 'There you were, working away every night after your day's work in school *and* reading to Sophie. Going through all those stories you'd collected, looking at the patterns and themes and producing a manuscript. You didn't just send them stories, you made '*a valuable analysis of the patterns and form*'. That's what they say here,' she said, looking back at the letter.

'My goodness, John.' She paused to make the tea. 'What a labour of love, and by lamplight as well, for most of the time. No wonder you got upset when there was no response. So, what will you do now?' she went on, surprised that he was taking an actual offer from a publisher so calmly. 'Would you think about going to Dublin and looking for a research post? With your first book behind you, you should be able to find something that would pay you to go on with what you clearly are so good at.'

'No,' he said firmly, looking at her directly for the first time. 'My job is here. I'm not giving that up, but now,' he added, with a wisp of a smile, 'I'm not giving up the stories either. If someone doesn't do it, they'll be lost,' he went on steadily.

'As Daniel always says: *Once they're gone, they've gone forever.* That's why I was so angry — I thought no one cared any more about our history and traditions. It was like my father all over again, just thinking about the present, and about money. That's why I avoided Dermot Donnelly, to begin with, when I heard he was trying to find Johnny a place as a servant. Servants aren't exactly given time to 'paint wee pictures' are they? But just think of what a talent would have been lost if his father had managed what he wanted.'

Hannah watched him carefully. She'd never noticed that he'd avoided Dermot, who had by now become a good friend of both Patrick and herself. She tried to remember back to that day when she'd first gone to speak to Johnny's mother and Dermot had appeared at the door later with the packet of drawings. She would never forget how distraught the poor man was when he admitted he couldn't see any way of feeding his family. Once that anxiety was taken away, his whole personality seemed to change.

She wondered if there was any way she could remind John that Dermot was a very different person now, that anxiety can change and distort how a person thinks and behaves.

'Are you going to tell your father about your book?' Hannah could hardly believe she'd spoken the words that had shaped in her mind.

'I was going to ask you that,' John replied promptly. 'What do you think I should do?'

Hannah pressed her lips together as if regretting her question. John had asked so, of course, she must do her best to reply. But there was no simple answer.

'John dear, have you any idea why your father didn't ask you what you wanted when it came to the time for further schooling? I got the feeling that he just acted.'

'Yes, that was the trouble. I didn't know what I wanted to be, like some people do, but I probably knew what I didn't want to do. But when I tried to say anything, he just thought I was being awkward and he got angry.'

'Did your father always want to be a coastguard himself?'

'I don't know, Hannah,' he said, shaking his head. 'He never talked about his family. I know from my mother that his father was a coastguard, but he was drowned long before I was born, and then my grandmother died too.'

'And did they have other children?'

'Yes, I think there were seven of them, but they all went away. Some to America, some to New Zealand.'

'So, when you visit your grandparents, those are your mother's family?' she said sadly. 'And you have five sisters?'

'Oh yes. And they never stop talking,' he said, shaking his head. 'I miss them terribly.' The small smile that had appeared momentarily disappeared completely.

'It is sad, John. I wish I knew more. I think your father meant well, but we can't know what anxiety he might have had. Probably he wanted to be sure he did his best for you, like Dermot wanted to do what he could for Johnny. Do you think that might be possible?'

'When I stopped being angry, I sometimes thought that, but then I'd think about home and my mother and my sisters and it would all start up again,' he admitted reluctantly. 'When I got no reply from the publishers, I even tried to blame him. And I know that wasn't fair.'

'But John, when we are hurt we are often not fair. We strike out, or look for someone to blame . . .'

'You'd never do that, Hannah,' he said sharply.

'Only because I was so fortunate with my family. Many people thought my father a hard man, but he was fond of me and never hurt me. Just think how he must have felt when I told him I wanted to marry Patrick, a Roman Catholic, when he was a strict Covenanter and only a poor labourer, when there were . . . well, others more suitable . . . ' she finished up awkwardly.

'But not suitable to you,' he replied with a great, beaming smile.

They both laughed and Hannah 'squeezed the pot' to give them each a last half mug of tea.

'I can't know why he acted as he did. I'm sure he did it for the best,' John said slowly. 'Perhaps, thinking about Dermot, I ought to give my father the benefit of the doubt. What do you think?'

'I think there's nothing to lose if you do. But you must promise to tell me if it seems to go wrong.'

John nodded slowly, then began to speak rather hesitantly.

'I remember you telling me when I first came here and was going on about the English, that your father once told you never to be bitter, always to take comfort from God and your friends. Bitterness, you said, was damaging. You were right, of course. I've been bitter time and time again in all these months of waiting. I've learnt that much at least. Your father was right and I must make contact with mine. Will you read my letter for me, Hannah, when I manage to get it down? Please,' he added softly.

He drained his tea and stood up.

'Hannah, I don't know what I'd have done without you. I hope I haven't tired you out.'

'Not a bit of it,' she said, standing up and hugging him. 'I shall be celebrating your good news for a very long time. I'll think about it every time we have bad news or another problem. Congratulations, John McCreedy. Sleep well. I'll see you in the morning.'

20

It was Daniel who explained to Hannah when she'd first moved to Ardtur why schools in Ireland always closed for the summer holiday on the last day of June and why they then had an additional holiday at Halloween.

'Well, you see Hannah, by July, all the older children will be needed on the land. First, there'll be the harvesting of the main potato crop and then there'll be preparing the ground for the next one. That late planting is harvested around Halloween, hence the extra holiday. In some places it's called 'the potato picking' because those potatoes have to be checked out and stored in clamps. It's a big job getting it all protected and under cover, as you can imagine. It's all hands on deck, as some might say.'

No big job this year, Hannah reflected, as she walked slowly home on a damp, grey June day after a Friday morning in school. There would be no crop to harvest at the end of June. The stalks, where they still stood above ground, were dark and bent, the potatoes in the ground all rotten. Not only were there none fit to eat, but there would be none available to plant for that late crop Daniel had mentioned.

This July, there would be no need for Rose and Sam to help her cut up 'seed' potatoes at the kitchen table for their near neighbour, Michael Friel, who always came to help plant the late crop every year, knowing that Patrick was away in Scotland. Because this year, neither Michael, nor anyone else the length of the valley had any potatoes to plant.

According to Sophie and the *Illustrated London News*, various experts had suggested ways of cleansing the soil so that a new crop could be grown. Of course, all their suggestions cost money, and with no crop to sell, there wasn't any money, neither for the rent, nor for meal and flour, never mind money for lime, or indeed for the purchase of imported potatoes uncontaminated by the airborne spores that various experts had blamed for devastated the crops throughout the whole country.

Without the usual summer pattern of work, Hannah, Daniel and John were well aware that the holiday might not be of much benefit to their pupils this year. To begin with, the loss of lunch-time pieces, breakfasts if needed, and meal and flour for those families who were short of an evening meal, would be sadly missed when school closed. Apart from some children who could help with turf cutting, most of their pupils would have little activity for the six-week break.

A 'holiday' was one thing, they had all agreed, but this length of time in the present circumstances might well see their pupils become bored and frustrated. It might even set back the very good work the last year had set going so successfully.

'Well, it's no hardship to me to keep going another couple of weeks,' said Daniel, 'but it's a different matter for you two.' He turned to

Hannah and John who sat with him in a welcome patch of pale sunshine, on a Saturday afternoon a week later when they'd agreed it was time to make a decision.

'Well, I must admit, I think it would be good for Rose and Sam to have company, other than just the children here in Ardtur,' said Hannah promptly. 'And what's good for them, might well be a help to other parents as well. But that's hardly fair to John,' she added.

Hannah was only too well aware that John's thoughts were very much focused on Galway and his need to visit his parents. He had managed to write and tell them about his research into folk-lore and storytelling and his good news about his forthcoming publication, but he had not yet had a reply. She knew how anxiously he was waiting for a response.

Daniel promptly took up the point she'd made.

'Maybe, John, you've planned your summer already,' he began. 'You'll not want to stay here working at school when you're fully entitled to your six weeks.'

'No, Daniel, I've not plans made yet, though I shall probably go to Galway at some point. What I'd been thinking about, when we agreed we'd meet today, was what we had at my old school in Galway, before I was sent to Dublin, that is. Some of the teachers called it a holiday school. That was where we did things we didn't normally do, like making toys for our little brothers and sisters.'

He paused and shook his head. 'They taught us how to cook on a campfire and I was no good

219

at all at that. But then, after that, there was a man came and showed us how to carve wood and I got quite keen on that. The girls, I know, did needlework and I think they made clothes.'

He laughed. 'I've just remembered one year we all helped to paint our own classroom. That was not a great success, I'm afraid, but we did enjoy ourselves doing it. Of course, most of us had fathers in the Coastguard Service, or who worked on the ferries, or fishing boats. I can see now there just wasn't the need for help that other areas would have had with the harvest. We certainly *did* do some useful things, that we didn't do at school,' he said firmly. 'And it *was* great company.'

'I like that idea of *holiday school*,' said Hannah thoughtfully. 'Particularly the idea of doing things you wouldn't normally do, like your wood carving, John. It could even be we might discover talents out there we haven't the time to look for . . .'

Hannah broke off as she saw a figure come striding up the track towards them. For a moment, there being no familiar Neddy and cart, she wasn't entirely sure at this distance that it was Dermot Donnelly. Then, as he came closer, he waved and smiled.

'Am I interruptin' you good people?' he asked, as soon as he had greeted them. 'This looks like a teachers' meetin', an' I can well come back another time,' he added, before they had time to reply.

'Sit down, Dermot,' said Daniel firmly. 'Maybe what we need is a parent's opinion on what we were talking about.'

'Maybe we all need a mug of tea as well,' said Hannah, as she stood up.

'Why don't I make the tea, Hannah?' John asked, looking at her and then glancing towards Daniel.

Amazing as Daniel was, dealing with people whom he couldn't see, John always noticed how very easy he was when Hannah was with him. He could see why. If ever Daniel couldn't 'see' what was happening, he would turn slightly towards Hannah. Sometimes, he did ask her a question, but more often he just waited to see what she might say. And it seemed that whenever he looked towards her she always said something that shaped his next comment.

John was well used to making tea in Hannah's kitchen, even when he had to mend the fire and coax it to burn up. Today, there was no delay with the fire, for Hannah had seen to it while John moved the fireside chairs outside to be ready for Daniel when he arrived.

A short time later, he carried out the mugs of tea. He'd put them on a tray, which he'd then placed on a stool. Placed beside Hannah's chair it provided a small table.

'It needs to cool a bit as we're low on milk,' he said, easily, noting that Dermot and Hannah had drawings and paintings on their knees and Daniel was looking pleased.

'So what do you think, Hannah?' Daniel asked steadily.

'Well I'm delighted, Daniel,' she began, leafing through the sheets of drawing paper on her knee a second time. 'Johnny has done it again,' she said firmly, turning round the watercolour she was looking at for John to see.

'This geranium jumps off the page, Dermot, as if I had just picked it,' she went on. She commented further for Daniel's benefit as she went through the paintings for a second time. 'A rich, deep red, Daniel, true to its actual colour, but he's used a wash behind it to suggest the mint leaves rather than paint them in detail. It looks wonderful.'

Daniel beamed. 'And what about the other one?' he asked. 'The one you said wasn't by Johnny.'

'The one John hasn't seen yet,' she said smiling, as she leafed through the remaining sheets.

Hannah found the one she wanted and held it up. It was clearly a child's painting, but once again the colour was striking, and this time the mint leaves were delicately outlined in green.

'What age did you say she was, Dermot?' Hannah asked, for John's benefit.

'She's only six,' Dermot said, 'but nothing would do her but that Johnny would lend her a brush. She said flowers don't like crayons!'

They all laughed as Hannah handed round the tea.

'It looks,' said Daniel, smiling broadly, 'as if you're the bringer of good news, Dermot. Maybe there's another artist in the family.' He nodded to himself.

He was silent for a few minutes as he drank his tea.

'Hannah,' he said, 'could we afford paint,

222

brushes and paper, if we operated a holiday school for a couple of weeks for our own pupils and all the young brothers and sisters within reach?'

Hannah saw John nodding and looking pleased, and thought of the men who had gone out and got drunk in Galloway and that incredible wager they'd won. She still asked herself how they could possibly have won so much money. It must have involved betting on a fight. How else could the stakes have been so high? It then struck her that if they did what Daniel was suggesting it could even be that some of those men's own children would benefit.

'Yes, I think we could manage,' she said, trying not to smile. 'And if we do, then I think it would help the families if we provide pieces as well. I'll check and make sure we've enough,' she added soberly, though she felt suddenly so elated, what she wanted to do was laugh.

★ ★ ★

The last days of June seemed to disappear even more quickly than usual and Hannah was grateful for the long evenings to catch up on her assignment of napkins. There was no doubt that daylight, even this misty daylight, was much easier on the eyes than lamplight, though she'd learnt long ago from her friend, Catriona, to use a glass globe full of water to enhance the lamplight on winter evenings.

She knew she had no real cause to be anxious about money, for Patrick was meticulous about sending a weekly postal order, but seeing so much need all around her made her want to put back 'under the bed' the few sovereigns she had used earlier in the year when things were so bad at school.

Although she now received a proper monthly salary for teaching three mornings a week, she still didn't want to lose her sewing money. Only if she could rely on putting *that* away, could she reassure Patrick if there was no work to be found for him in the coming winter. Even if there were the funds to go on delivering meal and flour, he would certainly want to share the job with Dermot Donnelly, unless Dermot had good news of the fishing boat being built in Port William.

Meantime, she was expecting Peter Gallagher, the draper from Creeslough, on one of the mornings when he knew she would be at home.

On the last Monday in June, however, it was not Peter who was standing waiting at her open door when she came back into the kitchen with rainwater for washing clothes from the barrel just outside the back door.

'Jonathan,' she said, delighted to see him. 'I wasn't sure when you'd manage a visit,' she went on, putting the buckets down. 'You seem to be very busy at the moment. You've been in Armagh and Dublin as well, haven't you?' She waved him to the armchairs.

He smiled wearily and admitted he'd had rather a lot of travelling to do, but then, once he sat down, he went on in his normal way to enquire about school and equipment and the distribution of meal and flour. He seemed particularly pleased at the success of Catriona's women's group who were making and distributing the clothes they'd produced from the flawed fabric he'd provided.

He laughed aloud when she told him the details of the drunken night out, a story that she'd felt she couldn't actually write about, even though she was sure he would understand.

It was as she was making tea, she looked back at him from the dresser and saw he was sitting motionless, looking into the fire. She realised with surprise that, for once, she had done most of the talking, telling him all the news, anticipating what he would want to know about, sharing good news they'd had in the valley with small amounts of dollars arriving from local people now in Boston, or Peterborough, Ontario, or New York.

There was still cake in the tin and Aunt Mary had sent down milk with a neighbour, so her task of making tea was easy, but the more she thought about it, and the oftener she glanced at him, the more sure she was that something was wrong.

'I hope things are going well with your own work in Yorkshire, Jonathan,' she began, as she passed him his tea and a small plate with plain cake. 'I know from my spies, as you call them, that there are problems in the textile industry with competition from India,' she went on, as lightly as she could. 'One of Sophie's papers said there were many weavers out of work in Belfast and other parts of East Ulster, and most of them didn't even have potato gardens in the first place.'

'Yes,' he agreed, 'there's a lot of unemployment there, I'm afraid. We're more fortunate in Yorkshire. There's more variety in our processing, so we're not facing quite the same amount of competition.'

The tone was unambiguously flat and now that he wasn't listening to her reports on progress, he seemed distracted. She was sure now that something was wrong, but she had no idea what it might be and how, if at all, she could do anything to help.

They sat in silence as they drank tea. Try as she might, she could get no clue. When he spoke first, she was almost startled, but very grateful.

'I'm afraid I'm poor company at the moment, Hannah. I've something on my mind that seems to keep tugging at me and won't leave me alone. I'm afraid I'm being rather silly.'

'I can't imagine that, Jonathan,' she said gently, 'but I wonder if you'd be the best judge of that.'

'Perhaps not,' he agreed, 'but who else is there?'

'Well, there's me for a start,' she replied. 'If I thought you were being silly I'd tell you so.'

'Would you? Would you really?' he asked, sounding surprised.

'Yes, of course I would. What's the point of not being honest? If I thought a friend was getting it wrong I'd tell them, unless, of course, they clearly didn't want to know. That's a different matter.'

There was the briefest of pauses as he took in what she'd said.

'I've met someone I've come to love, and I just don't know what to do,' he said abruptly, putting down his mug and clutching his hands together.

'Does she know that you love her?'

'I don't know. I've not said anything directly. We're good friends, we talk a lot when we meet, and we write ... ' He broke off, looking distraught.

'Is she married?'

'No, she's a widow. Her name is Sarah Hamilton. I met her at Castledillon and she copies letters for me on behalf of Sir George ... '

Hannah waited to see if he would go on, but clearly he couldn't.

'If you didn't have a wife, would you ask her to marry you?'

'Yes, yes, of course, I would.'

'And she knows about your wife, as I do?'

'But of course.'

'Do you know what I'd want if I were Sarah Hamilton?' she asked, trying to keep her voice steady.

'What would you want?'

'I'd want to know how you felt.'

'But what good would that do if I couldn't marry you?'

She shook her head sadly and looked at the hurt in his face. 'Jonathan,' she said, taking a deep breath. 'There is nothing more precious than the love of a good man. I know that. And I know I'd have waited even longer if I'd had to. I was only seventeen when Patrick came to the farm. He waited three years before he spoke. Yes,

I was young, perhaps it didn't hurt so much then to have to wait, but you and Sarah are not young. Don't deny her the love that you could share. Tell her, Jonathan. Tell her what you feel.'

'And what if she doesn't return my love?'

'Then you will stop feeling the anxiety you feel now.'

He sat silent, his face bleak. He looked as if he had lost everything he possessed. Hannah felt he was near to tears.

'I think you made a mistake once, Jonathan,' she said very quietly. 'You were much younger then. This time, you know your true feelings. You'll have to trust them. I think if you do, you'll find happiness.'

'Thank you, Hannah,' he said very quietly. 'I just hadn't realised how lonely I've been feeling. I haven't much family and I'm not close to my brothers. I do have some dear friends and many good colleagues, but loneliness is about having no one who would understand what you're feeling. But you do. I'll do what you say and let you know what happens. One way or another.' He gave a slight smile.

'Yes, please. Just as soon as you can. I'll be thinking of you.'

She knew that he needed to go and make some more of the visits on his list, but he did seem a little lighter in spirits. As she watched him walking down the track, she thought about Sarah Hamilton. She had lost the man she loved and Jonathan had lost the woman he thought he loved. She knew what she was hoping for, but it might take time, even if it were to happen at all.

21

Each day during that last week of June 1846, after Daniel had called the roll, John took out his list for the holiday school and asked if there were any other names to be added on. Hannah listened, as the names of both younger and older children were added each day to the existing fifteen pupils on the roll, who'd been asked to spread the word and invite any children they knew within walking distance to join them for the two weeks of holiday school.

Now, as John and Hannah saw just how popular the whole idea was becoming, she began to wonder how they could possibly cope with so many children for a week, never mind a fortnight.

Each lunchtime, Hannah, Daniel and John considered the new names and the new problems the extra numbers would generate. No doubt parents were genuinely glad to have something to occupy their children, already limited by the depressing grey, damp weather continuing since the late spring, but it was also obvious that when every spoonful of meal and flour had to be measured out each day, that the prospect of free lunches was an opportunity not to be missed.

There was enough money in the school funds to provide the necessary food, but what money wouldn't provide was enough space in Daniel's cottage to seat double, or possibly treble, their usual numbers. Even with the new tables and benches it was still a tight squeeze for the existing pupils. How on earth could they possibly accommodate all these extra children?

As Daniel said during one of their lunchtime conferences, in a better summer they could have sat outside, but at the moment there was seldom a day without misty rain, or low cloud. Some days, he insisted, it was cold enough that he for one was grateful for the prospect of a fire in the evening.

John suggested mixing pupils and visitors, splitting the names on his list and then having both a morning and an afternoon session. Hannah had already agreed to come every morning, instead of her usual three, but now she felt she must offer afternoons as well. She'd no idea how she'd manage all the things she had to do at home if she were out all day, but it just didn't occur to her to leave the afternoons to John and Daniel on their own.

Daniel suggested that both morning and afternoon sessions should be the same length, but shorter than normal school hours. He suggested ten till twelve and two till four. He then proposed that the four eldest school pupils might 'help out' as monitors, two in the morning, two in the afternoon. That, he said, would mean that Hannah could leave a little early in the morning and have time for a small 'catch-up' on her cooking and baking in the middle of the day.

It was still going to be hard work, but as

Hannah and John agreed after the first two days, it was so clearly worth the effort. Weeks ago, they had put in a special order for art materials. Now they were able to offer drawing, painting and sketching to everyone who was interested. They'd also acquired fabric and backing material from Jonathan Hancock so patchwork, rug-making and sewing were offered to both boys and girls. Hannah was quite delighted when some of the boys proved to be very good at pinning patchwork, even if they left the actual sewing in place to their sisters. She had spoken of the possibility of cradle covers for very young brothers and sisters and she was very touched by the number now under way.

While Hannah and John and their two helpers showed boys and girls what they could do with the various materials available, Daniel stood by listening to the new voices. Once everyone was at work he would tell a story.

Later, he commented on the devoted quality of the silence, both when he told a story and later, when John and Hannah took it in turns to read their favourite poems.

By the end of the first week, Hannah could hardly believe how easily all the children had found things they wanted to do, and, having chosen, how easily they tackled activities totally new to them. It looked as if the habit of 'sharing,' a standard part of everyday school, had simply stretched out from the regulars, as Daniel called them, to the newcomers. They were all delighted that the children were completely at ease with each other and with their teachers.

One of the most successful 'teachers' was young Johnny Donnelly, the boy who had moved from crayons to watercolour and whose pictures had enabled Jonathan Hancock to raise donations for the school. He was one of the four 'helpers' from everyday school and he not only encouraged even the young children to use both crayons and brushes as he had, but, by sharing his own pictures, and those of his six-year-old sister, he ensured that by the end of the week everyone in the morning group had at least one picture of their own to take home.

On that Friday morning, Bridget, the woman who made the lunches for everyone, came by request, bringing small packets of 'cookies'. Daniel had insisted that each person who had completed a project of their choice within the week should have a prize. It was Bridget's idea that 'something to share' would include other children who could not come. In fact, every single 'morning child' had earned a prize and from what Hannah could remember from Thursday afternoon, it looked as if there would be no leftovers from the second batch she had made for Friday afternoon.

The prize-giving was a great success. As children put pictures in folders to take home, to share with parents and neighbours, Hannah thought again of Jonathan Hancock and the first pictures he had given away and the donations they had brought to the school and to the valley. He'd be so pleased that some of that picture money of his had paid for the extra art materials, for the lunches and for the oatmeal for Bridget's little packets of cookies.

As she said goodbye to Daniel and suggested he rest himself at the weekend, she thought of all the former neighbours who had once listened to his stories. So many of them had since taken the Derry boat and now worked permanently in England or Scotland. They were one part of a long line who had made their way to Liverpool, or Glasgow, or anywhere they had contacts who would help them find work.

Surely they must miss their families and the places they once knew, just as she missed her father, her brothers, and sisters. She thought so often of the sight and sound of the waves on the Solway Firth, sweeping up to the beach at the bottom of their sloping fields. She wondered what images the emigrants from this valley carried in their hearts, as she carried hers.

Thinking of her brothers in Nova Scotia, she began to recall other emigrants she knew, like Marie and Liam, who had recently gone to New York, and a niece of Sophie's who had left for Boston. She wondered how they would feel if they got a picture of their home valley. Would it make them glad to be remembered, or sad to be reminded that they probably would never go back to their first home?

Producing pictures for all these people would be no trouble at all judging by this week's output, Hannah reflected as she set out for home, Sam and Rose running ahead of her and John having a final word with Daniel. A letter to accompany each one was a different matter. Only a few older children in each group could write well enough to produce even a short message. But then, Hannah thought sadly, few of the people who would appreciate pictures of 'their valley' could either read, or write, themselves.

They could probably not even write their own names. Just like the group of Irish harvesters Hannah had offered to help when she was seventeen and still a monitor — when one of her pupils was her own dear Patrick.

★   ★   ★

When Hannah had a sudden idea, like sending out pictures to former residents of their valley, 'taking one of her notions' as Patrick always called it, she found the details of her plan went round and round in her head until she had either solved all the problems involved with the idea, or wore herself out in the process. But this time, having 'taken this notion' at the end of the first week in July, neither of those things happened.

She had no sooner arrived home from holiday school, made up the fire and begun making tea for John, Sam and Rose, when Sophie from next door arrived in a flurry of skirts, clutching a letter for John.

To Hannah's great surprise, Sophie immediately said, 'No, thank you, Hannah dear,' to her offer of tea, and then suggested that Sam and Rose come over and read to her, just as soon as they had finished theirs.

As they exchanged glances, Hannah saw John's face lose not only its usual animation, but also its colour.

The long-awaited letter had come at last. John had written to his father, sharing his good news about the publication of his book on storytelling and now, after weeks when he had waited as patiently as he could for his reply, the envelope lay on the table, the Galway postmark quite unmistakable.

'Don't stay too long,' Hannah warned, as soon as Rose and Sam finished off their bread and jam. 'Sophie might like you to read to her for a little, but she sometimes gets very tired when she listens,' Hannah explained, knowing that Rose was indeed paying attention, even if Sam was not.

The moment they disappeared, she handed John the letter and watched him rip it open.

'It's not from Da,' he said abruptly, before he'd even unfolded it. 'It's from my sister, Clare. So something's wrong,' he added as he struggled awkwardly to pull out the single sheet of notepaper.

Hannah felt her spirits fall, the weariness of the day now taking away the pleasure she'd felt in the success of the week, the smiling faces of the children who had departed carrying pictures, or sketches, tiny patchwork cot covers, or packets of brownies. She sat finishing her tea, trying to stay calm and preparing herself for whatever might emerge from the torn envelope. John dropped the letter on the table and burst into tears.

She stood up, put her arms round him and felt his warm tears splash on her bare arms.

'Oh, John dear, what *has* happened? Please,

tell me what's happened.'

'I'm sorry. I'm being ridiculous . . . here, read it yourself,' he said thrusting the single sheet towards her. 'It's my eldest sister, Clare. She's not a great writer and her spelling isn't up to much,' he added, making an attempt to wipe his tears and collect himself.

The writing was indeed somewhat erratic but the message was clear enough. There had been an accident on board the small coastguard boat. A young man, a trainee, had been hit on the head and gone overboard. Their father, knowing the man was unconscious, had immediately gone after him and kept him afloat until help came. The young man was all right now, but Da was still in bed with pneumonia. He had been very poorly but seemed to be a little better today, his sister wrote. Clare had put no date on the letter and the postmark was smudged. Only one thing was clear to Hannah. Whatever the difficulties between John and his father, she knew for certain that he couldn't bear to lose him.

★　★　★

They talked quietly for a little while, John explaining to her how a man could be knocked unconscious if he were not entirely familiar with the movements of sheets, and booms, and other pieces of sailing equipment Hannah had never heard of before. What she could grasp easily enough was that going into the water uncon-scious could be fatal, if he fell face down. Clearly, John's father, a strong swimmer, was taking no chances. So, he had gone in after him. John remembered now that his father's Number Two was a good seaman, but not a good swimmer.

As John reread the letter again, some further details did emerge that he'd simply not registered in his first anxious reading. It was now clear the two men had been in the water a long time. There had been no help near at hand and the two remaining crew of the coastguard boat could not simultaneously manoeuvre their boat, hold her steady and carry out the rescue. They'd had to wait some time before a fishing boat saw their flares and came to their aid.

In just over a week's time John would be free to go to Galway and find out for himself exactly what was happening. Right now, Hannah encouraged him to write to his sister. If he took his letter to the post first thing next morning, he just might get a reply within the week.

Hannah reckoned that it would help him to be able to act. He would certainly not be the only one watching out each day for a possible reply.

★ ★ ★

But there was no reply that week. As day followed day, they both knew there was no point trying to guess what was happening in Galway, or even what might already have happened.

John, who clearly felt bad at having showed so much feeling on the subject, concentrated on the remaining week's work. It was only when he asked her how she felt about what they had done in running a holiday school and if she'd achieved what she'd hoped from it, that she suddenly remembered all the thoughts that had come to her when she saw the pictures being carried home.

'To tell you the truth, John, any thoughts I had went clean out of my head, as my father would say, when Sophie appeared with that letter from your sister,' she said. 'I think I was about to have either a great thought, or a silly notion. Certainly, I'd registered all those pictures and thought of all the people who've gone from the valley since the bad times began.'

'Were there many went from here?' John asked. He knew a good deal about emigration throughout Ireland from Sophie's newspapers but he had never actually asked about the valley where he both lived and worked.

Hannah shook her head. 'I really couldn't answer that properly. Perhaps the only people who do know are the priests and the ministers.'

'I could certainly ask the priest in Churchill — he's been very kind to me. Doesn't even insist on my going to Mass as I thought he would.'

Hannah smiled. There were some priests who had taken a hard line with their flock, some of them repeating the phrase that had made John so angry: '*The famine is God's judgement on the idle Irish.*'

But not all were like that. Catriona, another Covenanter's daughter like herself, had nothing but admiration for the priest in Ramelton. She said the only problem with the dear man was he had so little money himself and yet he still tried to help out those with even less.

It was while she was telling John about Catriona and the Catholic priest that she noticed he was looking at her very closely.

'Perhaps we should do what Jonathan Hancock did?' he said slowly.

'What d'you mean, John? I know he gave away Johnny Donnelly's pictures and then asked for a donation for the school. And we both know how much money we've had. All those books and paper and art materials. And money for pieces and bowls of meal for supper. But then Jonathan knows landowners and gentry,' she added gently.

'And we don't know *who we know*,' he said firmly. 'Most of those who went from this valley probably can't read a covering letter, even if all our holiday school pupils could write them, which most of them can't.' He echoed Hannah's thoughts. 'But we could get round that, Hannah. And it's not just those who've recently gone, there must be people from 1838 and back before that. It would be worth a try, wouldn't it?'

For a moment, Hannah felt confused. She hadn't seen John so animated in months, suddenly it seemed as if he had seen something he really wanted to do.

'Hannah, don't you remember the money that came from the Indian Army, and the story we read about the Choctaw Indians who'd had a famine themselves. We've no idea where a picture from this valley could end up. Can school afford the stamps and the envelopes?'

She laughed and thought again of the drunken men from the valley who had sent home an even

239

larger donation than most of Jonathan's offerings. She hadn't felt she could share the story with anyone in the valley, but, thanks to those men, they could indeed buy envelopes and post them anywhere in the world where they had a name and an address for someone who had once lived in this valley.

22

Hannah was indeed grateful when holiday school ended and she once again had time to catch up on both household tasks and on her untouched pile of napkins, but although she'd been looking forward to making amends for her unusually short, and often intermittent, letters to Patrick and her other correspondents, she admitted freely as July moved on that now she did have time to herself, she was feeling lonely.

She smiled wryly and looked around the empty kitchen. Rose and Sam had long since departed to play with the Friels and the other new friends they'd made in the first two weeks of July. There was no doubt it did look as if the holiday school had been a great success from the point of view of the children's new activities and the new friendships they had all made.

As for herself, as the later weeks of July moved slowly on, she admitted she was missing the daily contact with John, and Daniel, and indeed Bridget, who'd become such an active presence in all they did. But it was the lively atmosphere that had been created she missed most of all. Without the buzz of activity and the excitement of small successes that seemed to make the days fly by, she found herself thinking continuously of all the poor people who had not enough to eat and of those who were afraid they'd be turned out when they couldn't pay the rent. Families were being parted. Everyone knew how seldom any emigrant ever came back, even if they survived the long and perilous journeys that lay ahead of them.

Absorbed in her thoughts, she took a fresh napkin from the pile and made sure it had no flaws. It was never worth spending time hemming a napkin if it was going to be rejected by the checker. The small completion fee due would only be deducted from the next monthly payment.

She reflected again on that the second week of holiday school. It had been even busier than the first and it had managed to generate yet more problems, but despite that, it was full of a liveliness and excitement she now sadly missed. At the time, that liveliness and excitement had meant that none of the staff seemed to mind all the extra effort their activities had generated.

When they sent out a request for the names and addresses of people who might like to receive a picture of somewhere they'd once known so very well, they'd had a huge response from the families throughout the valley. Hannah had to smile as she thought of it. She'd never imagined the problems there could be just trying to make sense of a list of names!

To begin with, so many people had the same name. The list was full of McGinleys. She had heard a little about the McGinleys from Patrick and was prepared to find quite a few of them, but what she couldn't tell, when she studied the list, was if these were really all different people. She was familiar enough with nicknames, but how could she know what the person's official name was, if she also knew that no one ever used it? It had also occurred to her to wonder what use a nickname might be to a postman in Boston, or New York or Peterborough, Ontario.

Daniel, who had correctly predicted the problems with the children collecting addresses, had begun each of the first two sessions of the second week, by teaching them how to memorise and repeat the names they'd been given, as faithfully as they could. They had done their best. But if it hadn't been for Dermot Donnelly, who had by now got to know everyone on his delivery route for meal and flour, the task might have proved impossible.

Reading from Dermot's list mid-week, when they tried to make sure that no one from the valley had been forgotten, or confused with someone else, Hannah saw exactly what John had meant when he reminded her that County Donegal had precious little literacy. Only one in five, she'd been told. She had been interested in the figures and the difference between counties but she just hadn't grasped how few people that would mean in the length and breadth of the Lough Gartan valley.

On the other hand, she now understood more clearly why Daniel had wanted to run a school. Fifteen pupils might seem only a tiny drop in a large pool. It was a gesture, but over this last year she had come to see that small gestures could open the way for much bigger things.

With Dermot's help and much good humour, they finally got the list sorted. Daniel then composed and dictated a brief but warm-hearted message telling all the recipients they were not forgotten and their friends and family back in Donegal would be so pleased to hear from them, in Irish, or in English, whenever they had time to write. He ended his message with some words from an Irish blessing he was sure most of them would know.

As they had all agreed, what he made no mention of at all, was the present state of both hunger and illness, increasing week by week all over Ireland.

Daniel's message was written down by John and then copied out carefully by a few of their older pupils, and more laboriously, by any of the other children who could manage it. John and Hannah then made up the number of additional copies needed, inserted the names of the recipients, and took care of the packaging and addressing.

On Saturday morning, while Hannah was giving Rose and Sam their breakfast and Dermot was harnessing Neddy, John appeared with his small suitcase. It seemed strange to be parting so early, and so briefly, while Dermot loaded the carefully stacked packages, but once those packages were despatched, John would be setting out on his own long journey back to Galway, not knowing what he would find when he got there.

For Hannah that Saturday passed slowly indeed. She alternated her sewing with baking bread and fetching turf and water. It was a long time since she'd had to fetch either turf or water, for it was part of John's daily routine, a way of thanking her for making his supper every evening.

As the morning passed, she thought of him on his long journey. The worst part was not knowing what he would find. He'd replied to his sister's letter immediately, but they knew that even if she replied by return there was little hope of a letter arriving before he left. Together, they'd tried to face the best, and worst, that might emerge. They'd agreed the best plan would be to go to his grandparents' house first for news of his father before he even thought of going home.

Rose and Sam then appeared for lunch, in good spirits, full of news and questions. Sam, in particular, had started watching out for the blackberry crop, usually better further down the valley than close to home. Clearly, he wasn't impressed with the tight, red berries he'd seen today on the bushes down near the lake. What he wanted were large, black, juicy ones. Now that he was a little taller, and felt much more grown up, he had great plans for filling his bowl even faster than last year when the blackberry pickers set off after school for the first gathering.

★   ★   ★

'Are ye all on yer lone, Hannah?' asked Dermot, later that day, brushing the rain off his shoulders before stepping into the kitchen. 'Where's the wee'uns?'

'They went back down to play with the Friels a while ago,' Hannah replied, putting down her napkin and waving him over to the fire. 'I expect

Deirdre Friel is hoping the rain will go over so she can send them home dry . . . What are the chances?' she asked, doubtfully.

'Not great, not great,' he said, spreading his damp hands out over the comforting blaze. 'I think the rain's set in for the evenin' but sure you'd think we'd be used ta it by now. There's some says it's this weather that's brought the blight.'

'Yes, I've heard Bridget at school say that,' she agreed. 'But I've heard some other versions as well,' she went on. 'Daniel, of course, says that when nobody knows, you can have as many theories as you like.'

He shook his head wearily. 'Well, at least we've got your holiday job done. I don't think wee Sheila in the post office had ever seen so much mail for away, all at the one time, that is. Are ye hopin' to raise more money?' he asked, looking at her very directly.

'I don't know, Dermot,' she said honestly. 'We talked about it, but in the end we decided we didn't want to ask for money just at the moment. But we did decide what we needed to do was make contact. I don't think any of us had realised before how many people don't write home, because, of course, they can't. Perhaps what we've done is more 'casting bread on the water', if you know that expression. It seemed the right thing to do, to bring the valley back to the people who must miss it, and bring them back to their families, if only in thought. We're just hoping some good might come out of it. Perhaps something to lift spirits. And, yes,' she added nodding, 'if the odd few dollars are sent home to some of the families, it will leave more in the School Fund for those with nobody to help them out except the Quakers.'

'Like m'self, Hannah,' he said, quickly. 'What wou'd I be doin' by now if I hadn't had the few shillin's every week for the deliverin' of the meal and flour an' that money I had a while back from our Johnny's wee pictures. He managed a brave few more these las' two weeks, didn't he?' he said, with a sudden smile.

'He did indeed,' she agreed. 'And, even better, he got some of the newcomers really going. Did he tell you we were able to give everyone who wanted it some paper and paints, to take home on the last day? Maybe, indeed if things don't improve soon,' she added sadly, 'those wee ones might help us to raise funds like Johnny did. It's amazing how generous people can be once they realise there's a need.'

'Yer right there,' he said. 'A man was tellin' me yesterday that some newspaper he sees has a column where people can say thank you, for stuff they've received. Barrels of meal, and clothes, forby money,' he added quickly. 'An' sure on that list there was women from Derry an' women from Belfast, an' they knows the place all right an' what's goin' on here, but sure, wasn't there also some woman in a female seminary, whatever that is, in Washington, Pennsylvania, who can't know much about us at all, an' she'd sent thirty-one barrels of kiln-dried Indian meal.'

He paused, watching her face as she smiled and nodded her head gently.

'Any more word of the fishin' boats?' he said abruptly, suddenly focusing on the news that would most affect him.

'Not yet, Dermot,' she said, 'but I'm expecting Jonathan Hancock before the month's out. The first boat is nearly ready, as you know, but there's been some delay agreeing the money for the other two. Are you short at all?'

'No, thanks be t'God, we've more than most. It's just me wantin' full-time work. I'd like fine to be back at the fishin'. I'm sure yer Patrick woud be jus' the same if he were in my shoes.'

She nodded and stood up.

'Every bit the same,' she said, as she picked up the kettle. 'I need a mug of tea. I hope you do too.'

He smiled. 'Wou'd I ever refuse a mug o'tea in this house?'

* * *

When the damp, overcast weather continued in August and darkness came earlier each evening, people began to pass on rumours about it being a sign there would be a bad winter. Fortunately, there were also some pieces of good news, which were passed around just as vigorously.

When Hannah's neighbour, Sophie, was given a new batch of newspapers by her nieces she went through them slowly and carefully, now that John was no longer able to pave the way for her, as she called it. She was the first to share the news that a new Women's Group in Belfast had sent money to Connaught where things were much worse than in Donegal. She also found out, via John, that the priest with whom he'd stayed when he first arrived from Galway, had recently been given half the value of a cheque received by the local Presbyterian minister in Dunfanaghy.

There were many generous acts recorded in both local and national papers, but it was little to set against the overall picture. The local workhouse was almost full and more and more cases of fever were being reported. A fever hospital was being built near the workhouse in Dunfanaghy, but in other parts of Ireland the need had been so urgent that 'fever sheds' had been hastily erected. Even they were not enough. What was more troubling still was that it now seemed that even people who did have enough to eat were getting ill. From many areas the death lists included both doctors and priests, and those gentry who tried to take an interest in their tenants.

Now, it was no longer just the poor, or the hungry who died. Suddenly, no one was safe.

23

As the days of that damp and sunless summer of 1846 passed slowly by, Hannah did her best to keep busy and to stay as cheerful as she could. She told herself regularly that she had no cause to be either lonely, or apprehensive, but however hard she tried, she did feel oppressed.

Yet what had she to complain about? Unlike many people she knew, she had enough food. She had friends and a good fire on the hearth as well as a husband she loved and two lively children. She could go and visit Sophie, or Daniel, or any of her neighbours and would be welcomed. She could sit and write to Patrick as often as she wanted, and pass the time of day with Dermot when he arrived back with Neddy at the end of his day's work.

But try as she would, she still felt lonely and dispirited. She thought longingly of days long gone when she had her sisters for company, school friends to play with, her father coming and going from the fields, saying little, but a positive presence, sunshine and sea all around them.

Suddenly, sitting by the fire on a dim August morning she found herself in tears. She thought of Patrick working away with her father in those same gently sloping fields. When she shut her eyes she could almost feel the warmth of the sunshine on her skin, in her ears the soft ripple of tiny waves breaking on the wet sand, rolling fragments of shell up the beach, then sliding back again down into the dazzling expanse of the Solway Firth.

Why now? Why, after all these years when she had made this valley her home, cherishing the modest cottage on which Patrick had worked so hard to make it both robust and weather-proof, the whitewash gleaming, the thatch well mended every season, the eaves trimmed, the gutters below gravelled and sloped to ensure the rain-water ran away from the walls.

Yes, she missed him, but the more she missed him, the more aware she was of the passing months; almost five months gone, and only something over two months to go till the time of his return. Eleven years now since they'd said goodbye to her father and set out from the farm, now man and wife, when she was just twenty.

There was no romantic honeymoon like those she'd read of in the novels her sisters and their friends passed around between them. They had travelled back to Derry with the rest of the harvesters, finding on the way whatever lodgings, or shelter, they could. Only on one night did they share a double bed. That was when they had visited her brother in Port William. They had laughed together that night as they lay naked on clean sheets, remembering the corner of a dusty barn where they had made love, on the very first night of their long journey from Dundrennan to Ardtur.

Perhaps it was the weather, she thought suddenly. Was that why she felt such longing for sunshine and sea? There was so little sunshine this year that everyone looked pale. The sharp lines of the mountain were always muted, the lake misty, and for the first time in all her years in Ardtur, the handful of flowers she grew in the old pots she'd found in the barn had barely begun to open before they simply dropped their blooms to wilt on the damp grass.

Suddenly, she remembered the red geranium. Despite her hasty planting, it had grown and flowered. Perhaps that was the trouble. At the moment, she felt she could grow nothing, neither plants, nor ideas. Her life was confined to the everyday, the baking and cooking, the cleaning and washing, the hemming of napkins that ensured they would have food enough for the winter.

Even if Patrick could find no work when he came home and had only a half of the income from the delivery round Dermot had been doing since Patrick went away, she would still be able to provide food for the family from what she'd saved from his wages and what the draper paid her each month for her assignment.

She folded the napkin she had just finished, wiped her eyes and stood up. There was enough oatmeal left to make a batch of those biscuits Bridget had made for prize-giving at the end of the holiday school. If she made a batch this morning she could take some to Daniel when she went to see him this afternoon. Rose and Sam would certainly be delighted with such a treat at teatime.

'Hannah dear, is it yourself?' Daniel asked, even before she'd knocked on the open door of his cottage.

She laughed as she greeted him. 'Now, how did you know that? And me as quiet as a mouse?' she asked, as she walked across to the fire, pressed his hand and kissed his cheek.

'Well, maybe there was a bit of wishful thinking in my enhanced perception. Is it still drizzling?'

'Does it ever stop,' she asked vigorously. 'I think I would even welcome a storm. Anything to blow this weather away,' she said, as she drew up the other armchair to the fire. 'How are you, Daniel?' she asked, studying his face, and the set of his body.

'Sadly in need of distraction,' he replied. 'There's only so much time one can contemplate the human condition without becoming seriously critical of the whole enterprise.'

Hannah laughed again. However truthful and perceptive Daniel's responses might be, he had a practised irony, which seldom failed to raise her spirits.

He enquired about Patrick, about Rose and Sam, and about Sam's current ambition to be the best and fastest of the blackberry pickers. He then waved casually to the mantelpiece where she saw a couple of envelopes. Invoices for school materials awaiting her, or John, to deal with, she thought, glancing at them.

'Those are probably for you,' he said

dismissively. 'But much more to the point,' he went on, his tone softening, 'have you had any further communication from our young friend in Galway?'

She took a deep breath, knowing he would want all the detail.

'Yes, Daniel, I have, but I'm not entirely sure what to make of John's letters. He is very steady, very controlled. I don't think he means to cover up, or anything like that, but I still can't decide what to think from what he says.'

'But he does write, doesn't he?' Daniel asked.

'Oh yes. Regularly and at length. That's what is so confusing in some ways. He covers a lot of ground, or a lot of notepaper, you might say, but it doesn't tell me what I want to know.'

'Is his father still recovering?'

'Yes. That I can tell you. It does look as if he's made a complete recovery. He is back at sea as normal and has been up in Dublin on coastguard business. That should all be good news,' she began. 'But the bad news is that he's still either avoiding John, or actually refusing to see him.'

'And how is John taking that?'

'I can't entirely be sure,' she said. 'As I said, he tends to be very steady and calm in his letters and, of course, he's staying with his Cullen grandparents where he's made very welcome. What he did say quite clearly is that now his mother is unwell. He was planning to go and see her when he knew his father would be away in Dublin. But I haven't heard yet how that worked out.'

'It's hard on him,' said Daniel slowly. 'He talks a lot about his sisters but he's never said very much about his mother. What kind of a woman do you think she is?'

'Rather gentle and loving, I'd say,' Hannah replied, 'but unfortunately, I do get the feeling that John's father hasn't much time for gentleness. He certainly hasn't shown much towards John.'

'I find it hard to understand a man not able to appreciate a son like John,' Daniel said. 'I wonder if perhaps John resembles his mother. Certainly, John has a commendable empathy with his pupils; that is usually a more female gift.'

'Do you think his father might see that as a sign of weakness?' she asked, having not thought before of that possibility.

'It's possible. From what you've told me McCreedy Senior hasn't much time for those who can't stand up to him.'

'True enough . . . ' Hannah said. 'And yet he jumped into the sea after that young man who went overboard. It's clear now he saved his life.'

'Yes, it was an act of great courage,' Daniel said crisply. 'But that doesn't mean it was an act of compassion.'

'No, that's a fair point,' she agreed. 'I just wish John had more backing of any kind from his father, but then I can see the life of a coastguard would require very different personal qualities from someone who is drawn to teaching and is also a natural storyteller.'

'A bit more recognition of John's qualities and

considerable achievements wouldn't go amiss,' said Daniel. 'Has he told you when he's coming back to us?'

'No, I don't think he's thought that far ahead yet,' Hannah began, 'but he certainly asks for all our news and doesn't want to miss anything that's happened just because he's been away.'

Daniel sighed. 'It was a happy day when that young man found his way here. I have great hopes for him, Hannah. We must just try and give him the encouragement he should be getting from his family.'

He paused, glanced around the room again and then said: 'You better have a look at those envelopes on the mantelpiece, Hannah. Just in case we owe anyone money for supplies. That's your department, I'm glad to say.'

She reached up and brought down three assorted shapes, two rather battered-looking white envelopes with Dublin postmarks and a much larger, cream-coloured one with colourful American stamps.

'We've got one from America, Daniel. Did you know that?' she asked, as she opened it carefully, so that the stamps were not damaged and could be steamed off and added to the small scrapbook some of the older boys were keeping.

'Yes, I think Bridget may have told me, but I had forgot. Who is it from then?' he asked promptly.

'Goodness,' said Hannah, startled as she took out the single sheet and studied an impressive etching of a tall ship with three layers of sails. She read the address.

256

'It's from Boston, New England, the East Boston Shipping Company to give its full name,' she said, catching her breath as she scanned the short letter, written in a flowing copperplate. She then began to read it aloud.

15 August 1846
  Dear Hannah McGinley and John McCreedy,
  One of the many staff in our firm has brought to the works today a painting done by a pupil at your school. This has been much appreciated by many of the workers here, not just those many who have come from Ireland. I have been asked by the chairman's secretary to tell you that we appreciate your gift and we will be in touch again with you when all the staff have had the chance to view the picture, now on display outside the chairman's suite.
  I am,
  Yours faithfully,
  James Doherty

'What do you make of that, Daniel?'
'Well, well, well. What a coincidence if they got one of our Johnny Donnelly's pictures. We can guess, can't we, where a Bostonian James Doherty might have come from?' asked Daniel.
'Yes, I think we can,' said Hannah happily. 'But there's another gentleman's name on the letterhead as well, Daniel. It's under the engraving of the ship. It says: 'Chairman: Donald McKay'. Or perhaps it's pronounced Mackay.'
'A Scotsman, do you think?' he repeated

slowly. 'Wasn't your maiden name Mackay?'

'Yes, it was. But there are different ways of spelling it,' she added. 'My father always said it was the same clan, but people just wrote what they heard and different people pronounced it differently.'

'So we've found one of your countrymen on the other side of the Atlantic,' he said thoughtfully. 'I wonder how he came to be chairman, and to have a suite of his own and a large staff of Irishmen working for him, by the sound of it.' He smiled and was silent for a moment.

'The letter did say they'd be in touch again, didn't it?'

'Yes. When everyone has had a chance to see the picture.'

'Well, I shall be looking forward to that,' said Daniel, nodding to himself. 'Possibly another Donegal man and a Scots chairman . . . select company for Casheltown School, don't you think?' Daniel paused and then said abruptly, 'Hannah dear, much as I want you to stay, I've a feeling it's time you were going to collect the children?'

'Yes, I'm afraid it is,' she agreed. 'They're reading to Sophie and she does get tired quickly these days. But I may get up again later in the week,' she added, seeing the downcast look on his face. 'Meantime, I've brought you some prize-giving biscuits.' She took the small packet from her skirt pocket. 'Don't eat them all at once!' she said lightly, putting them into his hand.

'And don't you be long till you're back, as the saying is. It was so good to see you, Hannah.'

'And good to see you too, Daniel. I miss you

and John as much as I miss Patrick,' she said, grasping his hand. 'But we'll not tell him that. Will we?'

Still smiling, she stepped out into the dim afternoon and hardly noticed the thin drizzle as she walked quickly back to Ardtur.

★ ★ ★

Hannah did not knock at the open door until she had looked inside. Sophie had leaned back in her chair and closed her eyes as Rose read one of their storybooks. Sam sat gently rocking back and forward. He knew it was rude to fidget when someone was reading, or telling a story, but he and Hannah had agreed that as long as he made no noise, a little gentle movement wouldn't disturb anyone.

He looked up immediately, clearly relieved to see her. Moments later, Sophie opened her eyes and immediately offered tea. Hannah declined gently and kept their thanks and goodbyes to a minimum.

'Ma, what's a Relief Committee?' Sam asked, as soon as they stepped across their own doorway.

'Was Sophie telling you about them?' Hannah asked, as she moved to make up the fire and refill the kettle.

'She did explain what they were, Ma,' Rose began, 'but when she gets tired she talks with her mouth half shut and I thought it was best just to nod and agree.'

'Good girl,' said Hannah firmly. 'Sometimes

259

one just has to pretend, if it's the kinder thing to do.'

'Like telling a white lie?' asked Sam promptly.

'Yes, it's very like a white lie. As long as it doesn't do any harm,' she added, as she fetched milk from the cold stone shelf outside the back door.

'But you'll tell us what they are, won't you?' said Sam, as he watched her take mugs from the dresser.

'Yes, of course, I will, but some of these things keep changing. What I tell you today may change next week, or next month.'

'Sophie said they were stopping all relief,' Rose began. 'She said there was a man called Trevelyan in Dublin Castle who had no time for the Irish. He'd get rid of them, every one if he could. So he was going to close the grain depots and let people starve. Will we starve, Ma?'

'No, love, we won't. There is a shortage of food because we lost our potatoes, but we have flour and meal instead, and so do our neighbours. But there are some people haven't got meal or flour and we have to find ways of helping them. Relief means giving them food, or money, so they can buy food. There are different ways of doing it.'

'Sophie said they were forever chopping and changing,' added Sam, 'but then she just started muttering so Rose asked her would she like to hear another story.'

'And what did you read her then?' asked Hannah, glad that the kettle was beginning to sing.

Sophie was a dear soul, but not perhaps the best person to explain the complexities of famine relief to children. Perhaps she might just mention to her, next time she had a chance, that they were both very sharp, that they missed nothing and it might be better not to mention anything from the newspapers that would make them anxious.

'So, would you like a prize biscuit with your tea?' she asked, hoping to distract them.

'Like the ones we had at the end of holiday school?' demanded Sam.

'The very ones,' she replied, opening the cake tin. 'You can choose two each of the smaller ones. We must save the bigger ones in case we have a visitor, for I've no cake at the moment. That's a job for tomorrow morning. Now sit over to the table and I'll make the tea.'

'Ma, these smell lovely,' said Sam. 'I can hardly wait for my tea.'

'Well, you won't have long to wait, Sam. Ladies first, and pass your sister the milk, then it's your turn,' she said, wondering just what new developments there had been in the plans for public works and outdoor relief now the work-houses were filling so rapidly.

She would hear soon enough. Once John came back from Galway there would no doubt be a new selection of newspapers to read in the evenings and he would pass on all that was relevant, good or bad.

24

Hannah didn't get to baking the cake she had planned next morning. She finished making up the fire, swept the hearth and brought out her baking board, but just as she was about to put it on the kitchen table and start work, she heard voices outside. She listened for a moment and then heard Dermot thanking the children for giving Neddy such a good grooming before they went off to play with their friends.

Through the window, Hannah saw the children run off down the hill leaving Dermot standing looking at a scrap of paper he'd taken from his pocket. He was patting Neddy and looking thoughtful.

Probably the names of a couple more people who had nothing much to eat, she thought to herself, as she went and put the baking board back in its place at the side of the dresser.

Once Neddy was harnessed, Dermot would not want to pause for long, so she went to meet him at the door, already sure that he'd been using his very sharp eye for growing hardship. He was always quick to note the disappearance of any clothing with a bit of weight in it. When he saw that particular change in a woman's dress, he'd then look for the telltale sharpness of the nose and the dark smudges below the eyes. That was how he knew that either the family hadn't enough to eat, or that the woman in particular was not taking her full share of what food they had, but was giving some of it to the children, or even to an old person living with them.

Hannah knew that often enough he managed a casual question to a neighbour to confirm his observations, but as time went on he'd grown more confident. Now, he would simply come and tell her what he'd seen and what he thought.

Moments later, on this late August morning, the air already sharp with frost, she stood looking up at him before he began his day's work.

'Maybe they sold their turf to pay the rent,' he said, after he'd told her about passing the open door of a family that didn't have a fire. 'And come to think of it now, there wasn't even the smell of a fire about that house. There was a kind of dampness around it when I walked over as close as I could, without looking nosy.'

'I'm sure you're right, Dermot. Just add them to the list straight away. We've still got enough in the kitty to cover a few more and I'm expecting Jonathan, the man from the Quakers, sometime soon,' she said reassuringly. 'He'll already know about the state of the potatoes and if I know him, he'll have worked out something to keep us going.'

'Aye well, sure there's not much hope for anythin' from the main crop, not after what happened to the early. If the main goes the same way and the winter is any way hard it'll be desperate bad news for everyone,' he added, shaking his head. 'There's some I hear has been gettin' a bit of help from these public works, as they call them, but sure now they say the

Government is goin' to close them. They don't pay much, but sure there's thousands and thousands of people has nothin' else to look to.'

'Yes, I've heard that too, Dermot. We may have to see if we can get more help for ourselves. Maybe we'll have to write again to the people we sent the pictures to after the holiday school. We might have to admit things are no better and then ask them if they can help us a little.'

'Aye well. You'll always think of somethin' if I know you,' he said nodding abruptly. 'Now I must away on, for I'll have to pick up an extra bit of flour, or meal, or whatever I can lay hands on, wherever I can find it. Will I tell whichever man it is, to send you the bill?'

'No, you won't need to do that,' she reassured him. 'You can call on your way with my Scottish friend. I saw her last week so she'll have cash ready for you. Do you remember her? Catriona Ross at Ramelton?'

'Oh yes, I remember *that* lady all right. Indeed I do,' he said, nodding and beaming.

Catriona went to the bank regularly to draw money from Hannah's School Fund so she could provide Dermot with cash for the relevant merchant. What had made him smile, was remembering the way she always counted out the coins at least twice, if not three times, to make sure she'd made no mistake.

★　★　★

Hannah waved Dermot goodbye and came back gratefully to the fire, preoccupied by the sudden

264

remembrance of all she'd heard about the prospect of a very bad winter.

She felt sure that some of the people she'd heard speak about it were just repeating what they'd already heard, but there were others who referred to the very bad year of 1838. They had drawn some parallels with the unusual weather conditions that marked that year.

Distracted as she was by her talk with Dermot, she picked up her sewing and sat down by the fire, her baking board forgotten. Within minutes, she found herself doing sums in her head, something she'd always been good at in her school days. Thinking of Catriona reminded her of the sizable sum in the School Account. Most of it had come from that extraordinary affair of the drunken harvesters, but there had also been regular deposits from those good folk in the Yorkshire mills. They had been most regular in giving their penny a week. But, for how long might that continue?

There were other small donations too, a few dollars here and few more there, but these were not regular and might well disappear if things went on as they were going.

In most of what she had read or heard from John, it had been assumed that the potato crop would not fail a second time. But all the signs so far were that it had. It was true that other crops were perfectly normal, but having food available that one couldn't buy, because one had no money, was hardly going to solve the problem.

She was so preoccupied with her calculations that the fire began to sink low. Suddenly she felt the chill from the open door.

'Now then, Hannah, don't neglect the fire,' she said to herself, as she shivered in the cold air.

As she stood up, she caught sight of a tall figure striding up the rocky path, the tails of his coat flapping with the speed of his progress.

'Well, well,' she said to herself. 'You come most carefully upon your hour,' she whispered. 'Jonathan Hancock, I presume,' she added, smiling, as she made up the fire quickly before he arrived.

★   ★   ★

She went to the door to greet him and was surprised to find him looking distinctly cheerful. She'd always thought he had a handsome, yet very sombre face, but today that certainly didn't apply. As she held out her hand in greeting, she wondered if today it was perhaps her own face that was looking rather sombre.

Having walked so fast, Jonathan was not at all cold, but he admitted easily that he was thirsty and would indeed be grateful for the mug of tea she offered.

'Good,' she replied, 'that means I can have one myself, and we can finish off the prize-giving biscuits,' she said, grateful she had suddenly remembered them.

He settled himself by the fire and watched her move around, making the tea. She put the last of the biscuits on a plate, placed it on a stool and set it between the two armchairs by the fire.

'Do I detect a story behind these biscuits?' he

asked, looking directly at her.

'You do indeed,' she said, returning his gaze. 'Perhaps if I tell you the story of the prize biscuits you will tell me why you are looking so much happier than usual, despite the bad news we probably both have to share.'

To her great surprise he coloured slightly and looked so sheepish she began to guess what he had to tell her.

'You were right,' he said abruptly. 'I told Sarah Hamilton how I felt about her, one glorious summer's day when we walked together under the trees on The Mall, in Armagh. I don't think I shall ever forget it . . . '

'And . . . ' she prompted, when he stopped.

'She has given me her promise.'

'To marry you?' she said, wanting to be quite sure that the news really was as good as she'd now begun to hope.

'Yes, to marry me. She knows about my wife. She knows the doctors say she will not recover her mind but she may remain well in body. I've accepted that if she finds someone else who wants to marry her then I will have to give her my blessing and let her go. But you were right, just knowing how we both feel now is such joy. While we both live we do have hope and it so changes everything. And without your wise words, Hannah, I would not have ventured. I couldn't have found my way if you hadn't spoken,' he said, shaking his head vigorously.

'I'm so happy for you, Jonathan,' she said clasping her hands together. 'Please, may I tell Patrick? No one else, of course, but Patrick will understand and be as pleased as I am. After all, he had to wait three years before he felt he could speak for me. Though, fairly I was much younger.'

'It *has* made such a difference to me, Hannah. Just knowing that she cares about me. I have never felt like this before. Does it show?'

'Yes, it does,' she said, nodding. 'But probably only to someone who has seen you when you were sad. I don't think you need be afraid that you're wearing your heart on your sleeve.'

'I'm glad of that,' he said. 'It might seem sadly out of place in such a difficult time.'

'But that hope you now have will bring you encouragement for the work you do. And it will give her strength as well. If things go badly for us in Ardtur I shall think of you both and I'll wish you well.'

'I only have one problem now, Hannah,' he said, composing his face as best he could.

'And what is that?' she asked cautiously, wondering if he could be teasing her.

'How am I going to manage to keep my good spirits under control when we have to talk about matters practical . . . and make provision for what may be a bad winter into the bargain?'

'Perhaps your good news is sent to help us both,' she offered thoughtfully. 'We could look on it as an unexpected donation that we can call upon when we most need it. What do you think?'

'I think that is *just* what we need.' He nodded. 'I do have some good news, and indeed I have do have some bad, but our biggest problem will be if we have to cope with something unexpected. That really troubles me, but perhaps if we are both brave and speak of the worst that can happen then we will have the courage to try for the best. What do you think?'

'I think we need pencils and paper,' she replied promptly. 'Then we can write down anything that comes to us, good or bad, so that when we write to each other we'll have something there already, even if we don't need it. Wouldn't that be better than the other way around?'

They moved across to the table and it quickly began to look as if their good spirits did speed the work. What also emerged was that they now both had a good idea of how the other's mind worked. Hannah knew when to interrupt and ensure that Jonathan spelt out the details that he had omitted. He, in his turn, was familiar with her sudden silences. They always occurred when she'd suddenly see something he'd overlooked and for the moment didn't know how to put it to him.

There was a lot to think about. By the time Hannah insisted that they make a break for a bite to eat, there were sheets of paper spread all over the kitchen table.

★ ★ ★

They had lunch by the fire, went back to the table afterwards and were still sitting there, making further notes, when Dermot appeared leading Neddy by his halter, Rose and Sam walking one on each side of the empty cart.

'Jonathan, I'd like you to meet Dermot before

269

you go,' Hannah said quietly, as they saw the small procession pass in front of the house, on the way to the barn.

'He'll come in when the children start grooming Neddy,' she explained. 'He's been asking about the fishing boat and I know he'll feel easier if he hears the news on that from you. He's been so good with distributing the food. He's done so much more, way beyond the call of duty, as one might say, to make sure he finds anyone in need. But I know he's longing to be back at sea again.'

'I can only tell him the truth, Hannah. D'you not think it might discourage him?' he said, looking more like his sombre self. 'As I told you, it will be November before the new Quaker Central Relief Committee is set up in Dublin and it will surely be a few more weeks before they find two suitable people to come up here and assess the overall food situation.'

'But how can they do that in winter, if we're talking about fish?' Hannah protested.

To her surprise, Jonathan laughed.

'Hannah dear, assessors don't have to go and *count* fish, they have to find someone *they know they can trust* to *ask* about fish. They will probably already have made enquiries by letter. They just need to verify what's been said so that the funds can be allocated.'

★ ★ ★

'Dermot, this is Jonathan Hancock,' Hannah said, getting up and going towards him, the moment she saw him appear at the door.

'Pleased t'meet ye, sir,' Dermot said, looking awkward as they shook hands.

'And I'm glad to meet you, Dermot,' said Jonathan, shaking his hand firmly. 'And I do have some good news for you, but there's some bad news as well. Let's have the bad news first, shall we?' he said easily, as Dermot joined them at the table.

'I'm afraid the bad news is that it might be December before we get the go-ahead on the fishing boats, although the first one is just about ready. The real problem I'm afraid is that there are so few Quakers in Ireland.'

'Sure from what I heerd, I thought there must be a whole lot of yers,' Dermot replied, looking quite amazed.

Jonathan shook his head sadly. 'The only reason we've been able to help as much as we have so far, is that we are already organised to help each other. To begin with we couldn't provide much in the way of money ourselves, but we've had great help from Friends in America and many other places. The money for the boats, Dermot, actually comes from Nova Scotia, from Scottish emigrants long settled there.

'And, speaking of money. Here it is. I knew I'd put it somewhere safe,' he said, as he extracted three crumpled envelopes from his back pocket.

He handed Dermot a small envelope in which coins chinked and a larger brown one with his own name on it.

'Our usual terms for one of Johnny's pictures: a little for him, and rather more for his family,'

Jonathan began. 'The picture that went to America helped to raise £500 in Fort Wayne, Indiana, from a group of Irish emigrants, one of whom had already made contact with the Quakers in Dublin. That'll buy a lot of meal and flour,' he said, passing over the plain white envelope to Hannah.

Dermot shook his head and looked sad.

'An' to think that I tried to get him a job as a servant,' he said, looking really dejected. 'May God forgive me.'

'Well, I think you could say that He has. Don't you agree, Hannah?' said Jonathan quietly. 'You acted for the best — you were thinking of your family, not of yourself. If you hadn't acted when you did then Johnny's pictures might not have been recognised. The Lord works in mysterious ways,' he added smiling.

'Aye,' replied Dermot, 'an it was you that said, 'No we'll not sell them. We'll give them away and then see what comes.' That was your faith, sir, and sure with that behind us, Hannah and Patrick and I can keep this valley fed, and maybe, indeed, we'll soon be able to give them little fishes to have with their bread, whether its wheaten bread, or corn bread, or even barley loaves,' he added, smiling for the first time that afternoon.

25

There was frost on the grass in September, on the first day back at school, and before the month was out showers of hail and wet snow flurried round the houses. They dropped particles down the chimney so that the fire hissed and spat and Hannah, reading, or preparing schoolwork at the table, knew that within minutes of that first warning sound, the light would drop and the familiar picture of the track down the mountain framed by the front windows of the cottage would be blotted out by a sweeping curtain of sleet, or snow.

When the cold weather set in, she had put aside her work on the napkins to make a heavy pinafore for Rose to wear over her usual school dress. Then, to her surprise, the highly active Sam admitted that he too felt cold in Daniel's cottage, despite the fire, where they took it in turns to warm themselves. She puzzled for a whole morning and then made a garment, not dissimilar in style for him. She referred to it as a tunic and all was well.

But the chill of the worst days was not the hardest thing to bear. Much more chilling was the news that came day by day through newspapers, or by word of mouth. That was indeed far more dispiriting. Many of the worst cases that Hannah and Jonathan had talked about at the kitchen table were rapidly proving to be the case indeed. It was now official. '*There* are *only enough potatoes to feed the Irish population for one month.'*

In fact, there were no potatoes left at all in their valley by the beginning of October 1846. The sound potatoes, used for planting, by those who had them, had proved to be unsound after all. They had simply developed disease as they matured. Given the supplies of meal and flour, still being provided by the school and delivered by Dermot Donnelly, this was not the disaster it might have been, in the length of the valley, but elsewhere in Donegal starvation had indeed struck. Things were particularly bad in areas to the west of them, especially on the coast where there were no roads and the scattered mountain settlements were remote and difficult to access.

While the news was bad in Donegal, the news coming from much further afield was even more distressing. At the end of October the price of wheat, flour and oatmeal in Cork rose by fifty per cent in one week and at the same time Skibbereen became internationally famous for its death rate.

The workhouses were rapidly filling and the landlords, deprived of their rents for yet another year, were beginning to evict their tenants for non-payment of rent, leaving families not only without food, but also without shelter of any kind in the worst of weather.

★ ★ ★

'Well, my colleagues and friends, what should we do?' asked Daniel soberly, as they gathered by the fire, in the schoolroom, at the end of the second week in October.

Hannah had left Rose and Sam with Deirdre Friel and had come back to school to join John and Bridget in the empty classroom, the tables folded up against the walls, the benches left ready for evening visitors. Daniel had said only that he wanted to share his thoughts with them, but given all that had happened since the beginning of the school year, they were each, in their different ways, apprehensive about what he might have to say.

'There are those who might say, and indeed I think are already saying,' he began quietly, 'that we are *fiddling while Rome burns*. We are spending money on books and writing materials when there are people dying of hunger, though not, thank God, in this valley. Not yet, at any rate,' he added, his voice dropping, as he spoke the last words.

'We still have our pupils, we still have funds to keep the school going,' he went on more vigorously. 'We can still distribute meal and flour with money we've been given, but the question is, do we carry on with our educational work, or do we accept that the chances of survival are so slim that it is probably not worth the effort? Could it now be argued that what effort we may be capable of as individuals, would be better directed in other ways?'

Hannah exchanged glances with Bridget, who now not only looked after school lunches, but also prepared food to take to elderly people and to those who were sick. It was Bridget who found out when problems in the home affected their pupils. Her own family long gone, her husband working away like Patrick, she'd taken on the responsibility for knowing how things were with their pupils and doing whatever she could to help both them and their families.

John dropped his eyes and pressed his lips together. Then he looked at them both, saw neither of them about to reply, took a deep breath and began to speak.

'I think we should go on,' he said, baldly. 'We may not survive, or perhaps not *all* of us may survive, but what is the point of giving up when there is still hope? We're not just trying to educate a group of children and young people, we're also trying to help each other, trying to keep up life and spirits at a bad time. What's to be gained by giving that up? Nothing that I can see. I think we should keep going.'

'And what do the ladies think?' Daniel asked, his voice neutral.

Bridget looked down into the embers of the fire. She seemed anxious and uneasy.

'I agree with John,' said Hannah quietly. 'So much of the normal pattern of life in this valley has been torn away, but school is something that still goes on. It's not just for the pupils, it's a focus for everybody who has a child, or even an interest in a neighbour's child, coming and going every day. It's a known, continuing thing, at a time when most normal, everyday things are just not there any more.'

'Hannah's right,' Bridget said. 'Sure, hearin' those children out there at playtime laughin' and shoutin' wou'd put heart in you. An' look at all them letters that come back when they sent the wee pictures away after the holiday school last July. Sure, aren't there people out there, half the world away, wishin' us luck and hopin' we'll pull through. We can't give up an' let them down as well, can we?'

They were agreed. As they talked together in what proved to be a memorable, quiet hour, they acknowledged that Daniel had put into words the uneasy thoughts they'd all entertained in different ways. Now, suddenly, it seemed more possible to share one's feelings, to shape words, or to ask a question, rather than puzzle away inside one's own head.

'I'm grateful to you, colleagues,' said Daniel. 'I confess I often feel I cannot do my fair share of the work, but perhaps in the hours I spend in my chair 'doing nothing', I can gather up for us the possibilities. It is you who have to make these possibilities into reality, but at least my thinking is some kind of a start.'

'It's much more than just a start, Daniel,' John said vigorously. 'You're just like that man in the story of the two bottles, we all now know so well. You sit us down and say: 'Now do your duty' and lo and behold, a feast is served up.'

Hannah and Bridget laughed and Daniel nodded, as he always did when he was pleased. How often had the children performed the play John had written for them, based on the story he'd heard in Galway. Both in Irish, and in English, they'd taken it in turns to play the main parts. Suddenly, it seemed they'd been given something to help them.

They talked and laughed together as they hadn't done for a long time.

'Maybe, we've a wee bit of magic bottle ourselves, Daniel,' said Bridget, suddenly looking easy again. 'Sure look at the way money keeps turnin' up when we think we're runnin' low. If we keep goin' it'll encourage other people. Maybe, even if we were doin' nothin' else but that, it wou'd be worth doin', but you're doin' somethin else as well. Can't even the wee ones here at school write a bit and read the storybooks? That'll stan' to them, whether they stay or go.'

★ ★ ★

In the following weeks much of the news shared in the valley, and in the towns and villages nearby, was of people going. Thousands of families all over Ireland could see no possible future for themselves or their families. Some of them sold their remaining possessions to find the ticket money, some were tempted by the rock-bottom fares offered by individual vessels and some were helped to buy tickets by landlords who wanted to clear their land in the hope they could recoup the losses of the last years by moving their land to grazing and cattle-rearing.

Many of those individuals never reached their destination. Setting aside the losses from the wrecking of overcrowded ships, and the effects of the starvation diet on the cheap passages, survival was still doubtful on board ship where disease spread with the greatest of ease in the crowded and confined spaces.

Stories were brought back from Derry that told of queues miles long, of ships lined up at Gross Isle awaiting clearance to proceed to immigration, when no progress was possible with most of the passengers on board the ships either ill or dying.

★ ★ ★

A few days after Daniel's staff meeting, one of the harvesters who had travelled with Patrick to Mackay's farm arrived home, his right arm bound and splinted. He was well enough in himself, he said, he had been well looked after, but the weather in Scotland had been bad.

He'd been on the top of a haystack, he said, winding straw rope into a thatch that would prevent the stack being ripped apart in the winter storms. The hay was slippery, he had lost his footing, fell headlong and landed on a wooden rake.

It was not just the hay that was suffering. All the late crops were in a bad way, he said, many of them rotting in sodden fields. All the harvesters would be home several weeks early.

For Hannah, the news that Patrick would be back so soon was a wonderful surprise. She'd already been counting the weeks till he was due. Now she could count the days. But her joy was much modified when she began to think of the loss of income for farmers in Scotland, including her own father, and the loss of wages to so many harvesters from other parts of Ireland who would, like Patrick, now come home with significantly less money to tide them over the winter months.

'John dear, have you had any news from home?' Hannah asked one lunchtime a few days later as they sat eating their piece and keeping an eye on their pupils. 'I'm trying my best to keep cheerful as we all said we would, but I'm flagging. Is your mother still doing well? And have you found out yet about why your father's going to Dublin so regularly? Please, think of something?' she said desperately, hoping to make him smile.

'Well, something has just happened, but I can't really make sense of it. The letter only came yesterday and it was from my sister. She does write sometimes to save my mother the trouble. My mother usually doesn't mention my father, except to say: 'We are all well' in the last paragraph, but Kitty just let it drop in passing that my father is working for the Quakers!'

'John! How extraordinary. How on earth can that have come about? And what is he doing for them?'

'Well, I did read in one of Sophie's papers that the Coastguard Service was getting no credit whatever for the invaluable work they were doing. The article said there were coastguard stations all along the west coast of Ireland, a hundred and seven of them, if I remember correctly. Apparently, they are ideally placed for getting supplies into places with no roads. The service boats and cutters can get into even the smallest creeks and the permanent offshore

280

gunboats can carry fifty tons of supplies when they are needed.'

'But where is the food coming from?'

'I had no idea. But then, when Kitty mentioned 'going up to Dublin to see the Quakers', in her letter, I realised that my father is responsible for all the movements of craft at sea, in his area. If the Quakers have supplies to distribute, then he's the man who would have to authorise it, as well as organise it.'

'Is he now?' said Hannah quietly.

John pressed his lips together and looked so distressed she wished she could put her arms around him.

'Oh, John dear, that has to be good news,' she said, reassuringly. 'Perhaps something happened to him when he was much younger that means he can't cope with his feelings. He reacts angrily and then can't apologise. Or something like that. I wish I could be more help, but I haven't known all that many men, except my father and brothers. And Patrick, of course.'

'Have you heard yet when your big day will be?' he asked, smiling broadly.

'No, I'm waiting for a letter,' she replied, wondering if he was trying to change the subject.

'So am I,' he said, steadily. 'I've written to my father and asked him what I've done, or not done, and will he please tell me.'

'My goodness,' she said. 'Well done! That must have been a very difficult letter to write.'

'Yes, it was. I wasted a lot of paper, I'm sorry to say,' he replied wryly.

'John dear, it certainly won't be wasted. One

way or another it will help us both. I'd so like to understand myself what went wrong.'

'Well, you know you will be the first to hear.'

★ ★ ★

Counting the days until Patrick arrived home was one thing when it was months or weeks, but once a departure date arrived it became a matter of guesswork. Sometimes the party travelled by way of Stranraer; sometimes it was Cairnryan. That depended on 'doing a deal' with the captain of the vessel and sharing out the cost between them.

Then there was the problem of getting from Dundrennan to the coast, and, once in Ireland, getting from the east coast to Derry, or even Rathmullan. It could sometimes take a week, and with bad weather even more.

Hannah always tried to be very cool and steady about Patrick's homecoming. Sam, in particular, could get so excited by the prospect that he didn't want to go to sleep at bedtime in case he missed his father's arrival in the evening or even during the night.

At the end of October, after a short note with the departure date had already arrived, there was the first of a series of heavy snowfalls. Getting to school was difficult enough for both Hannah and the children, but as they 'picked their steps' through the most tramped places on the way, Hannah wondered what might it be like on the long road home for the band of men who had left the valley in April.

She found it hard to concentrate on reading and spelling on her three mornings at school. She kept thinking of what she could cook or bake, to welcome Patrick home. On the last Friday in October she was still preoccupied with his arrival as she came back up the track after lunch at school. She looked down and realised she was walking between the wheel ruts of the turf cart and following the unmistakable marks of Neddy's hooves.

Startled, she looked up suddenly and there was Patrick standing in the doorway.

He slipped and nearly fell as he ran towards her, put his arms round her and kissed her.

'I'm early,' he said. 'I saw Neddy in Ramelton and when I stopped to stroke him, Dermot appeared. He insisted on bringing me home.'

'Where is he now?' gasped Hannah, as he clutched her even more firmly.

'Making a pot of tea and pretending he hasn't seen us,' he said grinning, as he slipped his arm round her waist and drew her back up the slope to the front door.

'Welcome home, Hannah,' said Dermot, as he poured the tea. 'Your good man got here before you, so I made us a bite to eat. I hope that was all right,' he said, passing her the milk.

'As right as rain, Dermot,' she said, beaming at him. 'Have you looked in the cake tin?'

'No, I can't say I have,' he replied, cautiously.

'Well, pass it over and I'll open it,' she said, looking from one to another. 'Here you are. By special request of Rose and Sam, prize-giving biscuits to welcome their da home. Thank you,

Dermot, for your first-class delivery service. Even better than your service for meal and flour,' she said, as they helped themselves from the tin.

26

It was less than a week after Patrick's arrival home when the first of the heavy snowfalls came in the night. Waking to a white world the next morning, Rose and Sam were highly excited. Over breakfast, they talked of nothing but building a snowman, like the ones in their storybooks.

Sadly, their excitement quickly faded when they ventured out and felt the icy chill of the air around them. But the real disaster for them was the drift of snow they found piled up against the barn door where Neddy had his stall. They tried in vain to open the door.

It was not until Patrick had come and cleared the drift with a shovel that they were able to go and begin Neddy's usual morning grooming. They were neither of them pleased by the fact that they had not satisfied themselves as to his well-being, or presentation before their father, and Dermot came to take over and they had to go to school.

Now, as the exceptional weather settled in, it was not just food that was in short supply — keeping warm began to make a heavy demand on the turf stacks piled up against the most sheltered wall of each of the cottages.

Daniel, who still often got gifts of turf in lieu of the pennies pupils once brought on Fridays, admitted that he'd been amazed by the drop in his very generous turf stack after only a week of snow. It was dropping so fast, it would soon be as low as it usually was at Christmas. And that was still six weeks away.

Dermot and Patrick were now sharing the task of delivering the supplies provided by Jonathan Hancock's mill workers and the donations he'd raised with the help of Johnny Donnelly's pictures. The two men, now friends, had no difficulty whatever sharing the tasks, but Hannah had been concerned that having to share meant only a small income for each of them. She was aware that either or both of them, might feel that this small amount was a problem.

Patrick, when approached, said flatly that given there was no 'relief work' anywhere within range, it was better than nothing. The relief work he had heard about was backbreaking work, carrying stone and building roads that, as he put it, 'went nowhere'. It was also badly paid.

Happily, when she mentioned the drop in income to Dermot he quickly reassured her. 'Sure, won't I be going to sea when yer Quaker friend gets the go-ahead and that'll leave it all for Patrick. Amn't I grateful to have had it all over the summer when he was away. And then, ye remember I got that bit more for a wee picture as well.'

In the end, Hannah decided that she was worrying unnecessarily. But, just to set her mind at rest, and to make sure Patrick was easy, she decided to bring out the box from under the bed, where she'd been keeping the savings she'd made from his postal orders over the months he'd been away.

When she saw him prod the coins in their little

bags and shake his head, she had to smile.

'I just don't know how you do it,' he said. 'It's as if money sticks to your fingers,' he added, hugging her in the privacy of their bedroom, before he put the box back in its place.

But having resolved one problem, the snow did make everything seem more difficult. As the days passed, the tracks became more broken. Sometimes, when there was a slight thaw, ice formed. It was then immediately covered by the latest fall of snow. That made walking treacherous and both Dermot and Patrick had falls while carrying heavy sacks.

Realising how close they'd both come to breaking a leg, or an arm, they decided that dividing up the rations was now essential. They could no longer carry heavy sacks holding supplies to last for several weeks, but would have to do more work in a merchant's storehouse, or a cold barn, or a damp outhouse, to make a more manageable load that would last for half, or a quarter of that time.

Despite the snow, school attendance was good and progress was being made with both reading and writing and with learning English. Daniel had gone as far as to start pronouncing English words as if he had memorised them but had no idea what they meant. He then asked for a sentence in Irish using the 'unknown' English word so as to give him 'some idea of the meaning'.

'Teaching Daniel English' became one of the many games that Hannah and John encouraged, both to keep up spirits and to encourage trial and error without any fear of disapproval.

27

A letter had arrived that Hannah put aside until after their evening meal. In the end, it was Hannah's curiosity that got the better of her. Every time she glanced at the envelope sitting on the dresser, she wondered what it could possibly be. Once or twice, while she was serving the meal, she turned it over to see the castle Sam had pointed out. Then she'd look again at the postmark. Unsurprisingly, it still said Armagh.

Sam was quite right about the castle. There was a neat little one on the back of the envelope. Of one thing she was quite sure: it was not Dublin Castle. From all she'd heard, communications from Dublin Castle were likely to be bad news. She was hoping beyond hope that this might be good news.

'So, do ye think we may have a wee chile on the way?' asked Patrick, when they were finally alone by their own fireside.

'I can't be sure,' she said, surprised by the suddenness of his question. 'But I haven't bled . . . '

'An ye were feelin sick,' added Patrick. 'I thought I'd seen that poor wee pale face before,' he went on. 'Sure, an' I was right then. First Rose, then Sam. That's how ye looked when ye were carryin' them, but before ye showed anythin' at all round your belly. But, if I mind right, ye weren't sick for long, it were just right at

288

the beginning you went pale an' after that, then ye were as right as rain.'

'Was I?'

'D'ye not mind?' he asked, scratching his head.

She certainly didn't remember, but then it was more than nine years ago when she'd had Sam.

'Shall I open the letter?' she asked suddenly, as if somehow that would resolve the questions in her mind.

'Sure, why not,' he said. 'It'll hardly take a bite out of us.'

She laughed, as she opened the envelope carefully, not wanting to tear the paper where the little castle stood. She drew out the large, folded sheets, found there were four of them covered with a small but very legible copperplate and around them, a small sheet, half the size of the others with a short note in the same handwriting.

She unfolded the little note first.

Castledillon,
Loughgall Road
Co. Armagh
19 December 1846
Dear Hannah McGinley,

Your friend, or perhaps I should say, Friend, Jonathan Hancock, has asked me to copy this letter for you as soon as I received it from him. I do hope the bad weather, which we too have had in Armagh, has not delayed it too much. He told me of the work you are doing in Donegal and how important this letter would be for improving the food supply.

I hope this finds you and your family well.

Yours sincerely,

Sarah Hamilton (Secretary to Sir George Molyneux)

'My goodness, Patrick, I think this *is* good news,' she said, glancing at the opening lines of the main letter. 'Will I read it out to you, or will I read it and give you the gist of it?' she asked, not sure what to make of the look on his face.

'I think maybe, judgin' by the length of it, ye might need a mug of tea t' help ye along. Why don't you tell me who it's from and then I'll make the tea while you're readin' it.'

'Thanks, Patrick. Tea's a good idea. I seem to be very thirsty today.'

She looked at the date of the copied letter. *Dunfanaghy. 13th of the Twelfth month.* She'd forgotten that Quakers referred to the months by number and not by name.

So, it was almost two weeks ago when the two Quaker 'enquirers' Joseph Crosfield and William Forster had visited Dunfanaghy and made their report to the London Relief Committee. The Committee had sent a copy of the letter to Jonathan Hancock in Yorkshire. He had sent it to Sarah, so she could see it herself and then send a copy to Hannah. Given the state of the weather, the letter had done rather well.

The Quakers had written:

Owing to the depth of the snow, and a constant succession of violent snow-storms, we experienced much detention, and did not reach

Dunfanaghy until long after dark.

A portion of the district through which we passed this day, as well as the adjoining one, is, with one exception, the poorest and most destitute in Donegal. Nothing indeed can describe too strongly the dreadful condition of the people. Many families were living on a single meal of cabbage, and some even, as we were assured, upon a little seaweed.

Hannah paused. She knew that other areas were much worse off than they were themselves, but she had not known it was as bad as this. She started reading more quickly.

One of the local merchants had come to see the enquirers at their lodgings and told them what things were like for the worst off. The small farmers and cottiers had parted with their possessions to buy food and had nothing more to sell. Many families were subsisting on two and a half pounds of oatmeal a day made into a thin water gruel, about six ounces of meal for each.

She paused, looked up to see Patrick pouring the tea and said, 'You must hear the next bit.'

'Is it good news?' he enquired anxiously.

'It will be,' she said reassuringly. 'Thanks for the tea, love. Will you be seeing Dermot in the morning?'

'I wou'd expect so. Around the usual time.'

'Then listen to this,' she said. 'This is what he's been waiting for. It's no one's fault about the delay. Shemmie the fish man told me months ago, and I told Jonathan when he first came here, but they hadn't got the Central Relief Committee then, nor the London one either,' she

291

explained, as she found her place again in the letter.

Dunfanaghy is a little fishing town, situated on a bay remarkably adapted for a fishing population; the sea is teeming with fish of the finest description, waiting we might say, to be caught. Many of the inhabitants gain a portion of their living by this means: but so rude is their tackle, and so fragile and liable to be upset are their primitive boats or coracles, made of wickerwork over which sail cloth is stretched, that they can only venture to sea in fine weather. Thus, with food almost in sight, the people starve, because they have no one to teach them to build boats more adapted to this rocky coast, than those in use by their ancestors many centuries ago.

'So what do you think Dermot will say to that?' she said, setting the letter down carefully beside her and taking a long drink from her mug of tea.

'Ach, he'll be delighted,' he said, nodding vigorously. 'An sure, isn't one of the boats near ready? That'll do to start with till he teaches a few young lads ready for the next one. They were talking about three boats, weren't they?'

'Yes, that was the plan, but they had to get more money to pay for the other two.'

'An, d'ye think they've got it?'

'I don't know, Patrick, not till I read the rest of the report. But maybe that's as much as we can do tonight. I hope Dermot is early tomorrow. I'd love to see his face when I tell him, but if he's late, you'll have to do it for me. It's school in the morning,' she reminded him.

'Aye, an' you need your rest,' he said firmly. 'Though mind you, you're lookin' a queer lot different to what ye did this afternoon. You've got yer colour back again as well.'

* * *

Hannah slept well that night, waking only once when the wind whistled loudly in the chimney. But they were used to that. Patrick didn't stir, so she just moved even closer to him and fell asleep again immediately.

She woke early, the light bright beyond the thin curtains after a fresh fall of snow. She slipped out of bed, pulled a rug from the foot of the bed over her shoulders and made up the fire. She took up the letter where she had left off.

Most of it she knew, though the term 'conacre' was new to her. But she soon picked up that it meant the system of 'letting out' a piece of land to a tenant who had to manure it before growing his crop of potatoes. By this means, the enquirers wrote, a tenant farmer could supposedly support a family of from five to eight persons for at least six months on half a rood of land. The landlord benefitted by the manuring and working of the land.

'Half a rood?' she whispered to herself. She couldn't visualise it, but she knew it was very small.

But the next part of the letter she could understand and imagine only too clearly. She read it through quickly, then hearing no sound of movement, from either Patrick, or the children, she read it through again.

We were told that there were at least thirty families in this little town who had nothing whatever to subsist upon. And knew not where to look for a meal for the morrow. A quantity of meal was ordered to be distributed amongst them, and a sum of money left for their support, and also for a little turf, without which in this severe weather many would be frozen to death. The cost of turf is a very serious item on these poor creatures: and it would require sixpence per week, with the most economical management, to keep up the smallest peat fire imaginable. No public works were open in this district, although in this small parish there were, in the opinion of the rate payers, not less than 2,300 persons who were 'suffering from want of relief.'

Hannah put the letter down and stirred the fire, which had been recovering from being smoored for the night. Small flames rose where she had pushed in fragments of twig, gathered in summer and left to dry in the barn. Shortly the fire would be hot enough to hang the pot over it and measure out the oatmeal for porridge.

She shivered and held out her hands to the blaze. There must be more they could do up here in Ardtur. Dermot would soon be getting his call to go and collect the boat and start fishing, but more help was needed. No one here in the valley was as badly off as those poor souls referred to in the letter. She would have to give it more thought and ask Bridget and Daniel and John if they could do more. And Patrick would certainly help if he could.

28

The last three days of school in that December of 1846 were all bitterly cold, the tracks and roofs still thick with snow. Only for a short time at mid-day did large, shining drops pockmark the drifts of snow lying against the cottage walls beneath the overhanging thatch. The icicles went on growing every day while the turf stacks diminished rapidly.

At the end of school on Monday the twenty-first, Hannah, Bridget, John and Daniel pulled their chairs up to the fire in the now empty schoolroom. The tables and benches were neatly stacked against the walls to leave the space available for Daniel's regular evening visitors.

It had been a long term, made harder by the very cold weather and by the regular appearance of bad news, either coming from one of the children with illness in their family, or the Donegal or Derry newspapers.

Hannah was glad that at least she had something good to report.

Her three colleagues listened hard as she read the key passages in the Quakers' letter. They agreed the news about fishing boats would be good for the whole community, but what really delighted them was that Dermot would soon be going to sea. He had worked so hard distributing food up and down the valley and now not only would he be going back to sea, but he would have some local young men whom he would be teaching to fish. More food and a few more families with some real income.

Hannah did say lightly that she'd welcome a miracle for those 2,300 people in need of relief, but they all agreed that even miracles might take longer than the two school days still available, or even the four days leading to Christmas itself, on the coming Friday.

'The question then becomes,' said Daniel, 'short of a miracle, is there anything at all we can do to honour the so-called festive season?'

School would be closed for just over two weeks and they did all admit they were looking forward to the break.

'Yes, I think we all need a break,' said Daniel, 'and will be the better for it, but I'm not sure if that same break will do our pupils much good. What does everyone else think?'

'I think you're right there, Daniel,' said Bridget vigorously. 'What I'm wonderin' is how some of these families will manage for over two weeks with no pieces, and no bowls of meal for supper when their chile tells us it's had no breakfast.'

'Well,' said Hannah thoughtfully, 'we've had to accept we can't do anything straight away for those further afield who we know are in need, but we could certainly *do something* to allow our school families to still have what normally we'd provide for them.'

'I've no doubt, Hannah, you've done a calculation,' said Daniel. 'But can we really afford to give money, however little, if we have to multiply by fifteen?' he asked uneasily.

'Well, fortunately it only comes to eleven,' said Hannah, much to Daniel's amusement. 'We have three families with two children who are pupils, so they would only need three family gifts, not six. And Rose and Sam don't need any.'

'Oh, but wouldn't they feel left out?' Bridget objected.

'Yes, you're right, Bridget,' Hannah, said nodding, 'but that might be taken care of by my other idea. I was going to suggest that every child had a small gift they could share with their families. Again, it may not be possible, but I wondered if between us, Bridget, you and I could bake enough 'prize-day' biscuits tomorrow and Wednesday to make up a packet for each child. We *could* afford the oatmeal and it means they'd have something to share around at home. Perhaps, we might even suggest they could be saved up for Christmas Day itself. I wondered too if we might consider some pots of jam. If you thought that was a good idea I'd ask Dermot tonight to see if he can do a deal at Ramseys tomorrow.'

'I think that's a lovely idea,' said John. 'But it does leave you and Bridget doing all the work. What can Daniel and I do to help?'

'Don't worry we'll think of something for you to do,' said Bridget. 'Biscuits need to be counted out and wrapped and packed. And we could do with some kind of entertainment for the last afternoon while we're busy getting it all ready. You an' Daniel will hafta see to that, aye, an' maybe do some of our other jobs as well while

Hannah and I are bakin' and packin'.'

'Well, that sounds like a good plan to me,' said Daniel agreeably. 'I just happen to have in mind a new Christmas story from Galway, thanks to my colleague here. I was also going to propose we might get the children to write some Christmas rhymes, or short poems tomorrow. If they were written tomorrow, we could select the best to be read at the entertainment on Wednesday afternoon, couldn't we?' he asked, turning from one colleague to another, as he always did when speaking to them.

'What a splendid idea,' said Hannah. 'Perhaps if we get enough we could make some little folders, or paper books. We might even manage an illustration for the cover,' she added tentatively.

'And then perhaps in the New Year we could send them to the people who've sent us gifts, or messages of support when we sent out the pictures of the valley after holiday school,' added John. 'Can we afford all that paper and postage as well, Hannah? I remember it was rather a lot when Dermot and I took all the stuff to the post office back in the summer,' he reminded her cautiously.

'Aye, but sure, didn't we have a couple of packets of dollars waitin' for us when we came back in September?' demanded Bridget.

'Yes, you're quite right, Bridget. The postage *was* expensive but we'd still have enough money, even if those dollars hadn't come,' Hannah assured them.

She still found it difficult to appear cautious

298

when the sum in the school account was so high. But she'd promised, long ago it now seemed, not to give away the secret of last summer's drunken harvesters. Thanks to them, there was still a considerable sum upon which she could draw. Large as it was to her, she knew perfectly well it could do little, or nothing, for those 2,300 people 'in want of relief'. It was, however, more than enough to cover the plans they had just agreed, many times over.

★ ★ ★

The last two days did indeed fly by. Hannah and Bridget baked together in Bridget's kitchen while Daniel and John planned the entertainment as well as encouraging the production of rhymes or poems. Some children, when given the option of words, or pictures, chose to paint. So illustrations appeared and folders were made with New Year messages in very best handwriting. They would be completed on Wednesday with a choice of the best poems or rhymes.

On Tuesday evening, Dermot arrived back, very pleased that he'd done 'a good deal' for the jam with the chief shopkeeper in Dunfanaghy. He'd made sure to explain the pots of jam were gifts for the families of the schoolchildren up in Casheltown, and he was duly delighted when the merchant added two large bags of sweets as his own offering.

No pupil left school on Wednesday afternoon without a packet of biscuits, a handful of sweets, a pot of jam and an envelope, containing either money, or a collection of Christmas rhymes. There would certainly be a small treat to share on Christmas Day in every family.

As for Hannah and John there was no hurry on despatching the new batch of offerings from the valley. They would be safe in the drawer of the dresser where Hannah kept paintings at the request of Jonathan Hancock.

★ ★ ★

With the weather still so bad, John had decided not to attempt the journey to Galway.

Hannah did wonder if the weather was the real reason for his staying in Donegal for Christmas. It was months now since he had written to his father asking what it was he had done or not done, that he didn't write and didn't want to see him. He'd still had no reply to his letter.

His mother's letters were loving, but not very informative and his sisters, when they did think of writing, merely filled him in on their own preoccupations. So, he planned to spend most of his holiday copying up his scribbled records of Daniel's stories, so that he could study them more closely.

He also planned to visit the priest who had welcomed him to the valley and read the newspapers to Sophie. However bad the news was, she still seemed to thrive on knowing exactly what was going on in any part of Ireland. The *Illustrated London News* she considered a special bonus.

On their first 'day off' Hannah was touched

when John arrived and asked her if he could take Sam and Rose to visit their Aunt Mary. He knew perfectly well it would help her to have an empty kitchen while she baked and prepared for Christmas Day when both John and Sophie would be coming to eat with them.

The meal itself would be little different from usual, but there would be a pudding and a jelly, a particular passion of Rose, for whom it would be a surprise. She was also hoping to bake both bread and cake in case there were any visitors.

★ ★ ★

After all the hard work of that week, both at school and at home, there was a true sense of celebration over their modest meal. Afterwards, as darkness fell mid-afternoon, John entertained them by telling them Daniel's new Christmas story, which he'd been practising for weeks now.

That too was a great success, even if Hannah did confess to Patrick that she was so grateful that Christmas was all over. She had felt strangely apprehensive both preparing the gifts needed at school and then trying to make a small celebration at home on Christmas Day itself.

Patrick, as always, tried to comfort her. He reminded her how successful all her plans had been. In the end she decided she was being silly. It was as if she could not rest while she knew the plight of those 2,300 people in Dunfanaghy that the Quaker enquirers had recorded as 'knowing not where they would find a meal for the morrow'.

As far as Hannah knew, Jonathan Hancock had hoped to appear either with, or just after, the two enquirers, but she'd been disappointed. There was no sign of him and not even a note. Probably, she thought, the weather had complicated his plans which, of course, would have included visiting Armagh as well. Then, to her surprise, what she did have just after Christmas was a letter from Sarah Hamilton.

Hannah had indeed written promptly and thanked her for making that splendid copy of the letter from the enquirers and posting it to her so promptly. But she had not expected such a warm and immediate reply.

Drumilly Hill,
Loughgall, Co. Armagh
26 December 1846
Dear Hannah,
   I was so pleased to hear from you and to know that you have been able to give small gifts to the children at your school. My friend Mary-Anne and myself have been sorting through our stock to find items of clothing to give to a number of poor people in the city. In this bitter weather, they were so grateful. How I wish we could do more.
   I was most interested to hear that your friend, Catriona, had got a sewing group together just as we now have. Do you also have knitters? We have found some who do baby clothes, but Jonathan tells me that heavy knitting wool would be available from one of the mills if you had some women

who could make fishermen's sweaters or those lovely Aran sweaters I've read about.

I'm hoping Jonathan and I might see each other after Christmas. If we manage it, I shall pass on to him your news from school and ask him if he did manage to get to Donegal as he had planned. Do please keep in touch. I think perhaps you and I need to encourage each other. There is so much help needed and this awful weather makes everything worse.

Yours sincerely,
Sarah

Hannah smiled as she reread the short letter again, thinking back to that day when Jonathan 'thought he was being silly' and managed to confess that he didn't know what to do about his love for Sarah. How lovely it would be if they could marry and work together. She could imagine that given Jonathan's business contacts and Sarah's ability to organise, they could do great things and be happy themselves in the process.

★　★　★

The days often seemed long in that fortnight of holiday despite the very short hours of daylight. Patrick went off early to make use of the light and Sam and Rose, who had long since lost any enthusiasm for snow, liked nothing better than to play games at the kitchen table.

Hannah did encourage them to draw and

paint, but she was so grateful when John arrived and proposed an outing, even if it was just to collect the young Friels and walk down with them to see if there was ice on the lake.

Sometimes, he took them to see Sophie and then he would read to them all. At least when she knew John was reading, Hannah could relax. He would avoid all the bad news that Sophie had come to expect and so Hannah would not have to follow the visit with explanations and reassurances for the anxieties that Rose and Sam brought back.

For her own anxieties, many of which she could hardly distinguish for herself, never mind share with either Patrick, or a friend, she had no recipe, except the comfort of the night when warmth and love dissolved the burdens of the day and made the future seem less challenging than she felt sure it was going to be.

29

Pausing on the doorstep, a sharp breeze tugged at her warmest shawl as she closed the cottage door behind them. Hannah gazed across the unmarked white spaces that followed a fresh fall of snow in the night and tried to visualise a blue sky, with gleams of sunlight and opening buds on the hawthorns. She was unsuccessful.

However hard she'd already tried, she'd now decided there was little comfort to be had in this second full week of January, in general, and on this, their first day back at school, in particular!

She was grateful when John appeared promptly from next door, making a fresh track from Sophie's house to their own. Ahead of them now, the only other marking on the gleaming snow was the track left by Neddy and his turf cart when Patrick set off earlier for Dunfanaghy to collect cash from Catriona, meal and flour from the most reliable merchant in the town, and post, if there was any, from the office in the main street.

'Off we go then,' said Hannah, trying to sound more cheerful than she felt, as Rose and Sam moved ahead together, knowing she and John would want to talk about school and what they'd already planned together for the morning ahead.

It was perfectly clear that both Rose and Sam were glad to get back to school. They'd been missing their friends from the further end of the valley, too far to walk at the moment in such deep snow, and at the same time they had exhausted all their books, and puzzles, and board games. To Hannah's surprise, Sam confessed that what he missed most of all were Daniel's stories, while Rose couldn't wait to get back to the small school library, having long since exhausted the resources of her own.

'How is Sophie today?' Hannah asked, as Sam and Rose moved off quickly down the slope and John fell into step beside her.

'A bit better,' he said cautiously. 'She did sleep last night but she couldn't manage her bowl of porridge this morning. She says it's not the fever that's going round, this is some sort of tummy upset she's always had bother with.'

'Perhaps that's good news, John,' she replied quickly, thinking first of the child she was now quite sure she was carrying, and of the threat to their pupils if either she, or John, or Patrick, were to become ill. 'We might have to close the school if you or I picked up anything.'

'That's a sober thought,' he said. 'And there is a lot of illness going around. I read last night that there are now over 100,000 in the workhouses and they're just full of sickness. They're having to build temporary shelters in the grounds for those with fever. Some workhouses, apparently, have double the number they were designed for and are having to turn people away.'

'To die by the roadside, I suppose,' said Hannah sadly.

'That's seems to be the end of it,' John replied. 'Just about every English visitor who comes over to 'see for themselves' comments on that.'

They fell silent as they tramped carefully across the broken ridges of ice and crushed snow where the downhill track met the wider one that connected Ardtur with all the neighbouring town-lands. A fall here would not only leave clothes wet for the rest of the day, it would put one's bones at risk.

Daniel was waiting for them and greeted them warmly.

'Well then, did you divide up the work between you on the way?' he asked cheerfully. 'Which of you is going to do the session on New Year Resolutions? I haven't made any. That's my best effort towards not breaking them!' he said.

Hannah smiled and gave thanks for Daniel's good spirits. She had seen him at times look solemn and he was often deeply serious, but she couldn't remember when she'd last seen him in what she would call low spirits. He, who would appear to have good reason for feeling low, or limited, by his disability, seldom appeared to suffer from such an affliction.

She wished she could say the same of herself. But she could not. Despite all the comforts of her life, of which she regularly reminded herself, admonishing herself for not being grateful for all she was blessed with, she found that, in winter in particularly, she felt herself enveloped in a thick, grey cloud. When that happened, she felt she would never have an interesting thought, or a good idea ever again.

At its worst, her grey cloud manifested itself as anxiety; at its best, it was simply a nagging sense that 'something would happen' to take away all the things she treasured, beginning with Patrick and the children and the child she was carrying.

The negative feelings had grown worse over the Christmas holiday and despite all her efforts she could find no hope or possibility in the thought of a New Year. But the actual New Year itself had passed without incident. Today was the fourth of January, there was work to do and colleagues with whom to share whatever news might arise from the children, or from Bridget, their school mother as Daniel now called her.

The day began with Daniel's roll call. It was not the swift and automatic ticking of a printed document that Hannah remembered from her own school days. Daniel had his own technique. He called each individual name. When he received a reply, he then asked a question. Having listened to the answer and decided on the state of well-being of his respondent, he either announced 'present' in a firm voice, or asked a further question.

It was by way of Daniel's roll call many months ago that they'd first discovered children who'd had no breakfast, those who had illness in the family, or those who had a father, or brother, away looking for work. Hannah had listened and watched, totally absorbed, as Daniel put together the clues he had, with only a voice to guide him.

Today the news was good. All fifteen pupils were present. All had had breakfast. There was no illness at home to report. It was as good a start to a New Year as one could wish for.

★ ★ ★

Two weeks later, at the same roll call, Hannah had to admit to the first piece of good news in a long time. Johnny Donnelly reported that his father had had a message the previous evening and had left early that morning on his way to Derry. He was going to Port William in Scotland, to collect a fishing boat destined for Dunfanaghy. Two young Scots fishermen were 'being lent' to him until he had trained up some Donegal lads, Johnny told the class. By the summer, there would be fish to sell to those who had some money, and for those who had none, fish to give away, courtesy of the Quakers.

'And did you not think of going with your father, Johnny?' asked Daniel, who had listened carefully to every word.

'No, sir. My da asked me before the holidays if I'd like to come with him and learn to be a fisherman, but I said no. I don't think I'd be very good at fishin'. I hate killing things and I'm afeerd of storms. An' I'd miss paintin' the wee pictures forby.'

'I think you've done right, Johnny. What is right for one person isn't necessarily right for another. *Don't forget that, children.* You must try to think about *you*. Not in any selfish way, but because you are you and different from anyone else. If you don't make up your mind about you, *someone else* may make up your mind for you. That's not a good idea,' he added firmly.

'Johnny, I'm glad we'll not be losing you and I

hope you'll go on helping the younger ones with their pictures. You did a great job at Christmas with the illustrations on the covers of the wee books we made. *Present*,' he announced, as he made a tick on a sheet of paper for Hannah to copy to the official register later.

★ ★ ★

Despite the good work going on in school and the progress being made by their pupils, January and February continued to be physically taxing, bitterly cold and full of bad news.

John admitted to Hannah and Patrick one evening after supper when the children had gone to bed early, that what he'd been reading aloud to Sophie this last week or more was so dispiriting he needed to share it with someone. He said, awkwardly, that he still felt he should be able to cope with it himself.

To Hannah's surprise, before she had collected her thoughts, she heard Patrick speak.

'Ah, sure, John, there's nothing wrong with feelin' distress with the badness of things that happen,' he said gently. 'Sure, what sort of people would we be at all, if we weren't upset sometimes. Tell us now, like a good man, what you've been readin'. I'm not sure that a trouble shared is a trouble halved, as I've heard people say, but I for sure tell Hannah my worries and I think, I hope,' he said, pausing to look at her, 'she tells me hers.'

Hannah nodded vigorously and was pleased when John smiled broadly.

'Yes, John, Patrick is quite right,' she said. 'When times are hard, or one is feeling bad, you have to take any opportunity that comes to share. Now, do tell us what you've been reading about.'

'Well you both know there's been a wave of emigration, even this early in the year. I don't know where Sophie's copy of the *Drogheda Argus* came from, but I read it from cover to cover and I learnt a great deal about the place,' he began. 'I didn't realise Drogheda is such a very busy port. Apparently, some 70,000 emigrants left in February. That's bad news enough, whether they were heading for Liverpool, or hoping to go on to America, but what really got me was a report on women and children. It said they were 'competing with cattle for pieces of raw turnip lying on Steam Packet Quay'.'

'Aye, well,' said Patrick, 'That's no worse than those poor souls not so far away who are still livin' on seaweed. I hear the Quakers have sent a batch of big pots for making soup to a whole lot of places in Donegal. Creeslough has one, I hear tell, but the people organisin' the soup haven't got it goin' yet. It'll be a lot better than seaweed, even if it's only the one bowl a day.'

★　★　★

Hannah had been following reports on all the local efforts to raise money for those who were in such need. Sometimes there were indeed things reported that did raise spirits and helped one to

311

feel that there were many good people out there trying to do what they could.

She hadn't had the chance to visit Catriona herself since the snow came, but when Patrick called with her to collect cash, she'd told him about finding knitters who could work on fishermen's shirts. What she was hoping was that when they'd got used to knitting the shirts, they could try their hand on some of the fashionable craft items that would sell very well in England or America.

It was characteristic of Catriona that she would get on with something vigorously, while all the time looking out for something better. One of these days she'd have more good news from her, but in the meantime, Patrick did regularly hear from families in the valley who told him when they'd had a few dollars in the post and a note that had mentioned the 'wee pictures from school' that had gone out before Christmas.

But all these local activities were quite overtaken in the last week of February, in a way Hannah could never have imagined. Weeks later, she still had difficulty in believing what had come to carry them through the seemingly endless snow-filled winter, whose only variation so far had been ferocious gales and thunder and lightning.

'There's another letter for you and John with the same American stamps the boys came in and steamed off in my kitchen,' said Bridget in school one day, as she handed them their lunchtime pieces on small plates. 'Did you see it?'

'When did it come?' asked John, surprised.

'Oh, it was a couple of days ago, but it was left in the house the other side of the big drift. I don't know whether it was a postman brought it, or a neighbour. I do know our friend Dermot Donnelly always brings post if he's comin' home for a night or two. That and a bag of fish,' she said, laughing.

They never had to ask when Dermot was home between sailings because they had fish in their pieces next day.

'I left it in the usual place,' Bridget went on, 'but now I think of it, I forgot to tell Daniel. Maybe you've been so busy neither of you have even noticed it.'

'I certainly haven't seen it,' said Hannah, 'but then I only expect bills for supplies, not thank you letters or cards.'

'Well, I'll bring it out to yers when I go across for the children's plates. Knowing those ones, over there,' she said, nodding towards the closed door of Daniel's cottage, 'they'll have finished by now, an' not so much as even a crumb let fall on the floor!'

A little later she appeared, set down the piled-up plates ready to wash and took the letter from her pocket. She handed it to Hannah, who gazed at the colourful stamps as if they would tell her something.

But they didn't. It was indeed a similar envelope to the one they'd had last year, but this time the postmark had been obliterated. It looked as if it had been rained on or caught in spray.

313

She opened it carefully, unfolded a single large sheet and set to one side a printed card that had been enclosed with it. She recognised the writing and the secretary's name, James Doherty, and the engraving of the ship with the three masts. There were three sails on each tall mast.

As before, it was addressed to them both.

Dear Hannah McGinley and John McCreedy,
    Owing to bad weather, we did not receive your very welcome Christmas message until some weeks ago. Everyone here was pleased to have both another illustration and the rhymes and poems in the booklet you sent. The chairman, Mr Donald McKay, asked me to put this recent offering on display with the picture you sent some months ago.
    Knowing of the problems you are having in Ireland with the loss of the potato crop, he suggested that as a company we should send you a gift for the benefit of any people you know who may be affected.
    I have to tell you that he then discovered that each of the major departments in this large enterprise had already started an Ireland Fund and been collecting weekly subscriptions for some months. We have included a note of the amounts collected in dollars in each department and are now writing to ask you for details of a bank that you use. Should you think the sum rather large for your school to deal with, perhaps you could provide us with the name of a suitable person, or organisation, who would

ensure the money is well spent on your behalf.

Our contact with your pupils has given us great pleasure and we would wish to continue to support you while need arises.

I am,
On behalf of all at East Boston Shipyard,
Yours faithfully,
James Doherty

Hannah passed the letter over to John, silent tears running down her cheeks. He, having picked up the accompanying card was not surprised by her tears, but Bridget who had turned to look at them as Hannah read the letter, immediately came and put her arm round her.

'Ah, Hannah dear, what's the matter? Don't cry, love. It can't be that bad. Sure, whatever it is we'll get over it.'

Hannah managed a smile as she searched for her handkerchief.

'It's not bad news, Bridget dear,' she said, sniffing and then blowing her nose. 'It's the miracle we needed before Christmas. I don't know how much it is, but it looks enormous ... enough to feed all those poor people, all 2,300 of them.'

'Somewhere over £20,000 at a quick calculation,' said John, putting down the letter and looking again at the card. 'But it might be even more.'

Hannah looked at him and saw an expression on his face she could not interpret. He looked desolate, as if the generosity of these unknown people, many of them Irish, was more than he could bear.

She held out her arms to both John and Bridget, hugged them both and then, still sniffing somewhat, said: 'And how do you two propose we tell Daniel?'

30

As far as Hannah and her colleagues were concerned, there was no problem at all about disposing of the money. Hannah suggested they ask for a small amount for the School Fund so that they could continue to do what they had been doing for the last year or more, providing lunches, breakfasts when needed and supplying meal and flour via Patrick to any families in the valley that were in need.

As for the bulk of that large sum, which John kept recalculating in case he had made a mistake, that must go to the Quakers who had provided the fishing boats and the soup cauldrons and had made money available for the most destitute families when they came in December. With this money now available to them, they could both sustain the work they had already begun in Donegal, launch two more fishing boats and extend their plans for providing seed to small tenants, so that there would be other sources of food apart from the potato.

It was only a matter of writing to Jonathan Hancock, telling him the good news and asking him which bank would be most convenient for them to supply their work in the area.

Meantime, Hannah wrote back to James Doherty in East Boston, telling him how amazed and delighted she and her colleagues were at their generosity. She asked him if he could send some pictures of the ships they made, so that all the children would know what a 'clipper' was, what it could do, and where it travelled.

She told him that she was about to contact a Quaker man who had already done a great deal to help them and who would now be delighted to have the resources to meet the urgent needs of people in other parts of Donegal as well as their immediate location.

When she'd finished writing, she reread her letter and wondered if it was too long. It seemed to her these generous people were offering more than their hard-earned money. She wondered if many of them still missed their native land and felt some longing to be 'in touch'.

She thought of workers standing in the space outside the chairman's suite, looking at a picture by a young Irish boy, of a lake in a valley, perhaps like one they had once known, or had heard spoken about by an older generation. And she wondered if there were other people on the staff with a name, like James Doherty himself, that would be entirely familiar to anyone from this part of the world.

She decided to wait a day or two before sending her letter to the post with Patrick. Given the bad weather and the slowness with which the American letter had come, a speedy reply would hardly be expected. What she needed was a chance to have a quiet talk to John in the lunch hour on her next school morning and to see what came to her as she did her chores and sewed napkins.

The problem was, she thought, not with saying

thank you properly for such an incredibly generous gift, but of finding a way to offer in return something that would reconnect these people with what they were missing, the world they had once known themselves, directly or indirectly, through story and memory. That was what she wanted to do!

Meantime, she must write to Jonathan Hancock and tell him the wonderful news. She was surprised that she hadn't heard from him since the New Year when he'd apologised for not being able to visit Ardtur. He had indeed been in Dunfanaghy with his colleagues, as she expected, but the weather was so bad they'd agreed they must move on if they hoped to be back with their families for Christmas. He had, of course, ensured that she'd had a copy of that important letter that authorised the fishing boats and their upkeep, as soon as money could be made available.

Try as she would, having done the morning chores, she could not settle herself to sew. She washed and changed into her everyday clothes, made up the fire and moved across to open the cottage door.

She'd grown so used to the door having to be kept shut that she automatically prepared herself for an icy blast. But there was none. The wind had dropped. It was still cold and damp, but for the first time in months she saw the snow was melting. Sodden patches of grass were emerging under the hedgerows and there were now large puddles beyond the doorstep. They had not been there when Rose and Sam went off to school.

Grey clouds were moving at speed across the sky and for one single moment she saw a gleam of sunlight glint and fade on the wet thatch of the Friels' cottage down at the foot of the slope.

She shivered, but still did not move. Standing there, she thought of all the times she had stood resting in the sunshine, turning her aching shoulders towards the comfort of its warmth after she'd carried in the heavy buckets of water, or creels of turf. She felt as if she had almost forgotten what spring, or summer, could be like, her mind so filled with the snow and blizzards, the storms and wind of the last long hard months.

Spring would come again, but not yet. When it did, she and Patrick would already be waiting for her father's letter. He would go back to Dundrennan and she would stay here. By the time he returned there would be a brother, or a sister, for Rose and Sam. All being well.

It was ten years now since she had carried Sam, though there had been two miscarriages during that intervening time. But it seemed her body had not forgotten its previous experiences.

She felt perfectly easy with the changes and discomforts she now observed. She'd even managed to smile when she had to let out the waist of her better 'school' skirt, and she was touched by Patrick's gentle enquiries whenever they made love. July, or early August, as far as she could calculate. But she bore in mind Bridget Delaney's good advice: 'Just listen, an' the wee one will give you due warnin' if it's in a hurry.'

She was grateful for Bridget, for her presence, her support and her encouragement. Daniel was right. She was their school mother. With a large family of her own, now scattered across England and far beyond, she mothered both staff and children alike with her a lively and robust manner. Sharp she might be, but no one could miss her kindness.

She shivered again and knew she should go back indoors, but just then there was a brightening in the clouds. She thought for a moment there was about to be another gleam of light. She stayed where she was watching the sky, hoping it might come.

But it wasn't sunlight that suddenly caught her eye. At the very bottom of the track, a tall, dark-clad figure, wearing a hat, had just come into view. He was striding purposefully past the Friels' cottage and looking up the slope towards her. A few minutes later, he waved.

She'd only ever known one person to wear a proper hat in this valley, so she waved back, left the door open for him and went back inside to make up the fire.

'Jonathan Hancock, what a surprise,' she said to herself, as she put the kettle down. 'I wonder what brings you here, just when I have news for you.'

★ ★ ★

'Good morning, Jonathan Hancock,' she said formally, offering him her hand and smiling broadly.

321

'Hannah, my dear. It seems you have got news for me,' he said, holding her hand between both of his and looking her up and down.

'I have rather a lot of news for you, Jonathan, one way and another', she began, 'but I think you'd better sit down and enjoy your tea first. How did you manage to get rid of the snow for us?' she asked, laughing, as he parked his hat on the dresser and came to the table where the cake tin sat waiting.

'You're in luck,' she said, struggling with the tight-fitting lid. 'We had a birthday in school yesterday, so Bridget made prize-giving biscuits and John and I both got some to take home,' she explained, as the lid gave way and she held the open tin out for him.

'They do smell good,' he said, as she poured his tea. 'Ladies' news first,' he said, some minutes later, as he took a long drink of his tea, clearly thirsty after his vigorous walk.

Hannah smiled to herself. Now that the moment had come to tell him about the money, she really didn't know how to put it. Where did she start? Had she actually told him sometime last autumn about the holiday school mailing to East Boston last July? She certainly hadn't told him about the subsequent Christmas mailing.

'When is it due?' he asked promptly.

Hannah had to laugh. Here she was with this news of an enormous donation and he was waiting, beaming, for news of her expected child.

'Probably July, or early August. All being well.'

'That is wonderful news, Hannah,' he said, once again breaking into smiles. 'Sarah will be so delighted when I tell her, unless, of course, you've told her yourself. She said in one of her letters that she'd heard from you. She was really pleased about that.'

'Yes, I wrote to thank her for copying out that four-page letter from the enquirers. That was such good news for Dermot. You'll be glad to hear he is now back at sea and has three Donegal lads in training. The two 'borrowed' ones who came over with him in January were able to go back to Scotland last week and we get fish for supper every time he has a day off.'

'What splendid news!' he said enthusiastically.

She waited for him to go on, as he seemed about to say something. But he didn't.

She finally made up her mind to tell him about the American letter right away. She went to the dresser and took the little printed card bearing the note of the collection in East Boston from her school drawer. She set it down in front of him.

'We've had a rather large donation from some people to whom we sent 'wee pictures' last summer and New Year wishes this Christmas,' she began steadily. 'I need to ask your advice about where to send it,' she said, not able to read the expression on his face, as he turned the printed card over and over in his long fingers.

'Have you worked out how much this is in sterling,' he asked, staring at the printed card.

'John thought it was about £20,000,' she said, amazed that he seemed so unperturbed by the largeness of the sum.

'Probably rather more,' he said, smiling at last.

'Exchange rates have been somewhat volatile. We must make sure we get the best rate and the best bank. What wonderful news,' he said, a flatness in his tone she could not account for.

It was then it came to her. His good spirits when he arrived, the speed at which he was walking, the effort he had made to be enthusiastic over the money. Clearly, he had something he needed to tell her.

'Yes, it is,' she said. 'But I'm still waiting patiently to hear *your own good news*, Jonathan.'

He looked at her in amazement, smiled sheepishly, and then said: 'How could you possibly know I've had good news? I only found out a few days ago. I'm getting married in June.'

★ ★ ★

There was no doubt about it, Jonathan's news meant a great deal more to him than the huge donation from East Boston, though he later gave much energy to discussing what could be done to maximise it and get it in place as quickly as possible.

'Anyone I know?' asked Hannah innocently.

'A certain lady called Sarah Hamilton, who values your friendship and wants to come and meet you,' he began, now anxious to share her part in his happiness. 'Do you remember when I told you I thought I was being silly? And you gave me good advice. You said in particular that if I told her, she could then value the love of a good man. And I asked you what I'd do if she didn't share my feelings. You indicated that that would solve the problem, but in a different way.'

Hannah had the greatest difficulty remembering anything she had said to him, but she knew he would always recall accurately.

'I'm so delighted for you Jonathan,' she said happily. 'May I ask how this all came about?'

'Yes, of course. You, of all people are entitled to hear the story.'

Hannah was touched as he told her in detail what had happened. He explained how he had indeed come to Donegal as planned after a most terrible crossing of the Irish Sea, snow-storms in Donegal itself and an even slower journey back to Armagh.

'Sarah and I had lunch together just after Christmas. It was so lovely to see her,' he began, his face lighting up, as he told her about their ending up in one of the hotel's private rooms because they neither of them could bear the loud voices of some robust gentlemen at the next table.

'We had a plan to meet again the following day before I went back to England, but that had to be cancelled,' he went on hurriedly. 'I had visited my wife at The Retreat before coming to lunch with Sarah. She had had attacked me and I had a bruise on my forehead . . . You can still see it,' he added, brushing his hair back and displaying a short, but deep scar.

'Sarah tried to kiss it better when we met for lunch,' he went on sheepishly, 'but then, next morning, I had an urgent message to say my wife had fever. I was a risk to anyone I touched, or who touched me.'

He took a deep breath. 'You can imagine how I felt, Hannah. If I had infected the woman I so loved . . . '

'So what happened?' asked Hannah urgently, well able to imagine the consequences of such an innocent gesture.

'I had to send her a message telling her we couldn't meet, that I had been told to wrap up heavily and keep away from people and go straight home. We weren't even able to wish each other a Happy New Year.'

He dropped his eyes and looked at his hands. 'You know how bad the weather was in January. It was nearly two weeks before I had a letter from Sarah telling me she was perfectly well. And in the same post I also had two official ones,' he added quickly. 'One was to tell me my wife had died some three days after my visit. The other was the bill for her funeral, which had to take place immediately.'

'So you were able to ask Sarah to marry you?'

'I was. I asked her to name the day and she's now said it will take her till midsummer to find someone who can do her job for Sir George. So midsummer it is. We're planning to visit my cousins here in Donegal. Sarah, like you, Hannah, has never travelled in Ireland. She wants to see all the places she hears me talk about. I'd so like to bring her here to meet you in person. Could you manage that? You'll be near your time by then. But I'd be so delighted to see the two of you together.'

'All being well, Jonathan,' she said warmly, suddenly aware of how often these days she had need of this simple phrase. 'Send her my best wishes when you write and tell her I'll write soon myself . . . after I finish this thank you letter to our benefactors in East Boston. I could do with some help from you on that. If you have time.'

'Of course, I have time. After all you have done for me! Just tell me how I can help.'

31

The snow came back again within days of Jonathan Hancock's visit and with it the familiar biting cold, but as March moved onwards, the snow did retreat, though small patches lay for weeks in hollows and on the north side of cottages. It rotted rather than melted. But slowly, it disappeared, revealing, as always, that in sheltered corners and the bottoms of hedges, growth had begun, plants had moved slowly into life. At the first touch of sunshine, they responded immediately, sprang to life and unfurled, or even flowered.

With milder conditions it seemed that hope too was flourishing both in the valley and beyond. There were many people who said that the fierce cold of the winter would have killed off the blight, once and for all. There were many relief schemes all over Ireland only just getting into their stride. The long-promised public works were providing an income of sorts for 734,000 individuals. Relief Committees were encouraging further the Quaker initiative of distributing vegetable seeds to all those with space to plant.

Patrick planted the seed he'd helped to distribute and then bought some seed potatoes, none of his own from last year's crop having survived. He and the children prepared 'the eyes' as usual, and planted them one sunny afternoon as soon as they got back from school.

Meantime, Hannah and John were working on a small project for their friends in the shipyard in East Boston. Jonathan Hancock had thought her long letter to them would bring great pleasure to those who read it. He said he had no doubt at all but that it would be posted in the space outside the chairman's suite. He'd encouraged her to stay in touch with them, quite sure himself that there were many Irish emigrants who would be delighted to have her response, as well as the schools' thank you for the donation they'd received.

Jonathan had asked Hannah if either she, or John, knew any recent emigrants whom they could consult as to what would speak to their memories and longings and Hannah immediately thought of Marie, Daniel's niece, once a teacher at the school, now resident with her husband, Liam, in New York. What would it please Marie and Liam to receive from home?

But even before that particular letter was written, Hannah and John began to see further possibilities themselves. In one of their so-called staff meetings when they all drank tea together in Bridget's kitchen after school, they agreed that a school newspaper would both create an opportunity for the most literate of the children to write up local news, in both Irish and English, and also give someone like James Doherty in Boston something he could make available to anyone who might be interested.

It was a beginning. *News from the Valley*, the name they hit upon one Thursday afternoon, struck them all as a good way to keep in touch with the Irish staff in East Boston.

What intrigued Hannah when she reflected on that meeting, as she sat sewing by the fire next morning, was the way in which any idea one of them had seemed to grow, and generate into something much bigger, like a bonfire being fed and encouraged by a number of people.

She thought it was Bridget who had subsequently said: 'They might like stories.' It certainly was Daniel who mentioned *The Two Bottles* and John, who then pointed out that the proofs of his book, now in preparation, were already printed and readable. He could probably ask for an extra copy of the proofs, if the publishers knew it was going to be sent to America.

Meantime, as the gentler days of April moved on, Patrick and Hannah were only too aware of their imminent parting. Hannah noticed how seldom John lingered after he'd eaten his supper, fully aware as he was of how few evenings might remain to them, before the letter came with the ticket money and the date.

But there was one more evening in April when John did stay longer to share some good news with them both. As usual, he had discovered it when reading to Sophie the previous evening.

'Well,' he began, 'it seems that back in February when we were still snowed up, a band of Boston businessmen petitioned Congress to lend them a warship to deliver relief provisions to Ireland. You know that they're at war with Mexico at the moment. Don't you?'

Hannah wasn't entirely sure she'd known this,

but she nodded anyway, wanting to hear what happened next.

'For the first time in American history, the President, James K. Polk, placed a naval vessel under the command of a civilian on a private mission. Apparently, they started loading supplies on St Patrick's Day. It took them eleven days to load more than 8,000 barrels of food. Then a forty-nine-man volunteer crew sailed away under the Stars and Stripes and a white flag sporting a green shamrock.'

John paused and blinked a couple of times.

'Fifteen days later it was unloading in Cork harbour . . . and Sophie had a newspaper from Liverpool which said, '*The relief thus nobly sent may be regarded as one of the proudest events in American history.*''

John looked from one to the other.

'Sadly, however, the captain walked around the Cork alleyways. What he said was a lot less heroic: '*I saw enough in five minutes to horrify me.*' Hardly a happy ending', said John, holding up his hands. 'But we must give thanks for the good-heartedness of all those people who did contribute — 8,000 barrels of food. And they hadn't even heard of what we've had from East Boston,' he said, smiling. 'We don't ever hear the whole story, do we? We have to try to put the bits together and make up our own minds.' He rose to go.

'I thought I'd just stay a little longer tonight and tell you, in case you're busy packing tomorrow, or next day,' he said as he headed for the door.

'Sure, you're always welcome here, John,' said Patrick vigorously. 'An' I'm heart glad you'll be here over the summer, when Hannah will maybe need watchn'. Aye, an' there's that woman, Bridget, up at school, as well. The one I met when you ran out of meal, an' I had to bring you up a bag to keep you goin'. Hannah'll not go far astray with the pair of you to keep an eye on her,' he added, as if he'd just made up his mind and was now duly relieved.

* * *

It was only three days later that the letter from Duncan Mackay in Galloway came, and as always, there were preparations to be made. With Dermot back at sea, Patrick had been on the lookout for someone to take over the delivery of meal and flour. Happily, he had found a young man with whom he had once worked on a roof in Tullygobegley. He had already shown him round and introduced him to the people on what would be his regular round. Now, he brought him home and introduced him to Hannah, to Neddy himself and to his grooms, Rose and Sam.

A lively young man, with surprisingly blonde hair and blue eyes, he was another McGinley, one of the commonest names in the valley. Fortunately, his first name was Martin, and not Patrick, and from their very first meeting he got on well with both Neddy and his grooms.

But making him welcome seemed to take up a lot of time, or perhaps, as Hannah sometimes thought, time itself moved more quickly when parting was near. She had promised herself she wouldn't cry this time. But she did. Only, however, in the privacy of their bedroom.

When Patrick kissed all three of them goodbye at the cottage door, early one bright morning, she smiled and reminded him he'd need extra kisses when he came back. He'd need some more for a new baby, all being well. She was pleased to see him stride off looking easy, if not actually smiling.

* * *

There was real warmth in May. The May blossom, the hawthorn, which often didn't bloom till almost the end of the month in this part of Donegal, began to show white buds by mid-month. It looked as if it was going to be a good year for blossom and indeed, days later, the opening hawthorn flowers lay like snow on the fresh green of the bushes. Their perfume scented the evening air, especially if the day had been warm. The evenings grew longer and lighter.

Now, Hannah did shed tears in her empty bed, but as the days passed and the first letter came with remarkable speed, she began to feel her spirits lighten. It was too soon to hope that the blight might indeed have gone, but no one in the valley was as utterly dependant on the potatoes as once they had been. No one was going to starve in the valley with the resources they had and were using so carefully.

She and Patrick had decided that if they had a

girl they would call her Mary, after Patrick's aunt. If it was a boy, then Duncan, after her father. As the child began to move more vigorously, Hannah sat down oftener, taking her sewing out into the sunshine. She had to smile to herself sometimes when she discovered she'd nodded off and had done little for a whole morning.

Perhaps it was being with child, or perhaps it was the sunshine, or perhaps it was even the sense of having a dear husband, and friends, and work, and plans for the future, but Hannah began to feel more at peace than she'd felt for many a long day.

One of the continuing delights of the better weather was the speed at which letters came back and forth, not only between Donegal and Galloway, but between East Boston and Ardtur and between Ardtur and Castledillon in County Armagh, where Sarah Hamilton was preparing for her marriage.

Patrick was well and so was her father, the team of haymakers very much at ease, being mostly old colleagues. Across the Atlantic, James Doherty, the secretary in East Boston Shipping had responded vigorously to her initial letter of thanks and then to the first edition of the *Valley News*.

He told her that her colleague John McCreedy's suggestion of sending traditional stories had been greeted with great enthusiasm, that as a result, a number of friendship groups had been formed in the works. These groups planned to have regular meetings and hoped to share their own stories in return.

Daniel was concerned that Hannah might be over-exerting herself now that she was coming near her time, but Bridget reassured him that Hannah was carrying well. He had no idea what she meant by this, but he trusted her judgement and insisted only that Hannah did not carry books, or anything else, and that she sat down to do her teaching though she would always prefer to stand up.

★　★　★

As Hannah taught Monday, Wednesday and Thursday, Friday was a home day for her. A day to catch up on baking and cooking, and to make preparations for the weekend. There was always the danger of trying to do too much on a Friday when time was short and she admitted to having overdone it once or twice recently. She'd had cause to regret it. So, on Friday eleventh of June she made a point of doing some sewing both in the morning and in the afternoon. That was why she was able to watch John and the children coming home from school, before they even noticed her sitting just outside the cottage door.

Rose and Sam were alternately walking and skipping in their usual after-school way, but unusually, John was paying them little or no attention. His face was pale and immobile and he was walking as if he were half asleep. She'd never seen him look like this before. Immediately anxious in case he was ill, she got to her feet and stood waiting for them.

'Hello, Rose. Hello, Sam. Are you feeling all right, John?'

'Oh yes, yes, I'm fine,' he reassured her, noticing now that both children were looking at him as well. 'I just need my tea,' he said, dropping a bag of books on the ground by the cottage door, but continuing to hold on to a large brown, foolscap envelope.

Hannah knew something was terribly wrong, but she also knew she couldn't do anything about it until the children had gone out to play. She asked John to fetch another pail of water, made tea for them all as quickly as she could and questioned Rose and Sam about school while they ate their bread and jam.

The moment they left to go down to the Friels she turned to John.

'John dear, what's the matter? You look dreadful. Are you sure you're not ill?'

'I do feel sick, yes, but I'm not ill,' he said, his shoulders drooping as he gave up all pretence of coping.

'Do you know what that is?' he asked, pointing to the unopened packet he'd dropped on the dresser.

'No, John. I don't. What is it?'

'It's from my father. And you know how hard I've tried to go on without him since he didn't answer any of my letters. It was over. I tried. I really tried. I can't go through all that again. *I have no father*,' he said, breaking down and weeping.

She stood up and went to put her arms round him, only too aware of her protruding stomach.

336

She pulled her chair as close as she could and tried again. She felt his tears wet on her bare arms.

'And are you assuming the worst, John? What is the worst? What do you think he's sent you?'

'I've no idea, but it can't be good after all this time,' he said, wiping his eyes with a crumpled handkerchief. 'He's probably only wanting to have a go at me, telling me never to come near the place again not even to see my mother and sisters,' he went on, taking a great gasping breath. 'It can't be anything good after all these months. I've tried to forget about him and I thought I'd managed it and now it's all started up again. I can't bear it, Hannah. I can't bear it,' he said, dropping his head in his arms.

'John dear, whatever's in that packet, we need to know. When did you get it?'

'Just before we left school. Bridget remembered she'd put it up on the mantelpiece late yesterday, but Daniel had forgotten to tell me.'

'Well, it will have to be opened,' she said softly. 'May I open it for you, John? It has got to be done.'

He stared at her wide-eyed, his eyes still watering, his normally mobile face both pale and stiff. He nodded and looked away.

Hannah was aware of how slowly she was moving, as she went to the dresser and took her sewing scissors from their box. Awkwardly, she made access to the heavy envelope and then ripped it open. There was a letter written on small blue sheets of paper and a flat package in its own similar large envelope, which had been doubled over and stuck down. She set the package aside and took up the blue sheets, handwritten in black ink.

There was no address. It simply said *Dublin, June 1847* on the first sheet. She began to read, pausing to try to breathe normally.

My dear John,

You wrote to me some time ago and I did not reply to you. I am truly sorry for that and I apologise to you. I should have been able to do better than that. I do not want to make excuses for what I did, but perhaps that is now the only way I can explain. I do not have your gift with a pen.

I know you will be sad when I tell you that the woman you are so fond of and call Ma is not your mother. Your mother was a girl from County Down whom I met on my first posting. She was lovely in every way and we married at the first possible moment. You were born within the year, but she died a few days later. I have never got over her loss. She was the whole world to me and I would have done anything for her. All I had left was her son. Everything I did after that was done with what I thought she would have wished for you, our only child.

When I got my first senior posting to Galway I decided to remarry and thereby provide a mother for you. And this I did. I have recently confessed my bad faith to your stepmother. Good woman that she is, she

338

says she understands and she has forgiven me. I do not deserve such kindness as she has shown, but I give thanks for it.

You may wonder why after all these years and after my bad behaviour towards yourself I am now telling you this.

Some time ago one of my trainees went overboard. A splendid young man who reminded me so often of you. We were lucky to survive as rescue did not come quickly. A little longer and we would both have drowned. I was ill for some time and on recovery was asked to visit Dublin on behalf of the Coastguard Service. There I met with a number of Quaker enquirers. They were aware that the famine situation on the west coast was becoming ever more serious. Even where relief was available it could not be transported to those in need. They asked for my advice.

I have been working since then with these good people who listen to what I can tell them and value my detailed knowledge. I gave up all faith in God when I lost the love of my life. These people have made me question what I have done.

My work on the west coast is now much more dangerous than before. We are using our boats, cutters and even the gunboat to deliver supplies to villages that have no roads leading to them. Regardless of wind and storm, we are the only source of food. In some of the villages there are unburied dead and dying.

As I intend to go on doing this work, I have made provision for your stepmother and have now been forgiven by her. I would now ask you to forgive me also. Perhaps we may yet meet again in happier times.

I must congratulate you on your great achievement, your book, which I know about from your very good letters to your stepmother and sisters. The enclosed packet is doubtless your copy as it has a Dublin postmark and address. I shall buy my own copy when next in Dublin to meet my colleagues from the Quakers. I hope that you will sign my copy for me at some future date.

I am,
As ever,
Your loving father,
James McCreedy

Postscript

The Irish Famine did not end in the summer of 1847 though Hannah and Patrick, the new baby and many of the other characters survive. The story continues in 1861, when Hannah and Patrick's growing family are evicted and their cottage is demolished at the beginning of *The Woman from Kerry*.

Historians are still arguing bitterly over the numbers who died during the Great Famine, from starvation or the many diseases that were widespread in a population weakened by hunger. We have no record of the large numbers buried at sea or on arrival at a new destination.

All we can be sure of, is that five million people *did* survive and that many of them owed their lives to people all over the world who identified with their need and sent help, pennies from orphans in New York, ships full of grain from the Sultan of Turkey, huge donations from the Indian Army and the people of Massachusetts.

A long, long list of people of all kinds and conditions who '*did what they could, did it in love and saw that it was often even more than they could have hoped.*'

We still have need of such generosity in October 2017.

Anne Doughty
Belfast

THE BLACKSMITH'S WIFE

Anne Doughty

County Armagh, 1845. Married to the local blacksmith, young Sarah Hamilton spends her days looking after John and his apprentices at the forge. Her happiness is intensified by the steady love of her husband and the beautiful green landscape of her home on Drumilly Hill. But when tragedy strikes, her life is changed forever. As the crops across Ireland begin to fail and the textile industry struggles to adapt to new methods, Sarah isn't the only one enduring hardships. Along with her friends and neighbours, Sarah lives through loss and disappointment, but ultimately discovers love and the power of hope with the help of those dearest to her.

SUMMER OF THE HAWTHORN

Anne Doughty

Deirdre Weston, a London journalist, returns to her family home in Armagh to come to terms with the death of her mother. In her distress, she is comforted by a mysterious figure, a young woman, Deara, who seems to reach out to her from another age. Deirdre experiences some seventeen years in Deara's fifth-century life, a time as turbulent and troubled in Ireland as the late twentieth century has been. Both women discover the strength which flows from the love and support of the other, and this enables them to influence the world around them with far-reaching consequences.